PRAISES FOR WAYWARD PATRIOT: PRESERVING

"Riveting! Jack Mey tale of collusion and intrigue w f David Baldacci and John Grisha

— JIM HA....., Deputy Chief of Staff for the late Congressman Jim Hagedorn

"The book grabbed me from the beginning. Meyer combines action and suspense with a creative yet viable premise that left me wondering, 'could this really happen?' I'm looking forward to the next book in the *Wayward Patriot* series!"

— TODD HOPKINS, entrepreneur, founder of Office Pride and international bestselling author of *The Janitor, The Stress Less Business Owner,* and *Stop Using the "B" Word.*

"Meyer's first novel is a page-turning thriller with lots of twists and turns that will have you guessing until the very end. His character development is solid. He provides a balanced view on a divisive topic."

— MARTY FERRIS, Controller, Summit County, CO

"*Wayward Patriot: Preserving the Vote* is both entertaining and thought provoking! The premise is fascinating and the way it is written, it is hard to put down. It's exciting to consider a perfect election system but a cold splash in the face to be reminded that no system is perfect."

— MICK HARTLEY, Captain, Southwest Airlines (Retired)

"*Wayward Patriot: Preserving the Vote* is a story that could be the behind the scenes account of something that is emerging from some current headlines about tampering with our elections.

It is a story of two normal citizens who get caught up in a serious mystery that keeps readers attention from one chapter to the next. There is a natural desire to "get to the bottom of it."

Yet, there is a genuine twist at the end that brings it all to a startling conclusion.

As a person concerned about the integrity of our nation's elections, although this book is fiction, one can wonder if the story Meyer tells is more real than one's imagination."

— DENNIS JAMISON County Coordinator,
Election Integrity Project of California

"*Wayward Patriot: Preserving the Vote* takes the reader into the heart of what can happen in today's political process — the he said/she said, they said/we said back-and-forth/inside-out shenanigans political party players often resort to in the mad dash to cross the finish line in first place. The author employs countless twists-and-turns that keep his readers wondering what's going to happen next. When in real life, should it have happened at all? The book is immensely entertaining. Hope to see more 'wayward' action and intrigue to come!"

— REV. GEORGE SWANSON (Retired)

"In this era when election integrity is in question, this book brings to life the ultimate election fraud and forces the reader to consider its potential impact on America. It contrasts average Americans doing the right thing for the country they love with average Americans doing the wrong things for what they consider noble reasons. It is an exciting and intriguing roller coaster ride following the experience of people, no different than me, who have found themselves in over their heads. However, you're never really sure who the bad guys are until the very end. It is well written and thought provoking, considering some real and terrifying possibilities."

— DIANA LANTZ, business owner and 'Average American'

WAYWARD PATRIOT:
PRESERVING THE VOTE

The election is secure. Treason awaits.

Jack Meyer

First Edition Published in 2023 by:
3PPress Publishing Company
3609 Austin Bluffs Pkwy, #3 1/2
Colorado Springs, CO. 80918

3PPress.com

Copyright © 2023 by Jack Meyer

All rights reserved. No part of this book may be reproduced or transmitted in any form whatsoever without permission from the author, except in the case of brief quotations embodied in articles, reviews or books.

Names: Meyer, Jack (John Allan), 1955-

Title: Wayward patriot : preserving the vote / Jack Meyer.

Description: First edition. | Colorado Springs, CO : 3PPress, [2023] | Series: Wayward patriot series. | "The election is secure. Treason awaits."

Identifiers: ISBN: 979-8-9862931-0-3 (paperback) | 979-8-9862931-2-7 (hardcover) | 979-8-9862931-1-0 (ebook) | LCCN: 2023901487

Subjects: LCSH: Voting--United States--Fiction. | Election security--United States--Fiction. | Electronic voting--Security measures--United States--Fiction. | Blockchains (Databases)--Security measures--United States--Fiction. | Elections--United States--Management--Fiction. | Elections--Corrupt practices--United States--Fiction. | Legitimacy of governments--United States--Fiction. | Contested elections--United States--Fiction. | Computer security--United States--Fiction. | LCGFT: Political fiction. | Thrillers (Fiction) | BISAC: FICTION / Thrillers / Suspense. | POLITICAL SCIENCE / Political Process / Campaigns & Elections. | COMPUTERS / Blockchain,

Classification: LCC: PS3613.E953 W39 2023 | DDC: 813/.6--dc23

Editor: Carrie M. Cannella

Artworks: Lori Ehlke

Book design: Dreemer Designs

This is a work of fiction. The events described are imaginary. The events and characters are fictitious and are not intended to represent specific organizations, places, or people.

Printed in the United States of America

For my wife Barbara, who has supported me in so many endeavors throughout our life together.

PROLOGUE

The car sat idling with the lights off. The driver had parked on a street in a quiet neighborhood in view of a stop sign where motorists would pause under the street light before turning. This street, like many others, had been truncated on the other side of the road five years before when a new highway was built. A person couldn't see the speeding traffic because of the high wall that had been erected, intended to shield the residential area from the noise of cars and trucks as they flew by.

It was a chilly morning, and the humidity was high because of overnight rain. The temperature was just below fifty degrees, and the cool air penetrated the driver's light jacket through to the bone. Every so often a shiver would rise to the surface, as if the driver's body was objecting to the absence of a heavier coat. The bit of discomfort was necessary; both front windows were open so any surrounding sounds could be heard.

The night was made darker by cloudy skies, but silhouettes of houses, trees, vehicles, and other details began to appear as the lightening effect of the dawn developed, more pronounced in the eastern sky. The heady, sandalwood scent of a rainy night was still in the air.

The driver listened carefully, looking in all directions. There were no sounds other than the hum of the highway and the occasional roar of an eighteen-wheeler as it passed. No footsteps. Nobody walking a dog. No wind.

At the end of the block, the figure of a man appeared in the street light, running along the right side of the road perpendicular and heading east. The transmission was put into drive, and the motorist slowly pulled away. The car's headlights remained off.

At the end of the street, the driver turned right. In the distance, the man's figure appeared and disappeared as he jogged beneath the street lights.

The driver began to accelerate, slowly. Twenty miles per hour, thirty, forty. The drone of the engine was mostly swept away by the insistent sounds of passing vehicles from the highway. Fifty miles per hour.

The headlights came on when the runner was just twenty feet away. The jogger turned. His face could be seen clearly now. His expression was initially one of curiosity, but then his eyes widened. He planted his left foot, attempting to lurch to the right, but it was too late.

There was a booming thud as the car struck the man. In view of the headlights, the limp body flew forward from impact. The driver braked carefully to avoid the sound of skidding tires on the pavement, then paused as the airborne mass returned to earth, striking the roadway hard, tumbling, and finally rolling to a stop.

The driver maneuvered to the left to bypass the body. Three blocks later the motorist turned right and disappeared into the night.

Sometimes well-intended actions result in tragic consequences.
– Jack Meyer

WAYWARD PATRIOT
Series Book 1

CHAPTER 1

BRAD TILLMAN WALKED INTO PEACHTREE FREE CHURCH IN North Druid Hills, a suburb of Atlanta. The church was tucked back into a quiet neighborhood among the hilly terrain and tall pines that were common in the Atlanta area. It was a cool, cloudy day at the beginning of November. It seemed appropriate weather for the somber task at hand. Brad's wife, Barbara, was at his side.

Brad had been to funerals before, but he couldn't remember attending one for someone he knew so well. Before, he had attended to show his support for others who were grief stricken. Today was different. They would be eulogizing his best friend, Albert Johnson, who had died the previous Friday well before his time. Losing such a close friend so close in age to himself made Brad feel the fragility of life. As they entered the sanctuary, he thought that nobody was guaranteed a future. His great consolation was knowing that Al was a man of faith.

Brad and Barb walked up the aisle and saw that it was a closed casket. This was a relief to Brad, who always felt uncomfortable staring at the deceased. He and Barb approached the front of the church where Al lay. They paused, facing his casket, and prayed silently. Al had been in great health—forty-six years old, six-feet tall, trim. His sudden death was the result of a vehicle accident. He was struck by a car while jogging. Brad and Barb still couldn't believe it. They turned and went immediately to some open seats near several people Brad knew from work.

Brad Tillman was the epitome of a "normal" forty-seven-year-old man who carried a little too much weight for his 5'11" frame. Too much of that weight had settled around his midsection, and according to the charts, he was on the low end of the obesity scale. He himself didn't see it that way—he wasn't fat, he just needed to drop twenty pounds or so. His late buddy Al, a fitness junkie, had teased him about it. That and his shaved head. Brad wasn't completely bald, but his hair was thinning, so when the shaved head came into style, he razed it all off.

Al, an African American, was blessed with a full head of black hair and forwarded every advertisement he could find on hair growth products to his friend. Brad had countered with a recent birthday card to Al that read, "God only blessed some with perfect heads; to the rest he gave hair!" Brad's extra weight made his face round with few wrinkles. He kept his face clean-shaven, and his natural expression was one of thoughtfulness. Most would consider him reserved, as he was a bit shy in social settings, but he had a good sense of humor. When he smiled, he projected warmth and friendliness.

It was surreal to think that they were there to say goodbye to Al. Brad and Barb considered Al and his wife Linda their best friends. Al and Brad both worked at GC, Inc., a cybersecurity firm based in downtown Atlanta. They never interacted at work because they were in completely different fields. They had met at a company party a few years back only because their wives recognized each other from a baby shower for a mutual friend. The two couples hit it off immediately and regularly got together for a movie or dinner and card games. Brad and Al made it a point to eat lunch together at least twice a week, although they seldom discussed work, since neither understood much about what the other did.

Al was a project manager, working with software developers to implement sophisticated cybersecurity in new customers' computer systems. Not only was he a tech geek, but he was also often described as "anal" when it came to making systems secure. Al had told Brad many times that no system is perfectly secure, but that his job was to get as close to that as was humanly possible.

Brad, on the other hand, was a finance manager whose role was to keep the company lean and mean; in other words, profitable. He knew next to nothing about technology beyond how to use spreadsheets and the various accounting systems he had worked with during his career. He didn't like social media, but he had an account on Facebook. He figured it was a pretty good way of keeping up with his kids and grandkids.

Barb and Linda had grown close as well. Barb, a nurse, and Linda, a paralegal, regularly went shopping together. They shared an interest in craft work and scrapbooking. It was nice to browse for ideas and materials together without their husbands in tow. They had traveled together several times for weekend craft festivals in other cities. The men loved that there was someone to replace them on such outings.

Out of the corner of his eye, Brad saw movement and turned his head to see the pastor walking with Linda up to the front of the church. Behind them walked their son and daughter, both college-aged, clinging to one another. Other family members followed. Once they sat down, the pastor stepped onto the altar, welcomed the guests, and began the service. Brad found it hard to pay attention. Each eulogy would bring back a new memory that would recommence his mind wandering.

Barb nudged him when it was his turn. He didn't like public speaking, but it was the least he could do for Linda. He stepped up to the lectern and paused. He could feel a tingling inside the bridge of his nose and tears on the way. He took a deep breath to quell those feelings and smiled at the congregation.

"I'm sure everyone here knows what an amazing guy Al was. I feel so blessed that Barb and I have been such close friends with him and Linda. I'm not sure why Al and I hit it off so well, but I do know that nobody I know has more integrity than he did. He was always exactly the same, whether in the presence of close friends or total strangers. He always listened with a caring attitude and showed genuine interest in whoever he was with."

Brad spent a few more minutes talking directly to Linda. He promised that he and Barb loved her and would always be there for her. It was then that the tears came. He just couldn't help it. All he could do was squeak out, "Please forgive me," and return to his seat. He and Barb had been among the first people Linda called after the accident and were there for her immediately. When her family arrived, they withdrew and allowed them time to grieve.

When the service was over, most people went to the lunch reception in the church fellowship hall. The interment ceremony would be for family only, later that afternoon. Brad and Barb were the only non-family members invited.

After hugging Linda and the family, Brad went through the buffet line but didn't pick up much. He just wasn't hungry. As he turned away from the line, Jeff Unger walked up and extended his hand. "How are you getting along, Brad? I know you and Al were close."

Jeff Unger, a middle-aged man with wavy, salt and pepper hair, was more introverted than one might expect of someone who ran a multi-billion-dollar business. He loved to talk technology, but in social settings he was uncomfortable. Brad knew him to be a sincere man who cared about his work family, though. On more than one occasion, he had heard of Jeff helping out an employee who was having a difficult time. Once he had paid to have a single mom's car repaired when she had to deal with her daughter's emergency appendectomy.

"Yeah, this is a tough one, Jeff. I've never lost anyone so close. My parents and siblings are all still alive. I haven't been through this before."

"How did you guys become so close? You had pretty different backgrounds, didn't you?"

"It's hard to say. We just always seemed really comfortable talking with one another, about anything. I've never had that kind of bond with a friend before. Al was always so positive. He was encouraging and non-judgmental. I'll really miss our talks."

Barb joined them and held out her hand to Jeff. "Hi, Mr. Unger. It's nice to see you. Linda says you've been extremely helpful to her. We appreciate it."

Barbara Tillman was a trim woman with cropped hair. Though she was a year older than Brad, she looked younger. Her hair was just beginning to gray, but she never colored it. She was comfortable in her own skin and didn't feel the need to change her appearance. She seldom wore makeup. She wore a black pantsuit; she was not comfortable in dresses.

Jeff shook her hand. "Hi, Barbara. That's nice of you to say. But I wanted to thank *you* for being such good friends to Linda and Al. She told me she's not sure how she'd have gotten through last Friday without you."

"It's such a helpless feeling," Brad said. "All we could do was provide her a couple of shoulders to cry on until her family could get here. Linda told us she really appreciated your visit and all the company issues you handled for her."

Jeff Unger was the founder and CEO of GCI. He had started the company, originally called Gone Cyber, Inc., in 2003. Unger was a techie with an MBA and PhD in Computer Science. When the computer age exploded in the late 1990s, he quickly realized that capturing and storing information was a growing industry. He also recognized that information security was going to be important. During his college years, he had hacked into all kinds of systems without doing harm, just to see if he could. He knew if he could do it, others could too.

During the first few years of GCI's existence, growth was slow because few company managers could be convinced of their vulnerabilities. Cybersecurity seemed to be an unnecessary luxury, especially on the heels of all the money they had spent in preparation for Y2K. Jeff's big break came when he met a Department of Defense computer wonk at a backyard barbecue. They hit it off and regaled one another with stories of college shenanigans, including some involving Jeff's hacking skills. A couple of weeks later, Jeff got a call asking for a meeting to discuss technology challenges that the military was encountering in the war on terror. The enemy was getting more sophisticated, and it was becoming more difficult to get tactical information.

Jeff had been able to help, and GCI began winning military contracts. Initially they were to help with hacking various enemy networks, but they soon led to contracts to secure government systems as well. The company grew steadily and became quite profitable, but the government work was not always reliable, as administrations with differing priorities came and went. GCI needed to get back to developing the corporate side of their business.

The company's success in protecting government systems made the transition easier. Although most companies still didn't appreciate how vulnerable their IT systems were to hackers, GCI was able to land some large contracts. In 2016, when major corporations like Target began having electronic customer files stolen, GCI's growth exploded. Jeff, now in his early fifties, was unlike most entrepreneurs in that he was able to adapt and grow GCI seamlessly from a start-up to a multi-billion-dollar business. Brad thought about all of the many entrepreneurs who start a business, get it to the level of strong viability, and then sell it. They typically don't have the patience or interest in the bureaucracy that develops with a company of size. However, Jeff had surrounded himself with far-sighted corporate minds and was able to keep the company technically proficient while adding 6,000 employees to handle new business. They now had twenty-two offices around the United States, plus branches in London, Sydney, and Johannesburg.

Helping to manage that growth financially was where Brad fit in. He had always been a numbers guy. He was immediately drawn to finance with his very first accounting class in college. Accounting was too dry for him, but analyzing and interpreting the numbers to understand what they represented was what he loved. Jeff Unger had personally hired him at a time when GCI seemed to be losing control of its spending, and Brad had quickly tightened the financial sails. Yet, there were still opportunities for new ventures. Jeff himself personally led the Special Projects Division, a group of forty-five highly paid staff members who were technical and security heavyweights and worked hard to keep GCI on the cutting-edge of the cybersecurity field. Brad reasoned that it was probably strategically important to have such a team, but they sometimes burned through company money like it was kindling.

"Well," Jeff said, "Al was incredibly influential in staying ahead of the technology curve for us in the early years. I owe him so much. I want to make sure Linda and the kids are well taken care of. Again, I appreciate everything you've done for her. Let me know if there's anything more I can do to help."

Brad and Barb both nodded as Jeff moved along to talk with others. Barb wandered over to Linda now that the reception line had dwindled to a few and waited to avoid interrupting the last conversations. Brad saw two people who he knew worked with Al and greeted them. "Good afternoon."

"Hey, Brad. You did a nice job on the eulogy," said Chuck Gleason.

"It's good to see you," added Eric Blas.

"I guess you guys will miss Al on the third floor," Brad offered.

"Oh, you have no idea," Chuck said. "Al has been a key player in so many important development programs."

Blas disagreed. "Personally, I think we'll get things done more quickly now. Al tended to get too involved in other people's programs. I can't count the times we were approaching wrap-up when Al started asking questions and taking us off track."

Brad blinked. He was visibly taken aback by the comments and looked at Blas closely to see if he was joking. Blas was a wiry man, shorter than most. He showed little facial expression, but his manner of speaking seemed aggressive.

"Eric, you and Al together were the best we had," Chuck countered. "You didn't always agree, but you can't tell me that our work wasn't improved through Al's diligence."

"I'm not saying Al wasn't good at his job," Blas replied. "I just think he stuck his nose in where it didn't belong at times."

Brad could hardly believe his ears. "Look," he said as he stared at Blas. "Your comments aren't at all appropriate for this time and place. I'd appreciate it if you'd keep them to yourself."

Blas shrugged and walked away.

"Can you believe that guy?" asked Chuck. "Al's attention to detail saved his ass so many times that he should've been first in line to deliver a eulogy!" Chuck was a guy who was always positive and thought the best of people. That and his infectious smile drew people to him. Eric Blas could even turn *his* mood sour.

"Al told me that Blas was always in a bad mood, but I had no idea." Brad watched Blas across the room. "The least he could do is show some respect at a guy's funeral."

"I think he needs to turn off the news. He's always ranting and raving about the political right."

"Ah, one of those who thinks anyone right of center is a bigot?"

"Oh, that's putting it mildly!" Chuck said.

"Well, there are quite a few of those on the far right as well," commented Brad. "The political divide has gotten so bad in this country that I don't know if we'll ever resolve it."

The great divide seemed to fully manifest itself during the Trump presidency, when it seemed to Brad that conservatives had finally found their voice. Add Trump's inflammatory rhetoric to the mix, and the chasm grew wider. Then the Covid 19 pandemic seemed to put people even more on edge. More unrest came about with the Black Lives Matter movement, which seemed to spur anarchists to new levels of violence. Not to be outdone, white supremacists came out from the shadows, apparently believing Trump spoke for them.

Politically, Brad felt that those on the left seemed to think that all conservatives were racists, while those on the right claimed that liberals were trying to eliminate freedom and change the United States into a socialist country. Meanwhile, polls showed that most Americans considered themselves far from either extreme. The national media, however, seemed to overlook the foibles of some politicians, while taking every opportunity to caricature others as mean, bumbling, and bigoted. Unsuspecting citizens bought it all, and both party bases dug in and became more uncompromising than ever. Politicians even seemed to fear their constituents because they didn't know what they were thinking at any given moment.

"I wonder if it bothered Eric that Al didn't climb on the Black Lives Matter bandwagon," Chuck said. "He seems to think that every Black person in America should have the same point of view as him."

"I wouldn't be surprised," Brad said. "At least our elections seem to have calmed down a bit." He thought for a moment. "I think everyone is moving on. After 2020, I figured every election from now on would require two months of vote counting and an international tribunal to verify the results."

"I guess restoring confidence in the voting system settled things down a bit," Chuck said.

"There is but one man responsible for that, and we work for him," whispered Brad.

In 2021, Jeff Unger had stepped up and given every state government an offer they couldn't refuse, at least not under the circumstances. He promised to design, build, and maintain the most secure election system possible for the 2024 election—at cost. Jeff was not only considered a straight-shooting, nonpartisan patriot by Democrats and Republicans alike, but he had also shown GCI to be the best of the best in the cybersecurity industry.

Out of prudence, thirteen states of varying sizes took Jeff up on his offer. The system worked flawlessly, while saving those states millions of dollars. A law was passed whereby the federal government would pay for any state that signed up to use it. Since that time, elections had gone incredibly well. Politicians liked it because there were fewer contested elections, the media liked it because results came in quickly, and the public liked it because after the 2026 midterm elections, it seemed like election fraud was a worry of the past. Thirty-nine states had joined the system for that election. Now, the remaining states were committed and expected to be up and running for the upcoming 2028 presidential election, just a year away.

Jeff maintained a low profile despite all this. Nobody knew which way he leaned politically, or if he even cared about politics at all. He appreciated citizenship in a country where a person with an idea or vision could live out their dream. Brad was proud to work for the man.

Brad rolled his eyes. "Listen to us. Talking politics at Al's funeral."

"Yeah, I guess Eric Blas just brings out the worst in me," whispered Chuck with a big grin on his face.

Brad smiled and raised both his hands. "Enough! We're better than this!"

With that he strolled over to Barb and Linda. "It's good to see you two together. You support and complement one another so well. You're almost like sisters. I'm glad your family is here to support you, Linda, but I know Barb has been climbing the walls wanting to be there too."

Linda Johnson was a pretty woman who looked much younger than her forty-six years. Her hair was always perfect, and she wore understated make-up and lipstick that complimented her light brown complexion. Even in this situation, she was tastefully dressed. She stood tall and maintained her warm and caring demeanor.

"Oh, what would I do without our Barb? I want to thank you both again for the support you've given us over the past week. Al would appreciate all you've done so much."

"We're here for you," Brad said. "We plan to spend lots of time with you, so get ready!"

Following the interment service, the Tillmans headed home, consumed with sadness. Barb looked over from the passenger seat of Brad's Audi. "I don't know what I'd do if something happened to you."

"Well, you don't have to worry about that. I couldn't run to the end of the driveway, let alone four miles a day like Al."

Barb's jaw dropped down in a mock look of astonishment. She slapped him on the shoulder.

Brad thought it ironic that Al was the guy with the discipline to run every morning, watch what he ate, and otherwise take care of himself; yet he was the one who died early, struck by a car while running. He had taken such good care of himself, but it may have been carelessness that cost him his life. Linda told them that she nagged Al all the time to wear a reflective vest while running. After learning of his death, she had walked them to the closet to point out the vest still hanging there. Amid her grief, she was also visibly angry.

No one could be sure yet whether that had made a difference. The police told Linda that the driver left the scene. They interviewed all the neighbors and found no witnesses to the accident, which apparently occurred between five-thirty and six Friday morning.

That was it. Suddenly, Linda and her children were without their husband and father. And while there could be no comparison, Brad had lost his best friend.

CHAPTER 2

ON THE FRIDAY FOLLOWING AL'S FUNERAL, BRAD RECEIVED a call at work. "Hi Brad, this is Linda."

"Hey Linda. How are you getting along?"

"Oh, we're okay. You know," she said quietly, "the kids are going to stay home for the rest of the semester. They've arranged to finish their fall semester coursework from here."

"That's good news. You'll be wonderful support for each other." Brad could feel a tingling in his sinuses; he was nearly tearing up just talking to her. "I'm glad you called. Is there something Barb and I can do for you?"

"Oh, no. Not like that. But there is something work-related you might be able to help with."

"Anything!"

"Well, someone from GCI security came by yesterday and brought me all of Al's things from work. I gave him Al's work laptop, phone, and stuff like that. Then last night I ran across his briefcase, and it has some files and paperwork in it. I guess someone might need that. Would you mind stopping by to see if there's anything that should go to his boss?"

"Absolutely. I'd be happy to. How about two this afternoon?"

"That's fine. I'm not going back to work until Monday, so I'll be here."

Brad figured he'd leave around one-thirty and take the rest of the day off. He let a few people know they could reach him on his cell phone if necessary.

He pulled into the driveway and walked to the door. The front door was open, so he opened the storm door and walked in without knocking. This was a typical ritual at either home. They were almost like family. Their

10

doors were always open for one another, literally as well as figuratively. "Linda?" he called out.

"Hey Brad," she said as she rounded the corner from the kitchen. "Thank you so much for doing this."

"I'm glad to help, Linda." They walked back to the small bedroom Al had used as an office. "Has the family all gone home?"

"Uh-huh. Mom wanted to stay with me for a while, but I told her the kids will be here and it'd be better for us to adjust together. Here you go—it's a fine briefcase and Al loved it. I'd like to hang on to it. Michael might want it." Michael, their son, would be returning to Texas Tech in January.

Brad took the case and saw several manila folders on the left side. The center section was designed to hold a laptop, which Linda had already returned, and on the opposite side there was a single file folder. "All right, let me take a look. I'll make sure this gets where it needs to go."

"Thank you, Brad. Can I get you something to drink? Maybe a bottle of water?"

"That would be wonderful."

He sat at the small desk and pulled the folders from the left side of the briefcase. Each bulged with pages of material that seemed to be notes or reports relating to software development. On the tab of each folder was the name of a company, probably clients.

Linda returned with a bottle of water and some cookies on a napkin. "Here you go. Please eat some cookies too. I have so much food left over from the reception that I need all the help I can get!"

Brad grinned and set them on the desk. Even in mourning, she was thinking of others. "Thanks. And yep, I can already tell that Cathy might want some of these folders." Cathy Hoover was the Vice President of Product Development. Al's importance to the company was such that he was the only project manager who reported directly to a VP. "I'm almost done here, and then I'll get out of your hair."

"You're no bother at all, Brad. I appreciate a little company. The kids are with friends, so it's a good time to have you stop in."

At that, he turned in his chair. "Linda, how are you doing? Really?"

Linda teared up and leaned against the door frame. "Oh Brad, I'm not doing so great." Her tears turned into sobs. "I feel so ashamed. I was horrible to Al!"

Brad jumped to his feet and put his arms around her. "Hey, hey, what are you talking about? You didn't do this."

"But I was so ugly to him the night before he died. He'd been working for days on some project. It consumed him. I complained about it, and he said it was something that couldn't wait, that it was more important than him or me or anyone else for that matter. I told him his family is what is important and that I'd barely seen him for four days. I told him to get his priorities straight, and then I went to bed. Those were my last words to him. The next morning, he was gone before I got up."

"Linda, Linda. Couples fight all the time. Al knew you loved him. He was crazy about you! I had to listen to him gushing about you all the time." Brad smiled. "Al was wild about you and the kids. Nothing you could have said would've changed that. Hey, if you're up to it, why don't you come over for dinner tomorrow night? It's supposed to be cool with a chance of rain, but I can still throw some salmon on the grill, and we can relax inside. Fall weather, you know. Maybe we'll even light a fire in the fireplace."

Linda dabbed at her eyes and laughed through the tears. "I'll bet you haven't cleared that with Barb, have you? You're going to get yourself in trouble!"

"You know better than that. Barb would love to get some time with you. She gets off at three, so why don't you come over around four thirty? Bring the kids."

"On a Saturday night? They'll be out with friends, and that's probably what they need right now. But if you're sure it's okay with Barb, I'll be there. Oh Brad, I'm sorry I dumped all that on you. You must think I'm crazy."

He pulled a tissue from the box on the desk and handed it to her. "Not at all. You need to be able to confide in friends. You need to be told you're not crazy. Barb and I love you like family." Brad's heart went out to her. He and Barb occasionally had disagreements and exchanged some harsh words. He would hate to be taken in the midst of an argument before amends were made. He made a note to himself to be more careful with his words in the future.

When Linda left the office, Brad took a deep breath and wiped his eyes. He returned to the briefcase and pulled the lone file folder from the other side. It was obviously new and unlabeled. Inside was a single sheet of paper. Typed on the top left in bold was **"PENNSYLVANIA SPECIAL ELECTION."** Below that was the word "PRECINCTS" and a list of three-digit numbers in sequence. The next two columns over said "Democrat" and "Republican," each with its own list of numbers below. The fourth column, labeled "Other," contained much smaller numbers. Brad was looking at page two of seventeen. The columns only took up half of the page. On the bottom of the page was a large, hand-drawn question mark. The other side was blank.

Brad stared at the page. Precincts? Voter tallies? Al didn't work on the election side of the business anymore. That was compartmentalized and kept totally separate from everything else in the company. Could this have something to do with Al's "project"? As he stared at the document, he thought about what he needed to get to Al's boss. Was this information needed in Al's office? It was obviously on a computer somewhere. Al's only "value added" was the big question mark, and he may not have even scrawled it.

Brad closed the folder and placed it on top of the others. He left the empty briefcase on the floor beside the desk and walked out into the living room. "I'll get these into the right hands. I'm sure they'll appreciate you finding them, as it'll probably save someone a lot of work."

Linda stood. "Good. I thought that might be the case. Are you sure about dinner tomorrow?"

"Absolutely! We'll be looking forward to it. Until then ..." Brad paused. "Linda, Al loved you, and he knew you loved him."

"Thank you, Brad," she said softly. "I'll see you tomorrow. Have Barb let me know what I can bring."

As he drove home, Brad couldn't help but think about that single sheet of paper with the big question mark. If it was the thing that had consumed Al, why was he so interested in it? What was he questioning?

When he got home, Barb wasn't there yet. He fired up his laptop, keyed in his password, and opened his browser. He wondered if the numbers on the sheet he had found were drawn from a past election in Pennsylvania. Where could he go to learn about elections in Pennsylvania? He typed in "Pennsylvania election results." He clicked on one site that came up called "Election Results & Data." It was the Pennsylvania Secretary of State website. It looked like there had been a special election to fill an open US Senate seat. The special election had been just a few days ago, on Tuesday.

He clicked on "Special Election Results–Excel Format." It took about fifteen seconds to load. He clicked on it and found the Excel workbook with a worksheet labeled "US Senator."

On the left he saw precinct numbers. In the other columns, rather than Democrat and Republican, he saw actual candidates' names with their party affiliations. The last column was labeled "Other." He looked at the page from Al's folder and saw that the first precinct number was 032. He scrolled down to precinct 032. He looked across at the numbers in each of the three columns. He looked back at the single page. The numbers were the same. He went to the next line. Identical. All the way down the list, the numbers on the election results worksheet were the same as the numbers on the piece of paper in Al's file.

Brad looked back at the Secretary of State webpage to confirm the date of the election. Then, he sat back in his chair. How could that be? The election was this past Tuesday. He scrutinized the worksheet again. Could this be from a prior election? He looked back at the top of the worksheet at the title. There it was—Tuesday's date: November 2, 2027. These numbers were from an election that indeed took place this week.

That meant that the paper in Al's briefcase had to have been printed before his death. Al died on October 29th, four days before this election.

CHAPTER 3

HIS PHONE RANG. TOMMY SAW THAT THE CALL WAS FROM an unknown number. "Hello," he said.

A voice on the line said, "He just did an Internet search that concerns us. We may need to take care of him—do your homework and see what you think. I'll enhance monitoring systems."

"Will do," Tommy said and ended the call.

Brad closed his laptop and returned it to his briefcase. He closed the folder with Al's document in it and put it in the case as well. He went to the kitchen and checked the refrigerator to see if there was a clue as to what Barb planned for dinner. Nothing obvious. He pulled out his phone and sent her a text. "Can I take you out to dinner tonight?"

It was four p.m., so she was probably in her car. She usually wouldn't respond to a text while driving, so he was surprised when she answered right away. "Sure! Home in ten."

Brad didn't have a particular restaurant in mind; he just wanted to get out of the house so he wouldn't have time to think too much about what he'd just seen. It had been a rough week, and he needed to relax and spend some dedicated time with his wife. He decided not to mention his discovery to her. He wasn't sure what to think about it himself.

They enjoyed their evening out, a welcome respite from the stress of the week, over a shared bottle of wine and Italian cooking. Most of the conversation centered around their children. They had two daughters, both grown and married. Jill lived in San Diego with her husband who was a lieutenant, junior grade, in the Navy. She taught second grade in a public school. No kids. Their other daughter, Kristi, lived in Kansas City with her husband, who worked for a start-up software company. They had Brad and Barb's only grandchild, Hudson, who they didn't get to see nearly enough. After the baby was born, Kristi was able to return to her part-time job converting college courses to an online format at the University of Kansas.

When the conversation shifted to more recent events, Barb was delighted to learn that Linda would be coming over for dinner on Saturday. She was looking forward to some one-on-one time with her closest friend. They shared a special relationship, and Barb had been anxious to spend some time with her to see how she was doing.

But Barb was also a bit concerned for Brad. She knew that there would be a significant gap in his life with Al gone, at least for a while. She asked him, "I know you and Al went to lunch often and were able to confide in one another. How difficult is this going to be for you? Is there anything I can do?"

"Oh Barb, I don't know how it's going to be. Difficult, I'm sure. Just be here for me, like you always are. I appreciate the way we can talk about anything together."

"Absolutely. Even so, I'm sure there are things you would rather talk about with Al, uh, guy things.... I'm just so sorry. Just talk to me if you find yourself struggling."

Brad looked deep into her brown eyes. "Have I ever told you how much I appreciate you?" he asked. He had to blink a tear away.

"Yes, you have," she said, squeezing his hand.

Pulling into their driveway after the meal, Brad noticed a tall Sprinter van parked on the street a couple of doors down from their house. This was unusual, as the house lots in their 1970s neighborhood were generous in size with plenty of room for parking, although a person driving would really have to look to realize that there even were homes among all of the trees.

When they got inside, Brad thought about the van again and went to the living room window and pulled back the curtain. It was gone. Maybe a neighbor had some guests who opted to park in the street, he thought. He returned to the bedroom and went straight to bed. He and Barb were both exhausted, and she had to be at work early the next morning.

Saturday dawned. Brad felt lazy. There was plenty to do, but he didn't much feel like doing anything. He drove to the grocery store to pick up what they needed for dinner. Then he plopped down in his recliner and watched college football until Barb got home and they got busy with meal preparations.

The evening with Linda was pleasant. She was obviously tired, but Brad knew that Linda felt comfortable there. They had agreed not to ask about her future plans just yet. During dinner Brad asked, "Yesterday you mentioned that Al was consumed by something. He never let on to me anything like that. Did he say anything more to you about it, other than telling you it was a big deal?"

"No. That's it. It was just cryptic enough to make me mad. I don't want to go there again. Why do you ask?"

"Just curious," Brad lied. "I got to thinking that maybe I should have gotten those file folders back to the office on Friday."

"I wouldn't know about that. Someone probably would've called me if it was important."

Brad changed the subject. "So how are the kids getting their cars home from college?"

"They're both flying back in a couple of days to meet with their professors to get their remaining work for the semester. They'll drive back by the end of the week."

"It is wonderful that their professors are working with them.... Why don't you stay with us while they are gone?" Barb offered. "I'll bet your house is pretty lonely right now."

"Oh, you're such a sweetheart, but I can't. I'm going back to work Monday, and I need to start adjusting."

They played a few hands of hearts after dessert, and then it was time for Linda to go. As she left, Brad and Barb told her again that they were there for her if she needed anything at all.

CHAPTER 4

BRAD GOT TO WORK AT EIGHT-THIRTY ON MONDAY
morning. As promised, he dropped off the files with Al's boss, Cathy Hoover.

Cathy thanked him. "Oh, you have made my day. We were looking for files on all the companies Al had been working with last week
and, obviously, we couldn't put our hands on these. It would have been
embarrassing to require our clients to do some re-work with us if they
didn't show up."

Brad credited Linda Johnson for Cathy's good fortune. She asked
about how Linda was doing, and they talked about Al a little bit. Brad
could tell that Cathy was an impressive woman. Al had told him that she
was a technology genius and how blessed he was to be able to work for
her. She seemed to be a positive person, and for a techie, Brad thought her
communication skills were great. She was slender but obviously muscular.
Al also said she was involved in CrossFit and regularly participated in
fitness competitions.

Brad was always impressed by people who were good at their jobs
and also able to spend time staying fit. He could never get motivated to
exercise in the mornings, and by the end of the day at GCI he was wasted
and had no desire to work out.

He took the elevator to the eighth floor and settled in at his desk.
He still hadn't allowed himself to dwell on the precinct-level document,
but it was never far from his mind. At a quarter to ten his phone rang.
"Tillman," he announced into the speaker on his desk.

"Hey Brad, this is Eric Blas," he heard. The voice was flat and to the
point. "Cathy gave me the files you picked up from Al's wife last week. Are
you sure there weren't any others there?"

"Others?" Brad's mind went to the one file he'd kept. Had he misjudged by holding on to that piece of paper? He thought hard about it. If someone knew the vote count before the election, who was it and how did they know? Was there any legitimate explanation besides election fraud? If it was fraud, did someone know Al had that document?

"Yeah," Blas said slowly. "Cathy asked me to organize everything Al was working on so it can be reassigned to others in the department."

Brad decided to hold back. "No, is there something specific you're looking for?"

"No."

"Well, I gave Cathy the files that were in Al's briefcase."

"You're sure?" Blas challenged.

"Blas, if there's something you're looking for, tell me what it is, and I'll go to Al's house and see if I can find it."

"No, I'm just trying to be thorough. Later." He hung up.

Brad sat motionless for thirty seconds. *What was that about?* he thought. That back and forth felt like an elaborate dance with each of them trying to get the other to commit to something first. Neither wanted to disclose what he knew. A knot formed in the pit of his stomach. *What's happening here? Was that Eric Blas's document?*

He went back to work reviewing some spending reports he'd requested but couldn't concentrate on anything. He forced himself to make some phone calls. He found it easier to focus on work when talking to others.

He went to lunch alone, walking to a downtown cafe he and Al had frequented. He ordered a Reuben with chips, poured himself a Coke from the soft drink machine, and sat at a two-person table that barely had space for one. Between nibbles he gazed at his phone, not sure what he expected to see there. His mind was now completely focused on the precinct paper.

"Hi Brad," a voice interrupted his thoughts. "How are you doing? I'm sure you miss your lunch partner. We are all missing him a lot."

Brad looked up to see Jennifer Bradley standing in front of him, tray in hand. The only things on it were balled-up napkins and a cup, so she had finished eating and was on her way out. Jennifer was the administrative assistant who supported Al and several others on the third floor. They knew each other fairly well through conversations shared when Brad stopped in to pick Al up for lunch. Jennifer was in her early thirties and had a tattoo of a contemporary cross on the inside of her right arm. She wore a very thin ring on the left side of her nose. Al had told him that she was the kind of person who anticipated his needs and took action even before he asked. He described her as his "Radar O'Reilly," the super competent clerk on the old MASH television show. "The difference was," he had said, "that she was always upbeat and offered a kind word to everyone."

"Hi, Jennifer. I'm just fine. I saw you at the funeral last week and intended to say hello, but before I could you were gone."

"Yes, a group of us from the office were there together and couldn't stay very long."

He gazed thoughtfully at her for a second. "Have you got a minute? There's something I'd like to ask you."

Jennifer looked over at the woman she was with. "Sure, Brad. Tammy, you go ahead. I'll be along in a few minutes." She emptied her tray in the trash container and stacked it with the others already in place. Returning to the table, she pulled up the chair and sat on a corner of it. "What's up?"

"Thanks, Jennifer. I'd just like to ask you a few questions. But before I do, can you agree to hold this conversation in the strictest confidence?"

Jennifer cocked her head slightly and slid the rest of the way back into the chair. With a questioning look in her eyes, she slowly said, "Okay."

Brad looked directly into her eyes. "Thank you for your trust. Now, did Al seem distracted that week before he died? Did you notice anything unusual?"

"No, not really. He was very busy, but he didn't bring me much work. He did seem more serious than usual, but he got that way when he was up against a deadline or something like that."

"I know this is a strange question, but does anyone on the third floor seem to have a lot going on outside of work? You know, like outside calls that others can't hear?"

She rolled her eyes. "Oh, that would be Eric Blas. Everybody thinks he has some kind of tech business on the side and is trying to run it while he's at work."

"What makes people think that?"

"Well, he comes to work late a lot. He's always whispering on his cell phone. Sometimes he gets a call and closes his office door before he says much. I mean, everyone does that occasionally, but it's a regular thing with him. *And* he leaves early!" she added with a trace of disgust in her voice.

Brad reached across the table and touched her hand. "Thank you, Jennifer. Please remember what I said about keeping this between us."

She looked at him curiously. "Well, was what I said helpful?"

"I can't say right now, but I'll let you know if I have any more questions. The best thing for you to do is forget we had this talk. I'm kicking something around that could really stir up a hornet's nest if it came to light. I'd hate for that to happen if my intuition is wrong."

"Okay," she said hesitantly. "Anything I can do to help."

"Thanks."

"Well, I'd better get back to the office. It's good to see you, Brad."

"You too, Jennifer. Take care."

With that, Brad could no longer even pretend to work. He couldn't think of anything except the election numbers from the document in Al's briefcase. He returned to the office, packed up his briefcase, and headed home.

Tommy called the number given him. "He seems to stay pretty close to home and work. His backyard is mostly out of sight of the neighbors, and there are some big trees that could use trimming. If I can catch him at home alone, I could arrange an accident."

"Arrange it."

"Sir?"

"What?"

"How permanent do you want this to be?"

"Same as before."

The line went dead.

CHAPTER 5

AS HE DROVE HOME, BRAD THOUGHT ABOUT THE SCOPE and impact of his discovery. If someone could manipulate the results of a state election before the votes were cast, then they could pick winners and losers and potentially impact policy without ever running for office. He thought about the possibility of manipulating all election results: local, state, and national. It would take a mammoth organization to monitor and manipulate things down to the local level nationwide. He didn't know how something like that could exist in secret. One whistleblower on the inside would bring the whole thing down.

Suddenly a thought hit him that almost made him physically ill. He swerved into a shopping center parking lot and stopped. What if Al's death wasn't an accident? Might someone have discovered that Al had that document? Would they commit murder to keep him quiet? If they did have the potential for manipulating votes on a large scale, their power to manipulate the direction of the entire country would be extraordinary. If there was potential for being exposed, what other choice would they have?

He sat in the car for several minutes with his face in his hands. What had Al gotten him into? No, that wasn't fair; Al didn't give him the document. He thought that maybe before he got any more involved with this he should destroy the document and be done with it. He told himself to slow down and think. Who knows what this document really represents? Maybe the information on the website is wrong, or maybe the actual vote tallies were never entered.

When he had composed himself, he put the car into gear and continued home. He needed to talk to someone. He needed someone to tell him that he was making too much out of this. Once inside the house, he grabbed a beer from the refrigerator and sat down at the kitchen table. *What do I need to do to think through this clearly?* he thought. The chance that he'd stumbled across a national conspiracy leading to murder seemed far-fetched.

The doorbell rang, and Brad looked at his phone. 1:57 p.m. He walked to the front door and opened it. A lanky guy, about thirty years old, stood there. His long hair was in a ponytail, and he wore a t-shirt with the Atlanta Metro Utilities logo emblazoned on the front.

"Good afternoon," he began. "I'm from Metro Utilities, and our systems indicate there's a gas leak somewhere on this block. As a precaution, we're checking all the homes along this street to make sure there are no issues. May I take a look at the gas line in your basement? It'll only take a minute." Brad looked over the man's shoulder and saw a white Sprinter van in the driveway. It was like the one he'd noticed the night before.

"Why aren't you in a Metro Utilities truck?" Brad asked.

"Oh, that's a rental. Someone in the head shed started retiring old vehicles before the new ones came in. Makes you wonder how much of your utility payment goes to waste, doesn't it?" The man shook his head.

Brad thought about turning the man away but then convinced himself that he was overreacting and waved him in.

As the man bent down to pick up his toolbox, his left shirttail came up and exposed what appeared to be the grip of a handgun. *Don't let him in!* Brad's mind screamed, but the man was already past him.

Brad, you idiot! he said to himself. Al was murdered, and he was next. His mind raced, realizing that nobody was around to help him. He had to do something, and fast. He pointed at the door to the basement stairs and led the man to it. He forced himself to ask, "Do you always carry a gun when you work?"

The man came up close to Brad and stopped. He set the toolbox down and said, "Oh, you mean this?" He pulled up his shirt with his left hand to reveal a pistol tucked into a holster inside his belt. As he reached for it with his right hand, Brad shoved him as hard as he could. Going for the gun had shifted the man's weight toward the top of the stairs, and the extra force sent him tumbling down into the basement.

Brad didn't wait to see what happened next. He jumped over the toolbox and ran out the front door. Without hesitating, he leaped the three feet from the porch down to the lawn. He immediately ran to the right, around the side of the house and towards the trees in back. Their home street was at the west perimeter of the subdivision, and behind it was a steep hill with pine trees leading down to another subdivision. He half-ran, half-stumbled down the incline to reach the cover of the trees as quickly as possible.

Once there, he stopped and leaned against the downhill side of the largest tree he could find. His chest pounded, and he gulped in air. He covered his mouth. He clenched his jaw tightly as he tried to slow his breathing down. *One – two – three – four – five*, he breathed in. He tightened his chest as he tried to breathe out slowly, but it didn't work. As he took in and exhaled the breaths he needed, he listened carefully for the sound of footsteps. At first, the only thing he could hear was the pounding of his own heart, so he waited a couple of minutes more. Nothing but the whistling of the wind. He knew he couldn't return to the house, but where could he go? He couldn't hide beneath this tree forever. As his breathing normalized, he became aware of the strong scent of pine trees and looked down to see the needles he was standing in. He thought that he could move pretty silently in this, but the needles could also cause his feet to slip out from underneath him.

Brad navigated the remainder of the hill as slowly and quietly as he could until he found himself in the backyard of a medium-sized home. It was a ranch-style house with brick siding and lots of windows. He thought one was the kitchen window, as it extended out from the house and had several potted plants on the inside sill. He couldn't see any movement inside. He looked one way and then the other, seeing backyard after backyard, each butting up against the base of the hill. A few were fenced, but most were not.

The yards were typical of the Atlanta area, long and narrow, about three-quarters of an acre and sprinkled with tall pines. It appeared that the street these homes faced ran parallel to Larkspur, his street just atop the hill. He'd never driven through this neighborhood, but he knew that the entrance was about a half mile west of the entrance to his own. He climbed back up the hill a bit to make himself hidden. He looked at his phone, which had been in his hands from the time his doorbell had rung. It was 2:11 p.m.

He sat behind some brush where he could still see the street. He listened carefully but heard nothing. What should he do? He certainly wasn't going back up the hill. What if he'd killed the guy? Maybe he really was looking for a gas leak and carried a gun for his own safety. How would a defense attorney handle that? How would Barb handle that? *Barbara!* She gets off work in less than an hour. She can't go home. What should he tell her? He tapped her work number. Putting the phone to his ear, he waited for the recording to finish telling him to hang up and call 911 in case of an emergency. Finally, he heard, "Northside Critical Care," and in as composed a voice as he could muster he asked, "Hi, is Barbara Tillman available? This is her husband, and it's important that I speak with her."

"Sure, I think I can arrange that. Just a minute." The operator put him on hold. After a brief time, Barb came on the line. "Barbara Tillman," she said.

"Hi, sweetheart," Brad said in as normal a voice as possible. "I don't have much time, but I'm afraid I have some bad news. We won't be able to go home tonight."

"You're kidding! Why not?"

"It appears we have a gas leak. They said we need to stay out until we're given the all-clear."

"Oh, that's a bummer. Can I at least swing by and get a change of clothes? And my phone charger!"

"I'm afraid not. The fire department won't let you in."

"What if I promise to hold my breath?" she said sweetly, then asked, "Where are we supposed to go?"

"I haven't gotten that far yet. Tell you what, why don't you go to Linda's house? I'm sure she wouldn't mind. Just wait there until you hear from me."

"Okay, that could work. When do you think we can get back in?"

"Not sure. Gotta go. I'll update you as soon as I can."

"All right. You be careful."

"Will do. Bye." He tapped the screen to end the call. As he looked up from the phone, he saw the Sprinter van driving slowly along the street. He instinctively ducked further behind the bushes to make sure he was fully hidden. He could see through the bush well enough to know that the van had stopped. Why would he stop there? He realized this meant the man had survived the tumble down the stairs, and he wasn't sure how he felt about that. The thick brush ran along the hillside as far as he could see. Remaining in a crouched position, he jogged north as quickly as he dared. When he ran out of brush, he stopped and listened. All he heard was the whirring of distant traffic. He kept scanning the backyards in case the driver appeared. Nothing. Then it was there again, almost in front of him between the houses. It stopped, and this time he could see the driver. It was "ponytail," and he was on his phone.

Why did he stop? Brad wondered. It seemed like he knew exactly where Brad was. Just then his phone went "ding" as a text message arrived. *Shit!* he said, almost out loud. He put his thumb on the button to turn off the phone and pressed it so tightly he thought it might break.

He immediately started edging back the way he had come. As soon as he was out of the van's line of sight, he crouched down so low he was touching the ground with one hand. He scurried up the hill to a tight cluster of trees and brush. He turned and focused on the corner of the house where he'd last seen the van. Ponytail was limping slowly past the house and peering straight up at the hill in front of him.

Brad froze and dropped all the way to the ground. Keeping perfectly still, he used his peripheral vision to scan the area. His nemesis limped a little farther toward the hill and stopped, looking side to side into the backyard landscapes. He turned and limped back around the house, presumably to the van.

Brad was taking no chances. He sat there for thirty-five minutes and watched the van drive up and down the street six times without stopping. After twenty minutes without a sighting, he began to relax. As he did, the full weight of what had just happened came over him like a flood. He began shaking uncontrollably. Tears filled his eyes as he sat there. He didn't try to stop them. How could this be happening? He was being hunted like prey. He just wanted to go home. But home was the last place he could go.

CHAPTER 6

BUT WAS THAT TRUE? PONYTAIL SEEMED TO HAVE LEFT. HE or someone else could be watching the house though. Brad wasn't about to show up there by himself. What would happen if he called the police? He could report the intruder and tell them what happened, but if he mentioned his suspicions about election fraud, they'd probably think he was nuts. He wasn't about to turn his phone back on, as he thought they were tracking it somehow. He wondered if they could monitor his calls and texts as well.

Brad carefully traversed down the hill to the closest non-fenced yard and walked slowly between two houses to the street in front. He paused and looked up and down the street. Three doors down, a car was turning into a driveway. He walked briskly to the home and up the drive, flagging the driver down before he could close the garage door.

"Sorry to bother you, but it's an emergency. I live at the top of the hill behind you on Larkspur. A guy with a gun was in my house when I got home, so I just took off running down the hill. Could I use your phone to call the police?"

The man's eyes widened. "Of course! Are you all right?" He handed his phone to Brad.

"Not really, but thanks," Brad said as he punched in 911.

It took a minute to explain why he was calling about an intrusion into his home from a different neighborhood, but the 911 dispatcher assured him that a patrol car would pick him up there and drive him home. A car picked him up as promised a few minutes later. When he and the officer arrived at his house, the front door was open, and they saw that a second police car had beaten them there. The officers asked Brad to wait outside while they went in and checked it out. He wasn't enthused about standing around, exposed. He stood close to a tree and kept his eyes open.

Once the officers confirmed that the house was empty, they asked him to come inside and explain as best as he could what had happened. He told them about seeing the Sprinter van the previous night and then in his driveway when the man with the ponytail had come to his door. He described how the man talked his way in and the handle of a pistol sticking out of his pants. He finally explained pushing the guy down the stairs and bolting out the door and down the hill. One of the officers contacted Metro Utilities and confirmed there was no gas leak in the area, nor were any of their technicians driving a Sprinter van.

"Looks like you lucked out," the officer said. "Had that been a real technician, you'd be staring at quite a lawsuit."

The investigation took a little over an hour, after which the police formally reported it as an armed home invasion. The officers told him it was unlikely they'd find the perpetrator, but they would provide his description to all area precincts. They would contact Brad if they needed him to make an identification. After the police left, Brad quickly packed a bag and gathered everything he could think of for the next day or two, including Barb's phone charging cord. He locked the house and drove away, not sure when he might return.

He had driven about five miles, unsure of where he was going, when he noticed that a Honda Pilot had been behind him for a few traffic lights. He turned left into a subdivision, and the Pilot continued straight. After driving through the residential area for a few minutes, he left using a different street than the one he'd entered from. He watched carefully to make sure he wasn't being followed. He noticed no one. He drove down random streets to a grocery store a couple of miles away, where he parked and went inside. There was a small deli area, and he bought some fried chicken, vegetables, and a bottle of water, then sat down to eat and think.

He could no longer deny that he was being targeted. Whoever was after him may not want to kill him, or the guy would've shot him when he answered the door. They were apparently able to track his phone, so that needed to stay off. He wondered if they were monitoring Barb as well. He probably shouldn't call her, even if it was from another phone.

His mind went to that phone call with Eric Blas. It sounded like he was looking for that document. Could he be behind this? According to Chuck Gleason, Blas was something of a radical and had been on the team that designed the voting system. Maybe he was part of an extremist group that wanted to manipulate elections. And if that was the case, they may be willing to do whatever it takes to keep it under wraps, including murder. The thought chilled Brad.

Another piece of the puzzle fit, because if Blas was one of GCI's best at cybersecurity, he'd probably find it easy to track Brad. Then he could have others do the dirty work. Brad needed to avoid being tracked, and he needed to touch base with Barb. He had to assume they knew that Barb was at Linda's house and were monitoring it, so what could he do?

If he and Barb were going to communicate, they needed to do it face to face, in secret. Either that or on phones Blas doesn't know about. Brad had watched enough crime shows on TV to assume that a person could buy cheap phones where you paid by the minute to talk, but he wasn't sure if they could be purchased and have phone numbers set up without being traced to an individual. He noticed a woman with her phone out at the table next to him. When she looked up, he asked, "I know this is an unusual request, but I'm in a jam and need to check something on the Internet. Might you possibly allow me to google something on your phone quickly?" He bit his lip. "Sorry to ask."

She thought for a few seconds, then smiled and said, "Sure. I have to leave in a couple of minutes, though."

"Thank you so much! That's all it should take." She handed him her phone. Fortunately, it was similar to his, so he was able to navigate to the web function quickly. Using his thumbs to type, he entered, "Can you buy a phone without a name attached?" The first response at the top of the browser read, "Unlike standard cell phone plans, you do not need to undergo a credit check, give your full name and address, or show your ID. Buying and activating a prepaid cell phone can be completely anonymous. While buying your phone at the store, ask the store clerk to activate the phone for you." He scrolled briefly down the page and saw hyperlinks entitled "throwaway phones" and similar phrases.

He deleted his question and returned the phone to the woman. "Thank you so much."

Brad left the store and went directly to his car, thinking of places to buy phones for himself and Barb. He pulled onto a four-lane road that was beginning to clear from rush-hour traffic. Almost immediately, in a well-lit area, he saw the Pilot behind him again. Without thinking, he pressed the gas pedal and accelerated. The Pilot stayed with him. Though he had no idea where he was going, he put the pedal to the floor and his turbocharger kicked in. The Audi moved ahead quickly, blasting through the forty-five miles per hour speed limit. The Pilot accelerated as well, but the driver couldn't keep up.

Seeing the gap grow between them, Brad kept his foot on the gas and his speed grew to sixty-five, then seventy. By now he was weaving in and out of traffic, and his pursuer seemed to be temporarily blocked in by traffic from both lanes. He kept his foot down; as his speedometer reached eighty, he flew past a Gwinnett County police car. The lights went on and the cop followed in hot pursuit. The driver of the Pilot saw what was happening, slowed down, and made a U-turn.

It took a minute, but Brad finally heard the siren and saw the flashing blue lights in his rearview mirror. He had never been so happy to get pulled over. He let off the gas and checked his mirrors to see if there was any sign of the Pilot, but between the darkness and the glare of the flashing lights, it was impossible to see anything. Even as he continued to slow, his mind was running once again. They must be tracking his car. How could he get away from these guys? He turned right and stopped on the side of a residential street. The police officer pulled up behind him.

It seemed to take forever for the officer to run Brad's license plate. Though he didn't move, Brad's mind was still at ninety miles per hour. He wondered what would happen next. Was the Pilot parked nearby just waiting to tail him again? Whoever it was appeared to be getting bolder. What about Barb? They must know where she is. He thought through his options. He could tell the police exactly what was going on. Would they believe him? If so, what could they do? Escort him home? The people after him were probably watching the house.

He couldn't stay with the car. Could he just walk away after the police left? Where would he go? How would he get there?

Maybe he could drive away and park the car someplace else, closer to MARTA, the above-ground rail station, where he could catch a train. But what about Barb? If they were monitoring her phone, they could listen in on any call he might make to her. He couldn't tell her where to go. He couldn't tell her where he was.

Brad figured that with a story like his, there was only so much the police could do. Could he trust them to sweep up Barb as well and protect them both? He didn't really like the thought of walking away, leaving his $45,000 car abandoned for who knows how long. Could he arrange a tow?

The endless questions twirled and spun in his mind. He closed his eyes and tried to breathe.

The officer got out of his car. He couldn't hide his anger as he stopped next to Brad's door. "Are you trying to kill somebody or just yourself? I need to see your license, registration, and insurance."

"I apologize, officer. I don't know what to say," Brad said as he fumbled for the documents. "You probably won't believe this, but some guy in a black Honda Pilot was chasing me. I was afraid and maybe overreacted."

"Did you get his license number?"

"No sir."

Just then a second patrol car pulled up and parked in front of Brad. Once that officer stepped from his car, the first said to Brad, "Please step out of your vehicle." When he complied, the officer said, "Are you familiar with the Georgia Super Speeder Law?"

"No sir."

"Well, you're about to become very familiar with it. I clocked you at eighty-seven miles per hour." He glanced down at Brad's license. "Have you taken any medication recently, or have you used marijuana or any another substance that could affect your driving, Mr. Tillman?"

"No sir."

"Have you been drinking, Mr. Tillman?"

Brad thought to himself, *DUI?* That could get him out of here and get the car towed as well. He said to the officer, "I had a couple beers earlier."

The second officer said, "Mr. Tillman, would you please follow me?"

As they walked to the open space between the Audi and the forward patrol car, the first patrolman returned to his car with Brad's documents.

"Please look directly at my forehead, Mr. Tillman."

Brad did so. The officer then began to move his right arm up and down, out and back. He repeated the actions with his left arm.

Brad just stood there staring.

"Thank you, Mr. Tillman. Now walk toward me and follow my directions."

As Brad complied, the officer told him to turn left and then left again. He told him to turn right and then to stop. Brad figured he was looking for signs of intoxication, so he feigned a bit of awkward imbalance.

"Thank you, Mr. Tillman. Please stand still, pick up your left foot, and balance on your right." As Brad followed the directions, the officer told him to look above his head and then asked Brad to move one arm in front of him, then out to his side. Then the other arm.

Brad kept putting his raised foot down to steady himself, although he didn't really need to.

"Thank you, Mr. Tillman. Please stay here and lean against your hood. Keep your hands where we can see them. I'll be right back."

He walked to the other patrol car and spoke to his cohort for a minute.

Brad thought about what he was doing. Why didn't he just tell them the truth? He just didn't know what they would do. Would they just let him go and tell him to be careful? Right now, he needed to get away from his car safely.

Brad stood and turned around so he could see both officers. He paced a bit with his hands on his hips.

One of the officers said loudly, "Please lean against your hood and keep your hands where we can see them, Mr. Tillman."

Brad did as he was told. He leaned against his car, smelling the tar from the street and looking around at the surrounding houses. He didn't think that he and the police were drawing much attention. He could feel his heart racing, but he kept telling himself that he would be safe in police custody.

Both officers returned. The first said, "Mr. Tillman, we'd like for you to take a breathalyzer test to determine the amount of alcohol in your system."

"I will not agree to that, sir," Brad said, knowing full well that this was, in effect, an acknowledgment of guilt. The officer explained as much to him, but Brad still refused the test.

With that, one of the officers charged Brad with DUI. He read him his rights and put him in handcuffs. Brad was advised that his car would be towed to the police impound lot and that he would have to pay to get it back once he was released from custody. Brad asked about his briefcase and suitcase. The officer placed them in the trunk of the Audi and said they would be secure there.

When they arrived at the precinct, the police put Brad in a cell and then brought him out to make his phone call and for processing. Now he had to figure out how to get out of this predicament, but at least he was safe.

CHAPTER 7

ONCE HE'D BEEN PROCESSED, BRAD WAS ALLOWED TO make his phone call. He'd been thinking through this while in the patrol car. Whoever was following him would know the police had stopped him, so calling Barb to tell her where he was would give them no information they didn't already have.

He looked at the clock on the wall and saw that it was ten-thirty p.m. He dialed Barb's cell number and she answered immediately.

"Hi Barb, it's me."

"Bradley, where are you? What took you so long to call?"

"I'm fine, but I need your help. Don't panic, but I'm at the police station. I've been arrested for DUI."

"What?" She raised her voice. "You were out drinking while I've been sitting up worried about you?"

"Look, calm down. We can discuss this when you come pick me up. Right now, I need you to find an attorney. I'm at the Gwinnett County Police Precinct on Crescent Drive. Find an attorney online and send them here. Then head down, and I'll explain everything."

"How do I reach you if I need to?"

"You can't. Just call an attorney and come on down."

"Bradley, I can't believe you! I have to be at work at seven in the morning! What's gotten into you?"

"I understand. Try to calm down. I just need you to do what I said."

It took her an hour to get to the police precinct. When she arrived, she was unable to see him immediately. The police provided them with a private place to talk once the attorney also arrived.

33

Cynthia Goldberg was a heavy-set woman who was professionally dressed, yet her hair and make-up revealed the lateness of the hour. She introduced herself to Brad and Barb, and they all sat down around the small table.

Brad began to explain, "Look, I'm not under the influence of alcohol. I had about three swallows of beer at two this afternoon. I pretended to be under the influence to get arrested because I am in danger."

Both women raised their eyebrows.

"This is going to be a long story, but you need to hear it from the beginning." Looking at Cynthia, he added, "Unfortunately, most of this may seem to be irrelevant to why you're here, but you need to hear the background."

With that, Brad started at the beginning, describing the piece of paper he'd found in Al's briefcase, his discovery of possible election fraud, his suspicion that Al may have been murdered, and the apparent attempt on his own life.

"Whoever is following me seems to have the ability to track my phone and car. When I was trying to get away from them and the cops pulled me over for speeding, this was the only way I could think of to get away from my car and to a secure location." He hesitated and then said, "I faked some balance issues when they gave me the DUI drill and then refused the breathalyzer test."

Halfway through his account, Barb's eyes and mouth were open wide, her hands covering her cheeks. The tears began to flow as he finished, so he stood and pulled her to him, saying, "I'm so sorry, but I just wasn't sure about any of this until this afternoon."

"Oh Brad, I was furious when I came down here, but now I'm scared to death! You've told the police, haven't you?"

"Well, not really. I don't know what to tell them. Obviously they know about the guy at the house, and I told them someone was chasing me tonight, but I don't know enough about why these people are targeting me."

"They still need to know. Can't they put you in witness protection or something?"

Brad cringed and said, "I imagine it's a little early for that." As they sat back down, he looked at Cynthia and asked, "What do you suggest we do about this DUI thing?"

Frowning and shaking her head, the lawyer responded, "Congratulations, Mr. Tillman! You have topped anything I've ever come across in twenty years as a defense attorney. But the first order of business is to get you out of here. We won't need to make a plea until the arraignment hearing. That'll give us some time to sort this out. This afternoon's incident at your house should be in police files, so your story may not sound too far-fetched."

"Okay," Brad said. "I'll leave all that to you. Right now, I need to figure out how Barb and I can disappear."

Barb gasped. "You think they're after me too?"

"Well, I've been careful not to say anything to you about any of this when we've talked on the phone. However, if they think you know something, it's anyone's guess what they might do. We can't take any chances."

Cynthia got up and said, "I'm going to arrange for your release. It may require some bail money."

"Can I put it on a credit card?"

"Yes," she said as she left the room.

Barb fiddled with her hands. "What are we going to do?"

"We need to find someplace to go that they don't know about. That rules out family, as well as Linda's place."

They sat silent for a few minutes, then Brad sat up abruptly. "Do we know anyone who has moved, with their house empty and still on the market?"

Barb shook her head. He couldn't think of anyone either. After a few more minutes Barbara offered, "A coworker of mine and her husband are going to visit his family in Peru. Maybe we could offer to be house sitters."

"When do they leave?"

"Tomorrow night ..." Barb looked at her watch. "Tonight."

"Do you know how to reach her at home? We can't get anyone at the hospital involved."

"I have her cell number."

"That could work. You could tell her about our "gas leak" and ask if we could house sit for them. Kind of a win-win."

"It's after midnight. I can't call her now."

"Okay, let's see if Cynthia can help us get someplace where we can't be found tonight." Brad thought for a moment. "On the other hand, we can't just walk out of here, even with Cynthia. They must be expecting that."

CHAPTER 8

BRAD AND BARB TALKED WHILE THEY WAITED. HE TOLD her to turn off her phone. She had trouble grasping all that Brad had told her—they weren't people who interacted with criminals. Brad being threatened and chased was simply beyond what she could fathom. She asked question after question.

This was new to Brad too. However, he was an accountant. He knew how to think logically. He also knew that they needed to stay hidden. He and Barb tried to prioritize what they needed to do once he was released. They needed to find someplace safe to go and a way to get there without being followed. They needed new phones.

"Money," Brad said. "If he can track us through a cell phone and my car, could Blas monitor our financial transactions? If we use our ATM card, will he know where we're using it? What about our credit cards?"

It was well after midnight. Brad rubbed his eyes. He was starting to lose focus. Barb said, "Look, we have to find a place to sleep tonight. We should talk about all this with clearer minds in the morning."

Just then, Cynthia returned. "Okay, bail has been set at 200 dollars because of your safe driving record up until now. Come with me, and we can get that taken care of. Then you'll be free to go."

Brad said, "Thanks, but we have another problem. Whoever is after me surely knows where I am since they saw me get stopped and, if they are tracking Barb's phone, may have heard my call to her. We can't just walk out of here."

"Well," responded Cynthia, "I don't know how I can help with that. You need the police." When Brad nodded, she added, "I'll see who can join us."

A few minutes later, she returned with an officer who they had not yet met. "This is Sergeant Swanson. He was just heading home but agreed to see you."

Swanson was tall and lean, his voice deep and rich. His face was friendly, but the size of him was a bit intimidating.

"Sergeant, thanks for doing this. My wife and I are in a very difficult situation and have reason to believe that our lives are in danger."

Swanson looked at them both closely for a moment and said, "I see. Can you tell me how you've come to this conclusion?"

With that, Brad began again. He walked through the entire story, making clear that the police files should be able to corroborate the possible attempt on his life the previous day. He even described the potential election fraud he had uncovered that seemed to be the catalyst for all of this, but he stopped short of mentioning who he thought to be involved.

As he described his decision to feign intoxication during the police stop, Swanson's face reddened noticeably. Brad could tell he was angry and wondered if telling him had been a good idea.

With a voice that did not reflect his rise in blood pressure, Swanson spoke. "Mr. Tillman, this police department is here for the protection of our citizens. You may have heard that, largely due to political antics, we have a shortage of officers on this force. You have just wasted the time of two officers and others in this precinct by acting out your little game."

Brad's heart sunk as he was declared guilty of something he had never even considered. He respected law enforcement and knew that they had been demonized to the point that it was difficult to recruit good people to the force. Though he felt he had a legitimate reason, he could understand the officer's point.

"Sergeant Swanson, I am so sorry. I didn't intend to be a distraction to your officers. I guess I was in a difficult situation and didn't have time to think through the impact of what I was doing. I really do feel threatened and think we need to disappear from these people's radar."

"Mr. Tillman, you might be surprised to know that police officers are able to handle the truth. Don't go anywhere." With that, he left the room.

Brad put his elbows on the table and his face in his hands. "Well, that went differently than I expected!"

Barb said, "I can't believe he talked to you that way."

"He has a very valid point," Brad said.

"They have an impossible job to do, and I imagine this type of thing suggests to them both disrespect and a lack of trust," added Cynthia.

They all sat quietly for a minute, not knowing what to do or say. Brad turned to Cynthia, "Might this mean there could be other charges coming my way?"

The attorney shrugged. Brad could tell she thought there could be but didn't want to add to the gloom of the moment.

After ten minutes, the sergeant returned to the room. "Mr. Tillman, I have confirmed the incident at your home yesterday afternoon. However, what you've described as a possible motive would make this an FBI matter. I can provide you with the local number. As for your DUI charge, you will have to address your defense with a judge. You are free to go once you have paid the fine."

"Yes sir, I would appreciate that FBI number. I'm concerned that this police station is being watched, even as we speak. Is there any way you could help us get away from here undetected?"

"Mr. Tillman, perhaps I didn't make myself clear earlier. Every time I pull officers away from their patrol, they are unavailable to respond to possible emergency situations.... Here is what I would do if I were in your shoes. There is a back door out of the precinct and a back lot that is not visible from the street. I would ask my attorney to leave and drive away as if she were going home. She could drive around for fifteen minutes or so to ensure she is not being followed. Behind the back lot, there is a three – or four-foot block wall that separates the precinct from the shopping center behind. In about twenty minutes, we can let you out that door. If you can manage getting up the wall and navigating some thick bushes, you could meet Ms.—." He paused and looked at Cynthia.

"Goldberg," she offered.

"You could meet Ms. Goldberg in the parking lot and be off."

Swanson turned to Cynthia and said, "In the meantime, if you think you are being followed, call the precinct, and we will dispatch a car to assist."

The attorney nodded.

With no further discussion, Sergeant Swanson walked out of the room.

Brad looked at Cynthia with pleading eyes, "Would you do that for us?"

With uncertainty in her voice Cynthia replied, "I suppose I could. Where do you want me to take you?"

"Well, maybe a hotel or something with a discount department store within walking distance. Someplace not too close to our house."

Cynthia got up from her seat and said, "I better leave now."

"Thank you so much, Ms. Goldberg. I appreciate you coming out so late at night and your willingness to help. But there's one more thing. Barb and I both need to call in to work to let them know we won't be in tomorrow. May we use your phone?"

"If they're watching, they may have already connected you with me. Do you think it might be better to use the precinct phone?"

A rush of anxiety swept over Brad. His voice wavered. "Oh, you may be right. I don't know what to do."

Cynthia took Brad and Barb into the clerk's area so they could pay the bail. She asked the clerk if the precinct phones were more secure than regular phone systems, but he didn't know. Cynthia found Sergeant Swanson and explained the situation. He took a deep breath, as if to say, "What now?" He gave her his cell phone for the calls.

Before dialing, Brad suggested to Barb that she say there's a family emergency that would likely keep her out for several days. No details now, but a promise to update them later. Barb called the hospital and spoke to the floor lead nurse, who promised to pass the message along to her supervisor at shift change. Brad called Keith Hughes, his boss, and left a message on his work voicemail box.

Cynthia looked at her watch. "I will meet you in the shopping center parking lot at a little after three." Then she was off.

Brad and Barbara walked over to Sergeant Swanson to return the phone. They asked who would be taking them to the back door at the appropriate time. Swanson told them to return to the conference room. He would have someone get them shortly. As promised, at 2:55 a.m., an officer came in and said, "Follow me." He let them out through the back door and pointed to the wall and hill that the Sergeant had mentioned.

Brad thanked him as they walked out. "Can you do this?" he asked Barbara.

She rolled her eyes, put her back to the wall, and hoisted herself up to a sitting position on the wall. She turned toward the hill and scrambled on her hands and knees up and into the heavy brush. Brad used his hands to jump up to a kneeling position on the wall and followed behind her.

"Ouch," he could hear her mutter.

As Brad got into the brush, he could feel sharp twigs scrape against him. He worried about Barb. He hated that she was involved now. He wondered what she was feeling. He was sure he would find out soon enough.

They got through the brush and stayed low as they approached the parking lot. Fifty yards away, they saw a car parked with no lights on. Brad looked at Barb and whispered, "I guess we should have asked her what kind of car she drives."

Barb gave him *the look*.

"Well, there is only one way to find out if it's her."

He took Barb by the hand, and they hurried to the car, running in a stooped position as if they were trying to stay below cover. Brad looked in the driver's window and was relieved to see the attorney. He opened the back door, and they crawled in quickly. Cynthia drove around the center of the lot to exit onto the main thoroughfare. Brad's heart beat rapidly as they watched for a sign of someone following. Nothing.

Brad told Cynthia that he knew of a hotel across the street from a store that would likely sell the phones Brad was looking for. They arrived within ten minutes, and Cynthia drove into the covered entrance and stopped. She turned to face them in the backseat and said, "You don't need me for anything else tonight. I'll need to be able to reach you, though."

Brad and Barb thanked her profusely for all she had done, then Brad added, "I'm thinking I will get several prepaid phones. I can send you one, along with our new phone numbers, so we can talk when necessary."

"Okay, let's talk very soon. We have an arraignment hearing to deal with.... You two take care of yourselves. I hope this gets resolved quickly."

"Thanks again," Barb said. "I'll make sure he gets a phone to you right away."

Brad was concerned about using his credit card at the hotel. He turned to Barb and asked, "How much cash do you have on you?"

"I think I have a little over sixty dollars."

"Good, I have five twenties."

They went inside and talked to the night clerk. Brad told her that they would be prepaying in cash. The clerk didn't see a problem with that. She calculated the payment and gave them an amount. They pooled their funds and paid the $105.27. At that point, the clerk asked for a credit card.

"Why do you need that?" Brad asked. "We just paid you."

"I need a card in case there are ancillary charges."

"Look, it's three-thirty in the morning. We don't have a credit card. I promise we won't incur any charges and that we'll check out first thing in the morning. There won't be anything to pay, but we have cash if needed."

The clerk hesitated, but Brad handed her his driver's license and assured her that they would take care of things in the morning. She took the license and gave them their keys. Brad and Barb took the elevator to the second floor and found their room. They washed up quickly and crawled into bed. For the first time in eighteen hours, Brad was able to let go. The last thing he heard was Barb whisper, "Poor Al. And poor Linda!" Within minutes he was fast asleep.

CHAPTER 9

BRAD WOKE UP AND LOOKED AT THE CLOCK NEXT TO THE bed—7:18 a.m. His mind immediately returned to their predicament as he got up, showered, and dressed. Leaving Barb a note, he quietly left the room and took the stairs to the lobby. He grabbed a banana from the breakfast bar and walked to the department store, trying to think through their phone needs. He and Barb would each need one, and he had promised to get one for their new attorney. He'd figure out how to get it to her later.

At the store's electronics section, he found the phones locked inside glass cabinets, so he located a sales assistant. He decided to buy four phones, just to be sure.

"These are for my entire family," Brad said. "We're trying something new."

"Great! Will you be transferring existing numbers to these phones?"

"Nope. Any numbers will be fine."

"Okay. It'll take about twenty minutes to get them set up, so you can do some other shopping while you wait."

Brad nodded and headed to the men's department, where he found some underwear and jogging clothes. Then he went to the women's section and picked out the same for Barb. He could never remember if she was a medium or a large. That could change based upon the type of clothes she was buying. He described her to the sales associate, who helped him decide.

He returned to Electronics. All the phones were ready with a label on each showing its number. He placed the clothing on the counter, and the associate rang up everything together. At that moment he thought about the credit card transaction.

"Do you know how long it takes for a transaction to show up in online banking systems?" he asked. "I'm trying to make this a little surprise for my wife."

"The system checks your credit availability immediately, but in my experience purchases don't hit the bank until the next business day."

"Great," Brad said, as he handed her his card. Once the transaction was finished, he thanked her and turned and headed toward the exit.

When he got back to the room, Barb was getting out of the shower. "I called Judy Alvarez. They loved the idea of having us in their home while they're gone. I also texted Linda to let her know we're okay but might be out of pocket for a few days."

Brad froze. "You sent a text? You turned on your cell phone?"

"Linda says she has morning staff meetings, so I couldn't call her. As far as she knew, I disappeared without a trace last night. I wanted her to know I was okay. I turned off the phone as soon as I finished."

"Did you call your friend on the cell phone too?"

"No, I looked up her number on my phone, but I called on the hotel phone."

"Has the hotel phone rang this morning?"

"No."

"Okay. Get dressed as quickly as you can. We need to get out of here. They're probably on the way if they aren't here already."

Barb closed her eyes. "I only turned my phone on for a minute to send a short text!"

"That's about fifty-nine seconds more than they needed," Brad said as he went to the window to look outside.

"Oh Brad, what have I done? I'm so sorry!"

"Don't dwell on it. We just need to get out of here, and we need to do it quickly. We also need to be careful, Barb. I know this is all new to us, but we should discuss things and be aware of consequences before doing anything. You'll probably keep me from making mistakes as well. Let's go!"

Tommy's phone rang, waking him from a deep sleep.

"Yeah," he answered.

"We just located his wife's phone at the Comfort Inn on Roosevelt and 103rd. He also just charged something at the store across the street from there."

"I'll get there as soon as I can."

"Let's be careful here. I don't know what his wife's involvement is, but things are getting a bit more complicated. Update me before you take any action."

Tommy hung up.

They grabbed the shopping bags with the phones and clothes. Before leaving, Brad picked up the room phone and called the front desk. "Do you have a shuttle that goes to the airport?" The operator said they did, but it was just getting ready to leave. The next one would be in an hour, at ten a.m.

"We can be down there in two minutes flat. Please hold it for us!" Brad begged. "I can't tell you how important it is that we be on that shuttle!"

The desk attendant said, "Two minutes is all we can do. Other guests have to catch flights too."

Brad slammed the phone down and they took off. Instead of waiting for the elevator, they ran down the stairs through the lobby and out the front door. It took just over a minute. They jumped onboard and thanked the driver and the other passengers for waiting.

As the shuttle departed, Brad looked out the window and watched as the white Sprinter van pulled into the driveway and parked. He turned away quickly to hide his face from the driver. It was Ponytail. Brad told Barb, and she began to panic.

He took her hand. "It's okay. We need to stay calm. He can't know we're on the shuttle. It looked like he was parking."

Tommy walked into the hotel and asked if there was a house phone he could use. The front desk attendant pointed to the phone on an end table next to the couch. He strode over, sat down, and picked up the phone.

The hotel operator answered.

Tommy said, "Hi, may I have Brad and Barbara Tillman's room please?"

"One moment please."

The phone began ringing and continued to ring with no answer. He put the phone down and thought for a moment.

Returning to his feet, he walked back to the front desk. "Hi. I was supposed to pick up Brad and Barbara Tillman this morning. I just tried their room but got no answer. Is there any other place they could be waiting?"

The attendant pointed to the breakfast area where there were only two people eating the continental breakfast and one employee bussing the tables. Then she said, "Wait a minute."

She looked at her call log to see where the urgent call to hold the shuttle had come from. She looked up at Tommy and said, "I'm pretty sure they're on the airport shuttle that just left."

Tommy pushed autodial on his phone and put it to his ear as he ran to the van.

"Hello."

"It seems they are on the shuttle to the airport. I am about five or ten minutes behind them."

There was a pause. "Any idea what airline?"

"No."

"I'll get back to you." The line went dead.

Brad had turned again and watched Ponytail walk into the hotel. He thought for a minute, then moved across the center aisle next to another guy on board the shuttle. "What airline are you taking?" he asked the man.

"Delta."

"Great!" Brad exclaimed in relief. "I'll bet your ticket has a phone number on it, doesn't it?"

The man held up his phone and pulled up the Delta app. He tapped the screen a couple times and found a phone number for Delta reservations.

"Perfect!" Brad pulled out a business card, turned it over, and asked Barb if she had a pen. Instead, the man pulled a pen from his shirt pocket and Brad wrote down the number. "Thank you so much!" He returned the pen and looked ahead to see the ramp to the freeway about half a mile ahead. He waved Barb up to where he was standing and motioned to the front of the shuttle.

"I know you're not going to believe this, but we need to get off the shuttle now, please," he said to the driver.

The driver gave him a peculiar look. "I'm not supposed to let passengers on or off except at the hotel and the airport."

Brad pulled out his wallet and handed him a twenty.

The driver pulled over and let them off in front of a convenience store and gas station. Brad grabbed Barb's arm and said, "Run!" They scurried into the convenience store and turned to look out the window.

"Sweetheart, I just need you to do one thing for me." He pointed to the spot where they'd just gotten off the shuttle. "Don't take your eyes off that street. If you see a white Sprinter van, tell me right away."

"A what?"

"A tall white van with no windows in the back."

"Okay, but where are you going? You'd better not leave me!"

"I'll be right here. I just need to buy our airline tickets."

"Where are we going? Why did we get off the bus?"

Brad grabbed one of the new phones and dialed the number on the back of his card. He raised his hand to Barb and pointed to the street.

He was on hold for five minutes. At the same time the reservationist came on the line, Barb tapped him on the shoulder and pointed at a white van passing by. It wasn't the right one, but he whispered, "Good, keep watching."

He said to the reservation agent, "Good morning. I'm at the Atlanta airport, and my wife and I need to get to Orlando as soon as possible. What's the earliest flight we can get?"

After a pause, the agent provided him with some options, all of which departed after three p.m.

"I'm afraid that's too late. Have you got anything going elsewhere in central Florida that leaves earlier?"

The agent informed him there was a flight to Daytona Beach that left in forty-five minutes, at 10:10 a.m.

"Perfect," he said. As he did, Barb tapped his shoulder again. He looked up to see the Sprinter van drive by without slowing down. He gave her a thumbs-up and mouthed, "Keep watching."

He provided the necessary information to the agent, including his credit card number. He assured her that she could email their boarding passes to him and that they'd make it to the gate in time. He ended the call, gave Barb a hug, and heaved a big sigh of relief.

"Why are we going to Florida?" she asked.

"We aren't, but hopefully the guy in the white van will think we are!"

Barb grinned broadly and squeezed his arm tightly. "That was some quick thinking!" she said proudly.

"Well, it's going to take more than that to get us through this, but maybe it'll throw them off our trail for a while. The second van you saw was the one with the bad guys."

His phone rang. "Tommy," he said.

"They just bought a ticket on Delta for Daytona Beach. There is nothing you can do at the airport. Let's back off and see what happens. I can monitor his card transactions."

"As you wish," Tommy replied and ended the call.

Brad and Barb spent a few more minutes in the store, using the restrooms and buying coffee and breakfast burritos. They ate their breakfast on a bench outside the front door of a nearby office building. Once they finished their meal, it was time to plan the rest of the day.

CHAPTER 10

BARBARA SCRUNCHED UP THE PAPERS FROM THEIR burritos and tossed them in a waste bin nearby. She returned to the bench and asked, "What now?"

Brad fished the receipt out of the clothing bag and turned it over. He asked Barb for a pen and something to write on. She handed him the pen and her handbag, which was soft leather but would do for now.

He said, "First of all, we'll need money. I have twenty-eight bucks left in my wallet. How about you?"

"I have a twenty. I gave you the rest last night."

"And the other thing is, we need to figure out transportation."

"Can't we use Uber?" They had occasionally used the service to take them to the airport or on a night out when they thought they may be drinking more than wine with dinner.

"I'd rather not. We'd have to use a credit card. I have no idea if they can access the Uber database and track our whereabouts."

"My car is still at the police station."

"It probably has a tracking mechanism on it by now. We can't take that risk. For now, we need to take public transportation, or maybe we could use your friends' car while they're away."

"Brad, I'd hate to do that. Why risk dragging them into this?"

"Okay, maybe we can find an old car to buy. I think our best approach is to find a private seller and pay cash."

They sat silently for a minute. "That means we're going to need a good bit of cash," Brad announced. "We'll have to access our money market account, which shouldn't be a problem except that Eddie's number is in my phone and I can't turn it on." Eddie Clanton was their financial planner and had been for more than ten years.

The prepaid phones he'd purchased weren't smart phones, so he couldn't look the number up on the web. He looked at Barb and said, "Do you have a paper clip in your purse?"

"Umm, I'm not sure." She fished through the bottom of her purse and was pleasantly surprised when she pulled one out.

"I remember when we went to Italy last year we exchanged SIM cards for a local European number. I'm hoping if I remove the SIM card, I can turn on my phone without it syncing to the cellular system. Then I could get to my address book."

He removed his phone from its protective case and looked carefully at all sides. He saw a narrow panel with a small hole in one end and decided that had to be the right place. "Wish me luck," he said as he straightened out the paper clip and inserted one end into the small hole. A little tray popped out, and the SIM card was exposed. He turned the phone over. The tiny chip dropped into his hand. He handed it to Barb and asked, "Can you find a clean, safe place in your purse to keep this?" She took the card and rested it in her lap while pulling a small notepad from her purse. She tore a sheet out, laid the SIM card on the paper, and carefully folded it with the chip inside. She tucked it into a small pocket on the inside of the purse.

Brad turned on his phone and was relieved to find that the service indicator showed "No Service," but that he was able to access his address book. He took out the prepaid phone and dialed Eddie's number.

"Good morning, Eddie Clanton's office. This is Lori. How can I help you?"

"Good morning, Lori. This is Brad Tillman. Can you tell me how much we have in our money market account?"

"Hi, Brad!" Lori said and asked him to stand by for a moment. "Let's see, you have $12,412.36. Do you need me to transfer some of that to your checking account?"

"Yes, that would be great—please transfer 10,000. Thanks, Lori."

"For that amount I'll need your wife's authorization as well."

He handed the phone to Barb, and she okayed the transfer. Lori said that the transaction would take two hours to go through.

Brad and Barb turned to their to-do list.

1. Arrange a meeting with the FBI
2. Pick up cash from the bank
3. Buy a car, if possible
4. Get to Judy Alvarez's house by four p.m. to get keys, etc.

The Alvarezes were planning to leave for the airport at half past four, so they would have to watch their time carefully. Brad looked at Barb. "If we can get all this done today without being discovered, we'll be doing good."

They returned to the convenience store and found a magazine rack displaying free issues of *Local Cars for Sale*. Brad grabbed one, and they returned to the bench and browsed through the "For Sale by Owner" section. They quickly scanned all the ads and were drawn to one in particular. It was a fifteen-year-old Nissan Sentra that supposedly ran well but had to be sold because the owner was no longer able to drive. The $1,750 asking price made it even more attractive.

Brad called the number and spoke with Tom, who had placed the ad. After getting satisfactory answers to a few questions, he offered to pay full price, sight unseen. He asked if they could pick it up at two p.m. Tom said that the car belonged to his mother and that he would be out at that time, but he would ask his wife to meet them at his mother's house with the title.

They crossed the street, feeling uncomfortably exposed, and boarded a bus headed in the general direction of Lawrenceville, where the car was located. While on the bus, Barb asked the driver which buses they might need to get to Lawrenceville. He didn't know for sure but handed her a card that provided a brief description of the various bus lines. She had a tough time deciphering the information and said to Brad, "Why don't we get on MARTA and take it to the Doraville station? Then we could take a taxi the rest of the way. Taxis still take cash, don't they?"

"That makes sense," Brad said after thinking for a minute. "And yes, I'm pretty sure taxis take cash."

They stayed on the bus, taking it as far east as it went. The bus route card showed connections to MARTA, so they were able to figure out where to get off. The stop was near a shopping center with a family-style restaurant. They went in and found a table for two. After ordering a light lunch, they asked the waiter if he knew if there was a branch of their bank nearby. They learned there was one a half mile north on Peachtree Road.

They took their time with lunch, wanting to give the bank transfer enough time. The conversation eventually turned to the suspected election fraud. Barb had a lot of questions, most of which Brad couldn't answer, but he was able to give her some background on Eric Blas. He shared what Al had said about him, what Chuck had said about his political activism, and his own experience with him at the funeral.

"It sounds like he could be your guy. But he must have a network of people willing to do anything, including murder, to keep his activities secret. Why don't you turn him in to the police?"

"I have no proof!" Brad said. "I can't figure a way out of this. Who knows how many people he can muster to look for us? What's worse, we have so little evidence that I wonder if the FBI will take this seriously." Suddenly he groaned and put his face in his hands.

"What's wrong?" Barb asked.

"The only evidence I have is in the trunk of the Audi in the police impound lot!"

"Well, at least it should be safe there."

"It's so little, Barb. I hope we aren't on our own in this deal."

"Don't be so negative. We need to arrange that meeting with the FBI."

Brad agreed, but they had other things to take care of first. They walked to the bank and waited in line to see a teller. The transfer was complete, and they withdrew 4,000 dollars in cash. He asked for twenty one-hundred-dollar bills and the rest in fifties and twenties. Barb took 1,000 dollars in smaller denominations. Brad took the rest.

They walked back to the bus stop and caught a bus on a different route that took about five minutes to get them to a MARTA station. From there it was fifteen minutes to Doraville. They got off the train and looked around for a taxi stand. There was a mixed line of company cabs, along with individual drivers for Uber, Lyft, and others. They found one who took cash and rode to Lawrenceville to pick up the car.

Buying the Sentra proved to be easy. The woman had the title signed by her mother-in-law, so Brad filled in the odometer reading and signed his portion. The woman was happy he seemed to know what he was doing and even happier when he handed her 1,800 dollars and told her to keep the change.

Brad nonchalantly added, "Oh, and we'll take these license plates off as soon as we register the car at the Department of Motor Vehicles."

"I'm sure that will be fine," she said.

As they drove away, Brad felt a surge of independence like he'd felt when he got his first car at eighteen. "Where does your friend live?"

"I'm not sure. I can call her, but her number is in my phone."

"Oh," he groaned. He pulled off the road, and they repeated the process of removing her phone's SIM card.

Barb made the call using the same throwaway phone Brad had used before. Judy gave her the address, and Barb jotted it on her notepad. After she hung up, Brad said, "How are we going to find it? These phones don't have GPS."

Barb let out a breath of despair. "We could try to buy a map, or if we can find a library, we can get on the Internet, but who knows where there's a library out here?" After a pause she said, "Should you be driving?"

"What do you mean by that?"

"Did you get your license back at the hotel?"

Brad gave another exasperated groan. "Well, they'll have to catch me to find that out!" And off he drove.

Feeling a little helpless, they started asking people on the street for directions to the local library. On the fourth try, they got someone who pointed them in the right direction. Once inside, they were able to find and print directions to the Alvarez house.

By the time they got there, it was 3:40 p.m. The Alvarezes lived in Smyrna in the northwestern part of Atlanta's sprawl in a modest, well-kept home. They had contemplated delaying their arrival so they didn't interfere with any last-minute trip preparations the Alvarezes might be making but decided instead to just be early.

Nick Alvarez answered the door and invited them inside. "Judy says you have a gas leak at your house. I'm so sorry to hear that."

"Thanks. Yes, it is a bit scary, but we're so glad we found it. Things could've been much worse," Barb said.

"Well, this worked out well for all of us. I'm sure you'll be more comfortable here than in a hotel, and we'll feel better knowing you're keeping an eye on our house."

Brad shook Nick's hand and said, "It's nice of you to let us stay here. We aren't sure how long it'll take to fix. They said it might be a week."

Judy joined them and they talked for a few minutes, but the couple was packed and happy to get an earlier start to the airport. They were backing out of the driveway a few minutes before four. Finally, the Tillmans were someplace where they could afford to let their guard down.

CHAPTER 11

BRAD FELT ANTSY AND A BIT CLOSED IN, SO HE WENT FOR a walk around the neighborhood. The gravity of their situation weighed heavily on him, and his pace quickened to keep up with his mind. He had never felt so helpless in his life, had never in his wildest dreams imagined being in such a situation. Now Barb was involved and depending on him to steer them through this maze. He did not feel worthy of her trust, at least not in this situation.

His mind jumped back and forth between Eric Blas and the guy with the ponytail who had talked his way into the house. Blas seemed to always be a step ahead, and Brad had no confidence in his ability to hide from or outrun the guy. Blas had people willing to kill to protect his secrets. He had only seen one of them. How many others might there be? He had no real way to defend himself or Barb.

As he thought, his pace continued to pick up. Was he being followed? Or was his mind just playing tricks on him? As he looked around, he realized he had not been keeping track of where he'd been walking, and a sense of panic overtook him as he began to wonder if he could find his way back to the house. He turned around, thinking he should at least head in the opposite direction. He realized he had not given Barb one of the phones or recorded the numbers of any of the new phones. In fact, he had walked out the door without any phone at all.

He hated himself for his incompetence. He began to jog in what he hoped was the right direction but couldn't remember if he had turned any corners. He questioned whether he'd be able to recognize the house they were staying in. The more he thought through his failures, the more panic he felt.

Did the house have trees in the front yard? What color was it? Which side was the driveway on? He thought about what Barb would do if he wasn't back soon. He felt keys in his pocket. The car! *I'll recognize the car!*

He stopped and looked up and down the street he was on. There were plenty of cars parked on both sides. He started jogging again but gasped for breath. As he pushed himself to keep running, he noticed a large evergreen planted too near the sidewalk. Its limbs and heavy foliage hung halfway over the sidewalk, but there was room to get by. As he approached, Eric Blas suddenly stepped out from behind the tree directly into his path.

Brad stopped abruptly, nearly plowing into the other man. He stood stock still, wondering what to say. Blas's right hand moved up, and Brad saw the biggest handgun he'd ever seen outside of a *Dirty Harry* movie. Its barrel seemed to be oversized, but Brad knew next to nothing about guns. He couldn't take his eyes off that barrel. Blas placed it against Brad's left cheek and pulled the trigger.

Brad's entire body jerked as his eyes opened wide. The darkness was complete; all he could sense were the sheets around him.

Barb was jarred awake by the sudden movement. "Brad, what's wrong?"

He was so frightened by the nightmare that he was physically shaking. His t-shirt was drenched with sweat. It took him several seconds to respond. "I'm sorry. I had a bad dream."

"Do you want to tell me about it?"

He glanced at the clock and saw that it was three-thirty in the morning. "No, it's okay. Thanks, though." He didn't want to scare her.

As he took deep breaths, he thought back to the night before. They had gone to a drive-thru to pick up hamburgers for dinner. After that, Brad had a wave of exhaustion overtake him and headed to bed at seven p.m. He hadn't heard or felt Barb come to bed.

He decided now there was no way he could go back to sleep, so he threw the covers off and headed to the shower. Barb wasn't far behind. After both had showered and put on their new sweats, they made a pot of coffee and sat at the small kitchen table to plan the day.

CHAPTER 12

BRAD LOOKED FOR SOME NOTEPAPER IN THE ALVAREZ house. It dawned on him that being in unfamiliar territory while trying to survive was a hassle. He found a 5x7" notepad in a junk drawer in the kitchen that the family probably used for making lists. Every once in a while it was nice to be able to jot something down on paper.

He looked at the phones he had bought and wrote down each number. Then he assigned a name to each one. He wrote "Barb" next to the one ending in 6574. The one ending in 3661 would be his. The one ending in 9985 would be the one for the attorney. The fourth would be held as a contingency. He tore another sheet of paper from the pad and used the edge of the table to tear it into the three smaller sheets. He added the three-person directory to each one.

Brad and Barb talked about the need to be careful about who to call from these phones. Linda Johnson, anyone at GCI or the hospital, or any other known connections would be off limits. Once Cynthia Goldberg received her phone, she could be contacted on that phone only. When in doubt, they would talk to each other before placing any calls. If Blas connected these numbers to them, they could be tracked again—something they desperately wanted to avoid.

They had forgotten to ask about the Alvarezes' WiFi password, so they weren't able to use the Internet with their regular phones. Besides, since they weren't sure if their phones could be tracked that way, they decided they would only log in from public networks such as coffee shops and fast-food restaurants. They drove to a hamburger place and looked up addresses for shipping outlets nearby. Their first order of business would be to send the attorney her phone and mini directory. He wrote a note to Cynthia and sent the phone to her by same day courier.

The time had finally come to reach out to the FBI. Unfortunately, both he and Sergeant Swanson had forgotten about the FBI phone number. They went into a coffee shop and looked up the FBI website. They weren't surprised to learn that the bureau had a field office in Atlanta that covered the entire state of Georgia. They took their coffees and returned to the car to make the call.

"FBI, Atlanta field office, how may I direct your call?" Suddenly, Brad was at a loss for words. He had failed to think through how he would explain their predicament to a receptionist.

"Uh, yes," he stammered. "I need to talk to someone about an election fraud issue that I became aware of."

"What county are you calling from?"

"Uh, I'm not sure. I'm in Marietta."

"May I have your address, please?"

Brad clenched his teeth and looked at Barbara. He held his hand over the phone's mouthpiece, wondering if it did any good at all in muting his voice. "What address are we staying at?"

Fortunately, Barb had the address memorized and gave it to him slowly as he repeated it to the receptionist.

"Are you unsure of your address?" she asked once he was finished.

"Well, we're currently staying at a friend's house because we're afraid someone is following us and wants to do us harm."

"I see. And what is your home address?"

Brad provided that information, which seemed to satisfy her.

"What is your phone number, please?"

He fished the tiny phone directory out of his hip pocket and read her the phone number he'd assigned to himself.

"Thank you, Mr. Tillman. One moment please."

As he waited for someone to come on the line, Brad tried to think through what he was going to say to this person. Again, he felt out of his element. He had never talked to an FBI agent before.

"Good morning, this is Agent James," said a female voice, pleasant but businesslike.

"Hello, my name is Brad Tillman. I have become aware of what may be a serious election fraud situation. We believe we're being tracked and need help."

"Mr. Tillman, you used the word 'we.' Who else is involved?"

"Oh, sorry. It's my wife Barbara and me."

"Can you be more specific with regard to the election fraud you have become aware of?"

"Uh, yes. After a recent special election in Pennsylvania, I found a document that had to have been printed before the election. It matched 100% with the actual election results in the state."

"Are you calling from Pennsylvania?"

"No, my wife and I live in the Atlanta area."

"Can you be more specific about the document? What sort of document is it? How did you come to have it in your possession?"

Brad was a bit perturbed by all of the questions. Didn't she hear him when he said they were being tracked? Then it dawned on him. He was talking to a call center agent who was screening calls. He took a deep breath.

"We have a friend who worked in cybersecurity who was killed last month in a hit-and-run accident. The accident was before the election. After the election, I was helping his wife by going through some of his things. I found this document that appeared to have vote tallies on it in his briefcase. When I compared it to the election returns on the Pennsylvania Secretary of State's website, I found that the numbers were identical. We believe my friend's death may not have been an accident, and now we have reason to believe someone is trying to kill us as well."

As he gave voice to that last sentence, Brad seemed to run out of breath. He had not said any of that in such impersonal and frank terms before. Was he right about all this? He hadn't been physically harmed. Was he making too many assumptions?

"Why do you believe someone is trying to kill you, Mr. Tillman?"

Brad provided her with a brief rundown of the past twenty-four hours.

"And you think this has something to do with the document you found?"

Once again, Brad began to doubt himself. But he could think of no other reason someone would track his whereabouts and potentially want to hurt him. "Yes, I do. I don't have any enemies and have no idea why anyone would be chasing me otherwise."

"Have you been in touch with local law enforcement? If so, can you please tell me which agency and who you have told about this?"

"Yes, we spoke to Sergeant Swanson at the Gwinnett County Police Department."

"Thank you, Mr. Tillman. Do you believe you're safe right now?"

"Yes, we think so."

"All right, I will provide this information to the appropriate agents in the Bureau, and you should receive a call by the end of the day."

By the end of the day? *We could be dead by then!*

"Okay, thank you very much." Brad ended the call and looked at Barb. "She said we should hear from someone by the end of the day."

"By the end of the day?" Barb repeated in astonishment. "What are we supposed to do until then?"

"Oh, Barbara! I wish I knew. I sure hope we're doing the right thing."

CHAPTER 13

BRAD, WHAT'RE WE GOING TO DO?" BARB ASKED AGAIN.
"We can't stay out of work forever. What if the kids are trying to call us? We have to get in touch with them…. How are we going to deal with this guy who's after us? Do you really think he wants to kill us?"

Brad chuckled in spite of himself. He knew she loved him, but it was clear she thought they were in way over their heads. "Well, if we can sit down with the FBI, we'll finally be able to talk through it all with someone who deals with this sort of thing for a living." Brad said.

"But didn't you say that someone chasing us wouldn't be in the FBI's jurisdiction?"

"I did say that, but with the way things are playing out, I think they just might be interested in working with local authorities."

Brad realized Barb was right, though. They really needed to connect with their kids. How could they do that without involving or frightening them? Their phones and email accounts were probably being watched.

"Probably the best way for us to contact the kids would be by email," Brad said. "We haven't received any emails from them, so they probably aren't wondering about us yet. We'll need to be careful about how we do it. A guy like Blas will be able to track us right to the router and computer that we send from."

"Maybe we should go back to the library and do it there."

"Okay, let's do that. Let's do it now," he said, hoping this would make her feel better. He looked at Barbara and saw a tear run down her cheek.

"Oh, Brad, who are these people?"

Brad was about to answer when he was startled by his phone ringing. This was the first call on the new phone. He answered with some trepidation. "Hello?"

A woman's voice on the other end asked, "Is this Brad Tillman?"

"Yes."

"Mr. Tillman, this is Special Agent Betty Finnigan with the FBI. I am following up on your call to the Bureau relating to election fraud."

Brad looked at Barbara and smiled and nodded his head. "Hi, Special Agent Finnigan. Yes. I'm afraid I don't have much, but what I do have seems to have been important enough for someone to die over it."

"Normally we'd refer you to the state election commission, but I think we should meet to see what we're dealing with. When would be convenient for you?"

Brad's heart fluttered. "Um, well, we could meet any time, but the evidence is in my car that is in the police impound lot. I would need to arrange to get it."

"The police have your car?"

"Yes, it's a long story, and I want you to hear it all.... Tell you what, let me arrange to get my car taken care of, and then we can meet. Would four o'clock this afternoon be too late?"

"I suppose not. However, sometimes these things take longer than you might think. Perhaps we should make it nine o'clock tomorrow morning."

"I would really like to talk with someone today. My wife and I are convinced that someone is trying to harm us. If I get my hands on the information sooner, could I call and set up a meeting for later today?"

"Certainly. Why don't you see what you can do and then call me at this number? Then we'll see how much time we have."

Brad paused. "Uh, just a minute." He wasn't sure where to find numbers on the new phone. He tapped some buttons, hoping he didn't accidentally hang up on the agent. Fortunately, he was able to move around intuitively until he found what he was looking for.

"Yes, I have your number. I'll call you as soon as I have the document."

"All right, we'll talk soon," Finnigan said.

Brad turned to Barb. "We have to get the evidence out of my car at the impound lot, pronto."

"Are you sure that's a good idea? What if they are watching the impound lot? Didn't you say they could be tracking the car?"

"Hmmm, yeah, that's something to consider. We could wind up putting ourselves right back into their crosshairs."

"Maybe the police would bring us the bags," Barb offered hopefully.

"I don't know. They didn't seem so happy with us when we left the other night. That and the fact that they're short-staffed makes me think we shouldn't count on it."

Brad remembered that the arresting officer had given him a card with the address and phone number of the impound lot. "Maybe they'd be willing to give us a hand if it didn't require a lot of extra time." He picked up the phone and dialed the number.

CHAPTER 14

"GWINNETT COUNTY IMPOUND, MURPHY," A VOICE answered.

"Hello, my name is Brad Tillman. I have a vehicle in the lot that I need to arrange to pick up."

"You'll need to pay 150 dollars, and you can drive it away any time."

"That's great, thank you. However, I can't get there today. Could I have a tow truck come and get the car?"

"That's a little unusual, but it's been done before. I would need you to either be here to show ID or have it towed to the address on the vehicle registration."

"That's fine—I can have it towed to my home," Brad said. "Officer Murphy, is there a towing company that you might recommend helping me with this?"

"I'm not an officer. But yeah, we have several companies that we work with. When the department requests a tow, we have a protocol to follow that spreads the business around. However, since you're the one doing the hiring, I'd recommend you call Fast Track Towing. Those guys are great to deal with." He paused. "Please don't tell anyone I said that. It could create a problem for me."

"My lips are sealed. Would you have their number handy?" Brad looked at Barb expectantly and motioned that he needed something to write with. She scrambled to her purse and quickly came up with her pad and pen.

Murphy read out the number while Brad repeated it back to him slowly so that Barb could jot it down.

"That's right," Murphy said. "Now, how are you going to pay?"

"If you take credit cards, I can give you the number now."

"We do. Go ahead."

Brad went through the process until the transaction was complete and then remembered something else. "Uh, Mr. Murphy, there's one more thing I could use a hand with. I know you're busy, but there are some things in the car I really need to get right away. If I were to send a cab there, would you mind pulling a small suitcase and a briefcase out of the car and giving it to the cab driver?"

"No can do," said Murphy flatly. "I would need to see some identification. Anyone could call and send a cab over here."

Brad groaned. "Yes, I suppose they could. Then would you mind pulling those items out for me, and I can come down sometime after the car is towed? I'll show you my ID then."

"Are you sure you don't want to just drive the car out yourself?" Murphy asked.

Brad hesitated. "It's a bit complicated. I'm afraid it might be dangerous for me to do that. I think someone who wants to hurt me may be checking the impound lot just waiting for me to show up. It wouldn't be good if they were able to follow me from there."

Murphy whistled. "Do the police know about this?"

"Ah, yes, sort of."

"All right, I'll pull your suitcase and briefcase for you. You'll need to pick them up by five p.m. because my shift ends then, and I can't guarantee their security after that."

Brad glanced at his watch. It was a quarter after eleven. "Thank you so much, Mr. Murphy. I can't tell you how much I appreciate your help."

Brad ended the call and looked at Barb with a self-satisfied grin on his face. "What do you think?" he asked, fully expecting her praise.

"You have obviously forgotten that you don't have an ID. You left your driver's license at the hotel the other night," Barb responded in a tone that was anything but congratulatory.

Brad let out a sigh and put his hands up. "When will something go right for us?"

He contacted the towing company and, as Murphy had said, they were very helpful. They promised to pick up the car within two hours and tow it to the Tillman's home. He asked them to park it in the driveway and leave it unlocked with the keys in the glovebox. He would arrange for a neighbor to retrieve the keys and lock the car. He also let them know that he would likely have them pick up his wife's car from the police precinct as soon as he could get them the keys.

Realizing that getting his hands on the briefcase was going to take a while, he contacted Agent Finnigan at the FBI and told her that nine a.m. tomorrow would probably be a good time to meet after all. He got the address of the local FBI office and agreed to meet her there.

Brad and Barb grabbed some lunch at a fast-food place and then went back to the hotel to pick up his license. Fortunately, after a brief search, the desk clerk was able to track down where it was being held for safekeeping.

By this time, the car should've been towed from the impound lot, but they were taking no chances. They assumed that any tough guys watching the lot would follow the car as it was towed to its destination. They made a quick side trip to the library and sent a routine email to their kids. Barb wrote that they were super busy but doing well. She also promised to call to catch up in a few days.

They had a cab pick them up at the library and take them to the impound lot. It was four p.m. and Murphy was still there. Brad went inside while Barb waited in the cab. He was surprised to find several people working there, including a uniformed police officer. He asked for Mr. Murphy and, interestingly enough, the man's appearance was pretty similar to what Brad had conjured up in his mind. Murphy was in his mid-fifties, balding, and dressed in business casual attire. He didn't smile much but seemed like an efficient guy. He brought the bags out from his office as soon as he confirmed Brad's identity.

Brad thanked him again and Murphy simply said, "No problem." Then he looked at Brad and added, "Good luck. It sounds like you could use some."

Brad smiled and replied, "You can say that again." He wondered what image Murphy might have concocted in his mind for Brad. All the man had to go on was a phone call and the information that he wanted his car but didn't want to drive it out himself. He wanted some bags but didn't want to get those himself, either. Walking out, Brad shook his head thinking about what image such information might generate.

CHAPTER 15

BRAD AND BARB WALKED INTO THE FBI OFFICE AT TEN minutes before nine. Brad had his briefcase with the Pennsylvania precinct document inside. The closer he got to sharing this with federal authorities, the more he doubted himself. It was only a single piece of paper with numbers on it. There was no sign of where it had come from. What would the authorities be able to do with it? Except for his own escape and his belief that Al may have been murdered, he might have forgotten it himself. Despite this, he held onto the hope that today's meeting might lead somewhere.

They checked in with the reception/security desk and had a seat in the lobby. Before long, they were approached by a pair of agents in suits. The woman held out her hand and said, "Mr. Tillman, I'm Special Agent Betty Finnigan. Thank you so much for meeting us here." Then her attention shifted to Barb. "You must be Mrs. Tillman. Welcome and thank you for coming."

Betty Finnigan appeared to be forty something with a trim physique. Her brown hair was short but framed her small features nicely.

"Of course. Please call me Barbara."

The gentleman following Finnigan offered his hand to both. "I'm Special Agent Chris Allan." Chris Allan sported a buzz cut and had a boyish look about him. It would be hard to judge his age. The agents led them down a hallway and into a well-equipped conference room. "Please make yourself comfortable," Allan said.

Finnigan began. "I think that the best way for us to approach this would be to have each of you tell us about your concerns in your own words. We will be recording our meeting for our records, and you'll also see us taking some notes to fill in the blanks."

"Uh, okay," began Brad. "This is all a confusing nightmare for me. I'm not sure what's in your jurisdiction, but I'll tell you everything I know."

"Yes, please," Finnigan urged him. "Don't concern yourself with jurisdictions and the like. That's our responsibility, and we regularly work with state and local officials. Just tell us everything you can about your concerns."

And so Brad began. He started with the death of their close friend, Al, and went on to explain everything he could remember up to the present time. It felt good to share it all. He was with people who were accustomed to dealing with this sort of thing, and he could finally just unload all that had happened on them. For their part, the agents listened attentively, but they gave no verbal, facial, or otherwise physical cues to show they believed his concerns were valid.

When he got to the part about finding the voter tallies in Al's briefcase, he fumbled around in his own case and gave the agents the document. As he did so, he reminded himself that it was a sheet of paper with numbers on it and nothing else, besides the hand-scrawled question mark. He began to doubt himself again. They glanced at the paper, and Finnigan said simply, "Go on."

"It must have been in Al's briefcase before his death and before the actual election was held," he said, leaning forward.

The agents simply nodded.

Brad continued for another twenty minutes, telling them everything he could think of—his suspicion that Al was murdered, his two encounters with "Ponytail," the van following them, and his belief that a tracking device was attached to his car. He explained it all in as much detail as he could. "I think that's everything," he concluded, looking at both agents.

"Thank you, Mr. Tillman. It sounds like you've had a frightening week. Mrs. Tillman, what can you tell us?"

"I've obviously been with Brad since Tuesday morning." She looked at him. "I can't believe it's only been two days!" She turned back to the agents. "I was not with him when someone forced his way into our house or when he was followed on Monday night. I feel like

I really haven't been affected in the same way as Brad or experienced this the way he has."

Brad saw the agents glance at one another as if to signal, *did you hear that?*

Oh great! Make them think I'm crazy! Brad thought. He said, "Barb, you saw the Sprinter van that followed us when we left the hotel, right?"

"Yes, that's right! Brad told me exactly what kind of van to look for while he was calling the airline, and there it was, just like he described it," Barb gushed, realizing that what she'd said before had not been helpful.

"All right, thank you," Finnigan said. She picked up the document Brad had given them and handed it to Allan. He left the conference room momentarily and returned without it.

"Mr. Tillman, you said you believe that Albert Johnson's death was not an accident. Tell us what caused you to come to that conclusion," Finnigan said.

"Well, as I was contemplating what the information on the document must mean, I thought about the power it would give someone to manipulate elections. I wondered how many people would need to be involved and how they could be trusted to keep such a secret. I wondered to what extent someone might go to ensure secrecy." Brad's voice trailed off. Then he said, "Al died in a hit and run, and they never found the car or driver. I was horrified when I thought that maybe his death wasn't an accident."

Brad paused again, then he added, "Naturally, it was just a suspicion, and I kept telling myself to calm down. I thought it was my imagination running away with me. But then when a guy carrying a gun showed up at my door pretending to be a utility worker, I had to conclude that murder was a very real possibility." He shivered to hear the word spoken out loud.

Allan followed up. "Do you remember the police officers' names who came to your house Monday?"

"Sorry, I don't remember. I was pretty shaken up, and my mind was all over the place. I'm not great at remembering names even on a good day."

"What time were the officers at your home?"

"Let's see, I got home around two o'clock, and the guy with the gun arrived about fifteen minutes later. I would say sometime between three and three-thirty. It could've been a little later."

"Who else have you told about this document?" Allan asked.

"Nobody! Barbara didn't even know until she came to pick me up at the police station." He shook his head. "Oh.... I forgot. I did tell the police sergeant and my attorney."

There was a tap at the door, and it opened to reveal a woman standing in the hallway. She was professionally dressed, but Brad couldn't tell if she was an agent or an administrative assistant. She had a slight frown on her face. She used her index finger to motion to Agent Allan. He excused himself and left the room, closing the door behind him.

He returned about a minute later with several documents that he handed to Finnigan. He looked at Brad. "One of our people just checked the Pennsylvania Secretary of State's website for last week's election results. The numbers there do not match the numbers on the document you gave us."

Finnigan passed the two documents to Brad. Brad's eyes widened. "That can't be! I looked at the site on Friday and they matched exactly!"

Now his head was spinning. He looked at Barb, who only wished she could say something to help. Finally, she asked, "Brad, could you have been looking at a different website?"

"No! This is the webpage I looked at!" He looked at the agents. "I don't know what's going on here, but I know what I saw. Someone must have changed the numbers on the website."

Brad was confused and angry at the same time. He didn't know what to do or say. "Why would someone be after me if it wasn't about this? These people are technically savvy. They must have changed the website!"

Finnigan finally spoke. "Okay, let's continue with the interview. We can't do anything until we get all the information. Mr. Tillman, do you have any idea who could be involved in such an endeavor?"

Brad was expecting this question. He had thought long and hard about dropping Eric Blas's name. He had decided that he needed to tell them everything. "Well, there is an individual that comes to mind. I have no proof, but he probably has the technical prowess to carry out what has been done, and I understand he has some fervent political views."

Brad explained who Blas was, where he worked, Brad's own experience with him, and what Jennifer Bradley had said at the café.

"Well," Allan commented, "there are a lot of high-tech people in the world who are both offensive and politically active. Few of them will commit murder for their cause."

"I understand," Brad responded. "I just wanted to give you complete information from my perspective."

They asked the rest of their questions. Brad's mind was everywhere except in the here and now. Several times they had to repeat questions for him. He responded as clearly as he could. He was genuinely impressed by their thoroughness, but at times he felt like he was being accused of something himself.

At 11:43 a.m., Finnigan looked at Allan and asked if he had any further questions. When he shook his head, she stood and announced, "Then we're finished here."

"Mr. and Mrs. Tillman, we'll spend some time reviewing this and doing some follow-up. Is the phone number I contacted you on the best way to reach you?"

Brad nodded and stood, then paused for a moment. "Could I get copies of these two documents?"

Finnigan looked at Agent Allan and then Brad. "I don't see why not. Chris, why don't you take Mr. Tillman to get copies, and Mrs. Tillman and I will meet you in the lobby."

Agent Finnigan and Barbara waited until the men had left. Before leaving the room, the agent stopped, closed the door, and turned to face Barbara. "I'm sure this is quite uncomfortable for you, Mrs. Tillman, but I need to ask you something. Is your husband active in or interested in any political movements?"

Barbara looked surprised. "No, not at all. He's angered sometimes about how divided the country is, but he certainly isn't obsessed with it. He's proud that his company is supplying a secure voting system to the country so there's less speculation about voting accuracy."

"Has he ever voiced conspiracy theories to you about current or past political issues?"

"Special Agent Finnigan, Brad is an accountant. He deals with hard numbers and data. His mind is wired that way. When he wonders about something, he approaches it by digging for facts," Barbara said firmly. After a moment she looked the agent directly in the eyes and said, "My husband is not a nut job. He did not imagine all of this!"

"I understand. Thank you, Mrs. Tillman."

Barb and Agent Finnigan headed to the lobby and met Agent Allan and Brad there. "Thank you for bringing this to our attention. We will contact the police departments involved and do some follow-up," Finnigan said again.

She looked at Brad. "Mr. Tillman, I realize you're shocked that we were unable to confirm the numbers on your document, but based on everything you've told us, I want to caution you about probing further. There very well may be people who don't want you to have more information. You've done the right thing by bringing this to us. Let us do the investigating. It's what we do."

Brad looked at her, momentarily unsure of what to say. "Then what should we do, Special Agent Finnigan? What should we do?"

For the first time, Finnigan's look changed to one of empathy. "I suggest you sit down with people from the police precinct where your armed entry was reported. They're in a better position to offer assistance or make suggestions. I would try to get your life back to some semblance of normalcy as soon as you can. If you continue to have concerns about your safety, you may want to consider hiring a security firm to help you."

Brad looked at Barb and then back at Agent Finnigan. "Thank you. That gives us something to work towards."

CHAPTER 16

ONCE THE TILLMANS LEFT, THE AGENTS RETREATED TO Finnigan's office.

Betty Finnigan was the lead agent on their team. She was recruited to the FBI out of college after attending UNC Chapel Hill on a softball scholarship and majoring in accounting. She had never considered law enforcement as a career, but during her senior year she was invited to do a one-year internship with the Bureau after graduation. She found that she liked the work and was good at it. She felt like she was able to make a difference in the world and, because much of the work was related to white collar crime, her accounting degree was well utilized.

"Chris, this is pretty weak stuff," she said. "It does appear that someone is at least harassing this guy. In the present political climate, we probably shouldn't dismiss it altogether. If it turns out there really is something to this, the last thing I want is to be accused of sweeping it under the rug."

"There are people higher up in the Bureau who would disagree with you," Chris remarked.

"Unfortunately, you're right about that. Tell you what, why don't you contact the Pennsylvania Secretary of State's office and get an official election results document? Not just what's on their website, but the certified results. Then give the police a call and track down all the officers this guy has interacted with this week. See what they have to say about him."

"Okay Betty, I'll get the ball rolling."

Chris Allan was ten years Betty's junior. Though he had been with the Bureau for almost a decade, he still looked like he was in his early twenties. He studied Criminal Justice at Ole Miss and was definitely not an athlete. He was a pudgy guy, the kind that looked like he enjoyed his downtime. He was an avid sports fan, though, and rarely missed an Ole Miss game on television.

Chris and Betty were very different. She approached her job seriously, and her manner generally reflected this. Chris, on the other hand, was a more colorful character, easily finding humor in things he saw or experienced. He used sports analogies on a routine basis. They balanced each other well. He paused, leaned against the closed door, and gave her a doubtful look. "Betty, I thought this new election system was fraud-proof. Aren't we wasting our time here?"

"Could be, but let's at least give it a cursory look. Maybe we can put it to bed quickly. I'm going to try to set up a meeting with someone at GCI so we can get a better picture of the new voting system."

CHAPTER 17

WHEN BRAD AND BARB GOT BACK TO THE CAR HE LOOKED at her and asked, "How do you think that went?"

Barb rolled her eyes. "How should I know? We've never done anything like this before. At least they didn't seem dismissive."

After a pause she added, "Brad, I'm so sorry if I gave them the impression that you were imagining things!"

"Don't be sorry. You *weren't* with me that first day. I never thought you doubted me, though. Anyway, I think it helped when you said that you saw the Sprinter van."

"There's something else I need to tell you."

Brad gave his wife a quizzical look.

"When you and Agent Allan went to get copies, Agent Finnigan asked me some questions about you."

"What kind of questions?"

Barb told him everything in as much detail as she could remember.

Brad thought for a moment and said, "I guess they had to ask. If I were them, I would have done the same thing."

"Well, what are we going to do, Brad?"

"I'm famished! Let's pick up some sandwiches and go back to the Alvarez's place. We'll talk it through then."

They swung by a sub shop on their way and bought two-foot-long sandwiches, chips, and soft drinks. They figured they'd get two meals taken care of in one stop. When they got to their home base, they sat down to eat and discuss what to do next.

"Agent Finnigan said we should sit down with the police. Are you going to call them?" Barb asked.

"I guess so, but which ones? The guys who came to the house, or the ones I lied to?" Brad asked with a shake of his head.

"The ones who came to the house!"

"Okay, I guess I should also call the other precinct to let them know we'll be getting your car out of there, though. We need to take a key to the towing company."

"Do you think the police would be willing to look at your car to see if there's a tracking device on it?"

"Good idea. I'll ask. We need to have them check both cars."

"Brad, what are we going to do about money? We need to get back to work. We're going through money like nobody's business. We need to get back home."

"I hear you," Brad acknowledged. "I wonder if those guys have backed off since we've been talking to the police. I kind of wish we had let them know, somehow, that we're also talking to the FBI."

"But wouldn't that make them try even harder to keep us quiet?"

"Who knows? Maybe they'd think we already told the authorities everything we know."

"Do you think that would keep us safe?"

Brad rubbed his head and said, "I wish I knew. I'll call the police this afternoon and arrange a time to meet."

CHAPTER 18

AT EIGHT-THIRTY FRIDAY MORNING, CHRIS ALLAN WALKED into Betty Finnigan's office. "I have the election results report from Pennsylvania."

"That was quick!"

"Well, the woman at the state office was very helpful."

"What did you find out?"

"It looks like we could be game on. The numbers on Tillman's document are an exact match to the actual results."

"Whoa! What's up with the website, then?"

"I told my contact about the mistaken information on the state site, and she looked while we were on the phone but couldn't explain it. She was told the results were posted on the website Thursday morning after the election," Chris explained. "She said that the person responsible for updating it is quite reliable and careful with detail. She is going to follow up with them to see what might have happened."

Betty stared ahead for a moment, thinking. "That's good information, Chris. It sure looks like someone is trying to cover their tracks. Why don't we get our IT people on it? If the system was hacked, perhaps the culprit left some identifiable information."

"Okay. I'll tee it up. Let's see what they can come up with."

"Good!" Betty said. "In the meantime, I'll set up a meeting with GCI. Why don't you give the Gwinnett County Police a call and find out who's working the illegal entry at the Tillman house? Let them know that Mr. Tillman may be in someone's crosshairs due to potential voter fraud."

"Will do," Chris said as he left the office.

CHAPTER 19

BRAD AND BARB RETURNED TO THE ALVAREZ HOME AND rested for the rest of the day. On Friday morning they found it hard to get going. It had been two weeks since Al's death. That, along with the past few days, had them pretty well tapped out. They talked about the process of getting back to their normal lives. They would return the chips to their regular phones before going back to work; they would never say anything on those phones about the situation unless they agreed to it first. They would hang on to the throwaway phones for private conversations.

Later, Brad called the police on his regular phone from the car. They had agreed that this might be a good opportunity to let anyone listening know they were working with law enforcement. During the call, he mentioned that they had met with the FBI.

He was pleased to learn that a detective had been assigned to their case that morning. They set up a meeting for the following day at their home. Brad asked if it would be possible to check their cars for tracking devices. The detective said he'd do his best to make that happen.

The next day, Brad and Barb decided to leave the newly purchased car at the Alvarez house for the time being in case they needed obscurity in the future. They boarded a bus going in the direction of their house and took a cab the final mile or so. They arrived ten minutes early for their meeting and checked that both cars were in the garage. They thought it would be best not to touch anything.

Soon, an unmarked police car pulled into the driveway. Two men, one wearing a business suit and the other in more casual attire, got out and approached them. The first introduced himself as Detective John Conner. He introduced Specialist Jim Engle, who said he'd be inspecting their vehicles.

Conner seemed like a nice guy. He carried a little more weight than he probably had when he was a beat officer. His head was shaved, but a shadow revealed that he would have a pretty full head of hair if he let it grow back.

Brad and Barb invited the detective into the house.

"This is the first time we've been back to our house since the day of the break-in," Brad said. "It sure is nice having you here."

"I understand," Conner said in an empathetic tone. "Why don't I look around a bit?"

The detective started to move through the house, and Brad and Barb went to the kitchen. There was a pungent odor from the open bottle of beer still on the table. Brad poured the beer down the sink and tossed the bottle into the recycling bin. Barbara opened the refrigerator to see if there was anything they could offer Detective Conner.

When the detective returned, he said, "There's nobody here. Nothing appears to be disturbed, but let's walk through it together. Tell me if you see anything unusual."

They did the second walk-through and found nothing out of the ordinary.

As they returned to the kitchen Barb said, "I'm afraid we don't have much to offer you. Would you like a soft drink or a bottle of water? I could make coffee if you'd prefer."

"I'd love a bottle of water," Conner said, trying to put her at ease. "I'll go ahead and have Jim sweep the house for bugs too, once he's finished in the garage."

"That would be great," Brad said with appreciation.

As Conner went to the garage to make his request, Brad and Barb headed to the living room to get comfortable. The detective returned, opened his notepad, and settled into a chair next to where they sat on the couch.

They mostly covered old ground but also talked about the FBI interview. The Tillmans were surprised to learn that the FBI had encouraged the police to take the situation seriously. The three of them discussed Eric Blas in some detail. Conner told Brad and Barb that the police would do a background check on the man and investigate more as needed.

He told them that there weren't many white Sprinter vans around, and they had a line on those registered in the state of Georgia. "At this point, my guess is that the van is registered out of state. Did you happen to get a look at the license plate?"

"No, I'm afraid I was more concerned with getting away than gathering information."

Brad took the opportunity to ask the detective if he thought they were safe now.

"Well," Conner said, "we can put your home on a regular drive-by status and inform our people that you have been placed on the security alert list."

"Do you think we should hire a security company?"

"That's really up to you. A comprehensive security company could review your situation and offer recommendations for home, automobile, and personal security. It wouldn't be a bad idea to see what your options are and how much it would cost."

"Do you think these people might still be after Brad?" Barb interrupted.

"Well, I like that you let them know you're working with the police and the FBI," said Conner. He leaned a little forward in his chair. "I can't say for sure, but most people would back off after realizing that law enforcement is involved. Also, since this appears to be solely about information you have, they probably assume that you've already turned it over to the authorities and that they would gain nothing by continuing to threaten you."

Barb found this comforting and said, "I agree. I think we need to get back to our normal routine. We can't stay out of work forever."

The detective was about to respond when his colleague came into the room. "I did find tracking devices on both cars. Pretty high-end stuff. I also found listening devices in the kitchen and bedroom. All have been removed."

"Good work," Conner replied. "This gives us another avenue to explore. I suspect there aren't too many places a person could buy high-end devices like that."

The detective stood and said, "I agree that you should return to your normal routine. But as a rule, try to remain in areas where other people are around. I'll let you know how things progress, or if I have any further questions."

After the two men left, Brad and Barb talked about what they should tell people. They agreed on a story about a medical scare for their grandchild that turned out to be a false alarm. No details would be given.

They took inventory of the food in the house, threw away some old leftovers, and made a grocery list. They each called work to say they would be returning on Monday. Brad went online and found a security company that seemed to have a good reputation. He called and was able to make an appointment for a salesman to come by on Saturday afternoon. Then, after a trip to the store, they spent the rest of the afternoon and evening unwinding and relaxing.

On Saturday afternoon, Brad and Barb sat down with a salesman from APT, the security company. They explained the kind of threats they were worried about. When he heard Brad's explanation, the technician put the brochure he had prepared back in his briefcase and took out a large full-color portfolio holder and opened it up. Inside each cover was a pouch with multiple brochures, each describing a different option for the high-end system that he recommended.

Brad found the experience stressful. On the one hand, he wanted to be sure they could be safe in their own home. He definitely knew that the need was there. On the other hand, the cost for high-end options was significant. He didn't want to use up all of their discretionary income on a home security package. He looked at Barb. She looked into his eyes and knew what he was thinking.

"I don't see that we have a choice," she said to him. "I don't want these people to be able to stroll in here and hurt us in our own home."

Brad knew she was right. They opted for an advanced system that not only provided perimeter and interior protection but also would alert them if someone was anywhere on their property. They also ordered the Pro-Star system for their vehicles so they could contact someone with the push of a button in the event of an emergency. They paid extra to have the system installed and activated on Sunday, the following day.

Brad felt like a victim all over again. He had just paid out 2,500 bucks for installation of a security system and committed another 450 dollars a month for at least a year. They could just as well have robbed his bank account.

CHAPTER 20

"MR. UNGER, THE PEOPLE FROM THE FBI ARE HERE," JEFF Unger's administrative assistant, Carol Behmer, announced over the phone.

"Thanks," Unger said into his hands-free system as he rose to meet the two agents waiting in his private lobby.

"Good morning!" he said cheerfully as he put out his hand. "Jeff Unger."

"Hello," said the woman. "I'm Special Agent Betty Finnigan of the FBI."

The two shook hands. "Special Agent Finnigan, nice to meet you."

The second agent offered his hand. "Good morning, Mr. Unger. I'm Special Agent Chris Allan."

"Special Agent Allan," Unger said.

Both agents showed Unger their badges, and he invited them into his office.

Unger closed the door and motioned for the agents to take a seat at the small conference table. His office was beautifully detailed with a desk, built-in credenza, and bookshelves that matched the mahogany table. In front of the desk was a multi-colored area rug covering the wood floor. Finnigan noticed two doors other than the one they had entered through. She thought one was likely a private bathroom. She wasn't sure about the other. They all sat down, and Jeff began. "How can I help you this morning?"

"Thank you for agreeing to meet with us, Mr. Unger," Finnigan said. "As I mentioned to you on the phone, we're doing a little fact finding relating to a complaint we received. Recently an accusation of voter fraud was made to the Bureau. As you can no doubt imagine, it is important that we take these matters seriously and get them resolved quickly. Our reason for meeting with you is to get a better understanding of the electronic voting system that your company has developed for elections. I hope you don't mind if we record our conversation, since we expect the voting system to be complex and somewhat foreign to us."

"I understand. I have no problem with you recording the conversation, as long as the details remain confidential. Obviously, a proprietary system becomes vulnerable when others develop an understanding of how it works."

"We're on the same team in that regard, Mr. Unger. I have an agreement that says that the details of our conversation will remain confidential unless it uncovers or supports evidence of a crime. If a prosecutor wishes to use anything we discuss in presenting a case, he or she would work with your company to decide how it could be used without putting the proprietary nature of your system at risk."

Unger read the agreement carefully. "I'd normally prefer to have my attorneys review something of this nature, but as you said, we're on the same team, and I want to help. I have a great deal of confidence in our system." He signed the paper. "What sort of information do you need?"

"Well, we're interested in gaining a better understanding about the system's security. The accusation we are dealing with suggests that the system was manipulated to force a predetermined outcome of a senatorial race in a specific state."

"Interesting," said Unger. "May I ask where such an accusation came from?"

"Mr. Unger, that is not something we can share. As I'm sure you can imagine, it's important for us to maintain strict confidentiality in any investigation to protect those making an allegation as well as the accused. If we find that there is not enough evidence to support an accusation, it's best for all involved that it is not made public," Allan said.

"I can certainly understand that. It's just that I'm quite proud of our voting system, and I would hate to have it disparaged."

Both agents nodded.

Finnigan continued, "The best way to avoid that will be for you to provide us clear information about the system's security."

"Of course," said Unger. "Where shall I begin?" He paused and proceeded to give them a description of the voting system. "When we designed the voting system, we were coming out of one of the most chaotic elections in our country's history. It was also a time when cybersecurity advancements could nearly eliminate the risk of hackers accessing systems to do harm. Another factor was that the transition to a fully computer literate society was nearly complete. Most people seventy-five and younger were comfortable interacting with computers, smart phones, tablets, and the like. So, we were able to design a system that was not only user-friendly, but efficient and secure."

Both agents scribbled notes as they listened.

"Hacking is still a big threat, Mr. Unger. How can you say cybersecurity is ahead of those wishing to penetrate our systems?" Allan asked.

"I said that cybersecurity advancements were there, yes, but they were only beginning to be implemented. Something called block chain encryption was developed in 2019 and 2020 to make computer transactions highly secure. To implement it into a large, existing system takes considerable time and programming. I'm sure you remember the Y2K fiasco. It took years for companies just to change the year field in programs from two to four digits. Imagine what it takes to implement block chain security! We developed the voting system from scratch, so we were able to integrate the most advanced technology."

"I've heard of block chain," Finnigan commented. "How does it work?"

"Well, in simple terms, it's a data processing structure that uses decentralization to make the system nearly impervious to outside attack."

"I see," said Allan, though the discussion was getting beyond his understanding.

"In addition, we developed a highly advanced system of securing the interaction of a person or computer with an electronic system. At that time, companies were just beginning to implement MFA, that is, Multi-Factor Authentication, to secure an interaction. I'm sure you've experienced this in online banking."

Both agents nodded, though Allan had a quizzical look on his face.

"When accessing your account online, you put in your password and then get a text or email with a dynamic six-digit code that you enter to confirm it's you knocking on the digital door. Data that moves through most secure systems use a 256K Advanced Encryption Standard. In computer jargon, we say AES 256. When you think about encryption, think of a computer translating the data into a new language that's difficult to decipher. At the time we began development, the 256K algorithm had not been broken, but we knew it was only a matter of time. We were completing the development of a more advanced 512K algorithm that would take hackers thirty to forty years to access a system using their current methods. I thought the electronic voting process would be a good place to implement it.

"We also utilize a more advanced type of security system to ensure that the voter's interaction with the system is secure. The 'handshake,' if you will, that connects the voter to the registration is not a chain of characters like a password, but a grid. The grid has thirty-six characters covering four rows and nine columns. To connect for the transaction, every one of those thirty-six characters must match perfectly. It would take years for someone to replicate the grid using random character generators. That's what makes the transaction so secure. In addition, we use an advanced version of block chain for linking a citizen's vote with their registration."

"Okay," said Allan. "And this method of encryption and handshake is used throughout the registration and voting process?"

"Basically, yes. Nobody can falsely tie into a registration that is on file to cast a vote for someone else. Likewise, nobody can capture and decipher data that is moving through the system due to AES 512."

Allan looked at Finnigan and then at Mr. Unger. "I don't want Special Agent Finnigan to look bad, so I'm going to take one for the team. I don't understand how all this is used in voting."

Unger smiled. "Well, the technology itself is highly advanced. I think the best way to explain it is to walk through the elements of the voting process. The first thing that takes place is voter registration. I presume you both voted in the recent past and had to re-register using the new process. Do you remember what that process was like?"

"Yes," Finnigan said. "I followed a link to a website. I had to get my driver's license and hold it up next to my face and click on a button. On the screen there was a line that moved up and down over my camera's shot of me holding it. Then it gave me an odd-sounding paragraph to read out loud. After I read it, the computer took a minute and then came back and said I was registered. I think I also got an email confirming my registration and party affiliation."

"Right. When you were holding up your driver's license, the system was using the camera on the device to scan your face and the picture on the license. If you recall, it also asked you if the address on your license was correct."

"I guess it did," Finnigan nodded.

"It reads the data on the license and updates a person's address in the system if necessary. In that way, it confirmed you were who you said you were. The system also checked the IRS database to confirm you had a social security number and were a citizen of the United States. With that information, it confirmed not only your citizenship but also identified what state and precinct you lived in. State systems supply information on addresses and precincts online for us to draw on. For an election, the state officials supply details, including candidates for each office and any referendum on the ballot. When it's time to vote, our system gives you a ballot with everything you are eligible to vote for."

Thinking about his own experiences Allan said, "So, the voice pattern is what matches the person's vote to their registration file."

"That's right," confirmed Unger. "When someone receives an email or text invitation to vote, the system asks the voter to read a series of sentences out loud, which sometimes seem nonsensical, to match that person's voice to their voice at registration. The system then collects the vote and shows that the person has voted, ensuring that multiple votes by one person are not possible."

There was a pause as the agents pondered all of this. Finnigan said, "What about those who aren't able to complete the process online? Some people are still not computer literate, and I would imagine many senior citizens would not be able to vote this way."

"Sure. Every voter has the choice of going to a polling place. Those who do are aided in the initial process and then left to complete the ballot. If someone is not able to click on their voting choice, the poll clerk can click on a button on the screen. The camera in the device will be activated, and the system will record the process as the clerk asks the voter who they would like to vote for in each choice. We have people who check these interactions randomly, in real time. All are recorded for audit purposes."

Finnigan nodded.

"For those in senior living centers, we certify staff in the centers to aid their residents in the same manner. In those cases, the same audit process is used for every vote cast. These staff members are also able to help in the registration process. We provide a questionnaire for the staff member to go through verbally with the voter, which is recorded and determines whether the person is cognizant enough to understand what or who they are voting for. The standards are very liberal in that regard. We recognize that many people vote with no idea who they want to vote for, other than name recognition. That is our country's system, so nobody else should be held to a higher standard."

Allan said, "So it sounds as though it would be nearly impossible for a fraudulent vote to be cast. How about the system being hacked and manipulated from the outside?"

"Correction," Unger said. "It *is* currently impossible to cast a vote without being the person registered with that name and address. It's also impossible to cast a vote for someone who has died, as the voice match will not be possible. Since the system is national, it will not allow a second vote by the same person with multiple addresses or registrations. Individual states handle their own elections and can opt out of our system, but I can't imagine why they would. Our demonstrated success and low cost make the decision a no-brainer."

"And the system is *not* hackable from the outside?" Allan repeated.

"We have protected the system from that as well. First, we use separate computers for registering voters and receiving and counting votes. Only the registration system remains online because the process must be available 99.99% of the time. The only interaction between that computer and the outside is related to the actual registration and collection of votes. The system has no email capability or other communication link. We're able to manage the registration process so information not verifiable through state and IRS files cannot be saved. When a vote is cast, it is encrypted and downloaded to the computer and must utilize the advanced handshake process I described earlier to connect the vote to the voter's registration.

"The vote counting system," Unger continued, "is never online. We have a direct link capability between the two computers. That link remains closed except for a few minutes during an election when the counting system collects the votes. It uses the advanced handshake again to ensure that the only votes collected come from registered voters. There are backup computers in three separate locations around the United States so that data and processing capability is fully backed up even if the primary computer is lost for any reason, such as weather or a terrorist attack. Additionally, there is a secondary computer for each application, and these computers are kept offline. We use them to update and test new software, security protocols, and the like. Those updates are downloaded only after careful scrutiny to determine if there is malware or other damaging software on the machine. Those downloads require the 512K encryption as well."

"I see," said Finnigan. "But how is voting integrity protected from someone in your company manipulating the system from the inside?"

"That is a very good question, Special Agent Finnigan. We had to think that through on the front end. A special team was used to develop the software and security of the voting system. Once the team finalized the software, they trained the operators and a few other developers on the system and then redeployed to other areas in the company. The team that manages the system is completely different, and most are operators rather than developers. The developers tasked with debugging specialize only in certain areas so that nobody is fully knowledgeable on the entire system. Of course, the code is security protected, and programmers are only able to access those areas they have clearance for. We have an intricate version control system that tells us what changes have been made to the coding and who made them. It also tells us who has tried to access an area they don't have clearance for. Finally, we have security specialists who monitor all this and identify concerns."

"Are all programmers from the original team still with the company?" asked Allan.

"As you probably know, good IT professionals are highly sought after and move around a great deal. Until a few weeks ago, we had just two remaining in the company. Tragically, one passed away recently in a traffic accident."

"I see. Would you mind sharing the name of the last remaining developer?" asked Finnigan.

"The one remaining is Eric Blas."

"And Mr. Blas, though he helped develop the system, has no capability to access it?" Finnigan asked.

"Correct. Again, the voting systems are offline, and even though they're in a building adjacent to our commercial business, the other systems are not able to interact with them. Physical security for the voting system is high, and it's impossible to dial in."

"Mr. Unger," Allan asked, "I notice that you have two computers on your desk. I presume one of those is for the election system?"

"No," he responded. "Even I don't have access to the system beyond going through my people who are working with it."

The agents took a couple minutes to look through their notes. Finnigan asked, "Based on your involvement in your company's development and operation of the voting system, can you think of any way that a highly knowledgeable person could manipulate it to pre-determine the vote count in an election?"

"No ma'am, I cannot."

They paused again and exchanged glances. "Do you have anything else?" Finnigan asked.

Allan shook his head, then said, "Actually, just one more thing. Is the state of Pennsylvania using your system?"

Unger said that it was.

Finnigan turned to Unger. "Do you have any other information that you believe would be helpful in our investigation?"

"No. I believe that whoever has made such an accusation is mistaken or perhaps has political motives. The system is completely secure. As we speak, developers are working on the next generation of security for the system so that it stays that way."

Finnigan stood and held out her hand. "Thank you very much, Mr. Unger. You've been extremely helpful. You seem to have an excellent voting system in place."

Unger shook her hand. "Thank you. We certainly believe that we do and are committed to assuring a secure and efficient voting system well into the future."

As they walked out of Jeff Unger's office, each agent handed him their business card. Finnigan said, "If anything comes to mind that you think could be helpful, please give one of us a call."

"I sure will."

CHAPTER 21

BRAD FELT A SENSE OF RELIEF RETURNING TO WORK. WHILE there was a week's worth of issues to be addressed, it was good to focus on something familiar and safe. It took the entire week to get caught up and back to his normal routine.

There was one source of discomfort, however. What about Blas? The only time he had ever seen him in the past was when Brad went up to pay a visit to Al. What if he showed up? What if he bumped into him by chance? Brad wasn't sure what he would do if he found himself face to face with Eric Blas. He wondered if Blas would try to keep an eye on him or avoid him.

On Tuesday he got a call from Cynthia Goldberg telling him that the police had withdrawn the DUI charge against him due to the extenuating circumstances. She promised to send him her bill in the next few days, but he told her he'd pick up the invoice later in the week and retrieve the throwaway phone at the same time. He nearly choked when she said the fee had come to $3,790.

The next day, Brad calculated how much money he and Barb had spent while on the run. When he added up the cell phones, food, unused airfare, and fruit basket they'd sent to the Alvarez family, plus the legal fees, the total came to $8,406. And that didn't include the car they'd bought, nor the registration or insurance for the car. He needed to decide on whether to keep the car and register it or to sell it. For the time being, he had arranged to park the car at a friend's property several miles outside the city.

During this time, he and Barb heard nothing. Not a peep from the bad guys and no calls from the police or FBI. He wondered if the police and FBI thought he was a nutcase and had consequently dropped the investigation. Several times he was tempted to call but didn't want them to think he was obsessed over it. Many questions kept popping up into his mind, but he was so busy at work that he didn't have time to dwell on them. He noticed nothing suspicious at the office or at home. It was as if nothing out of the ordinary had happened.

Barb's return to work followed a similar pattern. When at home during the evenings, the two mostly talked about all the catch up at work, their kids, and other normal things in life. They agreed it would be best not to share their experiences or their suspicions relating to Al's death with Linda. They didn't know enough to be sure about anything, and they figured she had enough on her hands to get through the grieving process with her kids while also working.

CHAPTER 22

TWO WEEKS AFTER RETURNING TO WORK, BRAD FINALLY received a phone call from Detective Conner. The detective said that they believed they had found the man who had entered Brad's home under false pretenses. He asked if Brad would mind coming down to the station to identify him, and Brad readily agreed to a four-thirty meeting that afternoon at the county Police Headquarters.

Brad arrived ten minutes early, not knowing what to expect. Would he be face to face with this guy? Would it really be him? All the anxiety associated with the experience began rushing back.

"Good afternoon, Mr. Tillman," Conner said with an out-stretched hand.

Brad shook the detective's hand. Then he said, "Detective Conner, I'm not sure how this is going to work, but I'm pretty uncomfortable about it. Am I going to have to meet this guy?"

"No. I understand your discomfort. You won't ever be in the same room with him. Follow me, and we can take care of this quickly and have you on your way."

Brad followed Conner to a medium-sized room furnished with tables and chairs. He thought it might be a conference room or perhaps a training room. At the front, there was a large screen that seemed to take up half the wall.

"Have a seat," Conner directed. "Can I get you a bottle of water?"

"Yes, that would be nice. My throat is a bit dry."

Conner went to a small refrigerator underneath a counter in the back of the room and brought back two bottles.

Another man entered the room. "Mr. Tillman, this is Brian Peterman. It's his responsibility to take you through this process. I'm not allowed to be present. These things are done very carefully, and there are good reasons for following procedures. I'll be right outside when you're finished."

"Okay," Brad said as he took a sip of water.

Brian Peterman sat down across from Brad, slightly to one side. "What we're going to do is turn on this screen, and you'll see photos of several people, one at a time. The camera will show you a wide shot, a close-up, and a profile view of each. After you've seen all four, I'll ask if you think the person who entered your house is among them. Do you have any questions?"

"Uh, I can't think of any."

The screen came to life. On it was a background that showed height reference lines similar to what Brad had seen on television. Peterman tapped the forward arrow on his keypad. The slide showed an individual standing, facing the camera with the same background. He had brown hair that was pulled back. The next slide showed a closer shot of the man from the chest up, followed by a profile view. As Brad studied the pictures, Peterman watched him.

This first guy was definitely not the one, Brad thought. His hair was about collar length and too thick to create the ponytail the guy was wearing that day.

Brad stared at another man in all three views, and then a third guy and a fourth. All had longer hair in various shades of brown. Brad's heart sank. He wasn't there. The police obviously had the wrong leads.

"Do you believe any of these men was the man you encountered?" Peterman asked. "Would you like to see any of the pictures again?"

Trying to be as careful as possible, Brad said, "I don't think so, but let me look at the third guy again."

The three photos of the third man were displayed again. He was the only one with hair fine and long enough to be combed back and pulled tight on his head, with the hair below the band hanging straight down. But the guy who attacked him was just starting to bald, unlike the man in this photo. Brad stared at the close-up frontal view. Was it possible he had done a comb-over to conceal any balding? No way, Brad thought.

"No, I'm afraid he isn't there," Brad said, somewhat apologetically.

"Are you sure?"

"Yes, I'm sure," Brad said as he started to stand.

Peterman held out his hand. "Hold on. Let's look at a few more." Brad sat back down as the picture changed again. He was shown a fifth man. Then a sixth.

"It's him!" Brad exclaimed.

"Just hang on a minute, please. Let's go through the full set."

All three photos of the sixth man confirmed that he was the guy. He didn't have a ponytail in the photos, but something more like a man bun. It was him though. Brad was surprised at the details he remembered of the guy's face. Kind of a crooked nose. A freckle or mole of some sort on his left cheek. A scar on the upper left side of his forehead.

The slides continued with another photo. A different person. Nope, he thought. An eighth subject was shown to him. "No, the guy I told you—he was the one."

Peterman went back to the slides of the sixth man, showing all three angles again. "Yep, that's him," Brad said confidently.

"Are you sure? This man doesn't have a ponytail."

"I'm sure. I recognize his face. When he was wearing a ponytail, his hair was pulled back on his head in the same way as this bun. It's him."

"All right, Mr. Tillman. Before you make your final decision, I want you to understand that this man's life might be changed forever, based partially on your testimony. If you have any doubt at all, you can express it now."

"I have no doubts."

"Mr. Tillman, are you prepared to identify this person as a witness in court, should a prosecutor ask?"

Brad paused. It wasn't that he was unsure. He was just thinking about the prospect of facing this man. "Yes," he said.

"All right, Mr. Tillman. Please wait here for a moment."

Peterman went to the door and motioned for Conner to return. As the detective came in, Peterman pointed to the screen and said, "This is the person that Mr. Tillman identified." As he did so, he handed Conner a card on which he had written the identifying number of the man.

Peterman left the room as Conner sat down across from Brad. "This is the man we picked up. His name is Thomas Everett. He owns a white Sprinter van registered in North Carolina. He works as a handyman."

"Great!" Brad exclaimed.

"Well, we seem to have your man, but I'm not sure what we can do with him just yet. He isn't telling us anything. We aren't sure how we would charge him. He entered your house at your invitation and had a gun on him legally."

"But he chased after me! He followed us the next day when we left the hotel!"

"I understand, but that's not enough to hold him on. At least we have some new information to explore."

"You can't hold him? What if he comes after me?"

"I doubt that'll happen. We won't tell him that he was identified by you. All he knows is that his van brought him under suspicion. He stammered a bit when asked about his whereabouts on the day in question. It will be easy to confirm with the utility company that he is not an employee, so we should be able to determine that he entered your house under false pretenses. So, we do have somewhere to begin," Conner said. "It is actually not a bad thing that he won't remain in custody. We can monitor him and learn more."

"What should we do in the meantime?"

"Nothing at all. You've been helpful. Just go back to what you've been doing."

Brad's face drooped. He felt let down. Still, he understood that the guy's actions didn't provide proof of intent. As he headed home, he found his mind cluttered with everything again. He hoped it was only temporary.

CHAPTER 23

BETTY FINNIGAN WAS DEEP IN THOUGHT WHEN THE PHONE
rang. "Finnigan," she answered.

"Hi Betty. This is Frank at the lab."

"Hi Frank. What are you analyzing today?"

"I was just looking at that vote tally document you sent down. I
can offer you a couple bits of information about it."

"Oh?" Betty wasn't really expecting to get anything from the
document, but she had sent it down to the lab as a matter of routine.

"I'm not sure if this will help, but it appears to be a copy created
from another document, and not a printout. If you like, I could analyze
the toner to determine the brand of copier used. I do know that it was
a large office machine and not an ink-jet printer."

Betty thought for a moment. "Yes, Frank. Please do that. Knowing the copier brand might prove to be useful."

"Okay. We'll take a look."

"Frank, it is possible to link a copy with a specific copier, isn't it?"

"Yes. You find the copier, and I can tell you if it's a match."

"Thanks, Frank. I'll look forward to hearing from you soon." She
hung up the phone and paused for a moment. Al Johnson may have
found the document, but it could have been someone else. Anyone
could have made a copy out of concern. They could have returned the
original so nobody would know it had been removed.

She picked up her phone again and called Chris Allan to discuss
the case. They agreed to meet at one p.m. to review all the facts.

After lunch, Chris walked into Betty's office and closed the door
behind him. "I don't have much more than we had last week," he said.

"I understand," Betty said. "I got a little more this morning and thought we should discuss it."

She filled him in on the new information about the document being a copy. "I thought we might review what we have. I'm still unsure whether there is enough here to go further."

"Well," Chris said, "We know that the document had final vote tallies on it. Tillman believes it was in Al Johnson's briefcase before he died, which would make it before the election."

"Right. Go on."

"At this point, all we have is Tillman's word that he found the document in that briefcase before the election. We need to see if there's any evidence to corroborate that. There could be another explanation as to how that document got into the briefcase."

"It may be time for a visit with Johnson's wife," Betty said.

"We know now that it's a copy, and we should know soon what type of copier was used," Chris went on. "If we can find out what machine the copy was made on, it could help us determine who made the copy."

"Keep going."

"We know that someone seems to have hacked into the Pennsylvania Secretary of State's website and changed the numbers from actual to fictitious ones. I got a call about this yesterday. There doesn't appear to be any evidence of outside intrusion into the system. That means that whoever changed those numbers must have had authorization."

"Did their office ever get back to you on what the person who posted the numbers had to say?"

"Yes. She said she posted the vote tallies at 9:13 that Thursday morning. She kept notes and a copy of the final vote report that she used to post the data. She's convinced there is no way she could have input all the numbers incorrectly."

"She would have had to be asleep or under the influence to get every single number wrong. The only matches between the original numbers and what they were changed to are the totals," Betty said. "I wonder if they handle their web security in house, or if an outside party is contracted to do that."

"I can check that out easily enough," Chris said, making a note.

"Okay, what else do we have?" Betty asked.

"The CEO at GCI believes their technology makes it impossible for someone to manipulate votes in his system."

"Yes, he sure made it sound like they have a tamper-proof system, inside and outside."

"Tillman gave us the name of Eric Blas, inside the company, as one he thinks could be involved. A review of his background indicates he's never been in any trouble. His Facebook posts show that he pays close attention to politics and takes the liberal side. He's volunteered on campaigns and such, but there's no indication that he's ever done anything illegal in his political activism."

Betty thought for a moment. "We sure don't have much to go on. It appears that someone may have panicked and changed that website. Had they not done that, we may have dismissed the whole thing altogether."

"Agreed," Chris said. "I'll check on who handles the security for the Pennsylvania technology. Would you like for me to contact Al Johnson's wife?"

"Yes, we should probably do that," Betty agreed. "But be really careful. We have no hard evidence that her husband was murdered, and I certainly don't want to upset her more."

Chris Allan stood to leave. "I'll get the ball rolling on all of this."

"And Chris," Betty added, "Maybe we should let the Tillmans know we'll be contacting Linda Johnson. She'll probably call them immediately. We should do whatever we can to keep her mind at ease with regard to her husband's character."

"I agree. I'll find out her schedule and arrange a meeting. I'll let them know about it."

"Thanks, Chris."

CHAPTER 24

BRAD WAS FINISHING UP IN HIS OFFICE FOR THE DAY WHEN he heard a phone ring. It took him a few seconds to figure out where the sound was coming from. Finally, it dawned on him that it was the throwaway phone inside his briefcase. He grabbed it and said, "Hello," as he walked to the door and closed it.

"Mr. Tillman, this is Special Agent Allan from the FBI."

"Special Agent Allan, how are you today?"

"I appreciate your deference, Mr. Tillman, but Special Agent is a bit cumbersome. You can call me Chris or Mr. Allan if you like."

"Thank you, Mr. Allan. Have you made any progress on our situation? I haven't heard for so long that I thought perhaps you decided not to pursue it."

"Well, what we do is a game of inches. Every detail matters, and we must establish factual information in order to be effective in our work. We have some information, though, and I thought I'd bring you up to speed on what we know."

"Thank you."

Allan hit the high points, advising Brad that his document did show correct vote tallies and that the website was changed between the time Brad looked at it and when he first met with the FBI. Allan told him they were exploring possible avenues for manipulating votes. Then he said, "Mr. Tillman, we think it will be helpful to talk with Linda Johnson regarding the document you found in Mr. Johnson's briefcase."

"I see," Brad said. "You should know that Barb and I have not told Linda anything about our experiences since I found the document. I just told her at the time that I had found some files that should be returned to Al's boss. We didn't want to bother her or upset her with anything more."

"I can appreciate that. Agent Finnigan and I agree that we need to tread lightly. We'll be careful to stick to pertinent questions regarding the document and the whereabouts of the briefcase just before his death. We anticipate that she'll contact you wondering what's going on, so I wanted to give you a heads-up."

"I'm glad you did," Brad said. "How will you tell her the document was brought to your attention?"

"Naturally, we don't want to mislead her. We'll explain that you found the document and, as a good citizen, handed it over to us."

"Okay," Brad said slowly. "Do you think I should call her and let her know?"

"You can be the judge of that. I'll be calling her tomorrow afternoon."

"Okay, thanks. I'll talk about it with Barb, and we'll probably give her a call tonight. Please be careful not to give her the impression that Al did anything wrong."

"We'll be as careful as we can. We understand what she's going through. Have a good evening, Mr. Tillman."

Brad pressed the *end* button and stared at the phone. He had hoped that Linda would not have to be brought into this. Reflecting on the situation, he understood that all the FBI had was his word that the document came from Al's briefcase. He doubted that Linda would know anything about it. He wondered what questions this would raise in Linda's mind. He hoped she wouldn't be too upset.

That night Brad briefed Barb on his conversation with Allan. She agreed that they should reach out to Linda before the FBI did. They would still not mention the danger they had been in as a result of finding the document.

At about eight p.m., Brad picked up his cell phone. After Al's death, he had changed the contact information in his directory from Al's to Linda's name and number. He felt a brief pang. He pressed the call button and waited.

"Hi Brad," Linda said. "How nice to hear from you."

"Hey Linda! How are you getting along?"

"Well, I've had some sad evenings. I don't know what I'd do without the kids here. It's difficult for them too, but we're getting through it together."

"I can't even imagine what it must be like."

"We're okay. I've been meaning to give Barb a call. I owe you guys dinner. I'd love to see you."

"That would be great. Yes, call Barb. Her schedule is the one that is typically the challenge," Brad said. "Linda, the reason I called is to bring you in on something Al may have been working on before he left us."

"Okay," Linda said slowly.

"Do you remember that afternoon you asked me to come by and go through Al's briefcase to see if there was anything that needed to go back to GCI?"

"Yes," she said, again slowly.

"I found the files I thought should go to Al's boss, Cathy Hoover, but I also ran across something I wasn't certain about. I took it along with me to ask Cathy about it."

"Did she need it? What was it?"

"It was actually a document that didn't appear to have anything to do with Al's work. It weighed on my mind a bit, so I did some exploring. The document appeared to show voting irregularities in a Pennsylvania special election. The more I looked, the more concerned I became. I actually contacted the FBI."

"Brad, surely you're not suggesting that Al was involved in something illegal!"

"No, as a matter of fact, I think he would have contacted the FBI, just as I did."

"What are you saying then?"

"Look, Linda, the document I found had results of a special election on it. But the election didn't take place until the Tuesday after Al's death. I couldn't understand how these numbers could be on a document that was in Al's possession before the election. Al wrote a big question mark across the whole page. This makes me think that it somehow came into his possession, and he didn't know what to make of it."

"Why are you telling me this?" Linda's voice was shaky.

"As I said, I turned the document over to the FBI. I found out today that they are going to contact you to see if you have any information about it."

"Information? How would I have information?"

"Perhaps it's more accurate to say that they want to know how and when the document got into the briefcase. You know, did Al always carry it to work, was there anyone in your house who could have slipped it into the briefcase, that kind of thing. The FBI has to be thorough in its investigation. Like you say, you probably don't know anything about it, but they need to explore every detail."

"Oh, Brad, I don't want to deal with this."

Brad felt awful that this had come to Linda. "I'm sorry, Linda. I understand. I certainly didn't want to upset you with it. That's why I haven't said anything. I'm sure it won't take long to talk with them, though. All you need to do is answer their questions the best you can."

Finally, the conversation came to an end with Brad telling Linda that she should expect a call from Special Agents Finnigan or Allan soon. Afterwards, Brad felt like he'd been beaten with a rope. He felt as much stress now as he had when he and Barb were on the run. He recounted the call with Barb, who clearly understood the distressing position this put her friend in. She wanted to call Linda right away, but they decided it wouldn't help. Hopefully, the FBI would call her tomorrow as Allan had said, then he and Barb could follow up with another call of their own.

CHAPTER 25

TWO DAYS LATER, CHRIS ALLAN TAPPED ON BETTY
Finnigan's closed office door. She was on the phone but motioned for him
to enter. He quietly opened the door and took a seat while she finished her
call. Turning to him, she asked, "What's up?"

"I've set up a meeting with Linda Johnson for tomorrow afternoon at four p.m. at her home."

"Great!"

"I also spoke with the Pennsylvania Secretary of State's office.
They use a third party to handle security for their systems. That party
is Gone Cyber, Inc.," he said, watching for her reaction.

She shook her head. "Well now, that piece fits conveniently into
the puzzle, doesn't it?"

"My contact put me in touch with their system administrator,
who said they've been really pleased with GCI because they never
have to take the system down for maintenance. They're able to work in
the background."

"Did you ask if someone from GCI might have the ability to
access the website and change content without authorization?"

"Yes. He said he's never been concerned about that, but he spec-
ulated that they could probably do so if they wanted. I asked if he
could see who accessed and made changes to data on the website, and
he said he couldn't, but that GCI could. He's asked them to change
information before."

"Isn't that convenient?" Betty responded.

"Looks like we are moving the ball up court!" Chris said. Betty
grinned and rolled her eyes.

They agreed to meet up the following day to visit Linda, and Chris returned to his office. Betty placed another phone call.

"GCI. Mr. Unger's office."

Finnigan had learned many years ago to take note of and re-member names of people she met during her investigations, no matter how potentially insignificant they might seem at the time. Remembering someone's name is a sign of respect, and people typically feel honored by it. It also tends to make them more helpful. Not always, but often enough.

"Hello, Carol, this is Special Agent Betty Finnigan with the FBI. My partner and I met you last week when we visited with Mr. Unger."

"Yes, I remember!" Carol beamed.

"Thank you. Is Mr. Unger available to take a phone call?"

"I'm sorry, but he's out of the office today. Is it urgent, or could I have him return your call? Perhaps there's something I could help you with?"

"Yes, please have Mr. Unger give me a call. It's not urgent."

"Is this the best number for him to call?"

"Yes it is. Thank you so much, Carol."

"You're welcome!" Carol said warmly. "Have a lovely day."

Betty knew that the question she had would be more appropriate for someone well below Unger in the organization. However, at present he was the only person they had talked to, and it would create quite a stir for an FBI agent to make a cold call to some underling and ask for information. He could delegate the task easily enough or put her in touch with the right person.

She picked up the phone again and pushed a speed dial button.

"Frank," announced a man's voice.

"Hi Frank, this is Betty. I hate to press you, but were you able to identify the type of copier used to replicate that document I shared with you?"

"Hey Betty. I was actually going to give you a call this afternoon. Yes, the toner used was from Yosheti. I can't be more specific than that because they use the same toner in all of their machines, just packaged in different cartridges. I'll have the completed report on your desk in the morning."

"Thanks, Frank."

Betty hung up the phone again. On a lark, she dialed Brad Till-man's number. The phone rang a few times; eventually she heard, "This is Brad," in a tentative voice.

"Hello, Brad. This is Special Agent Finnigan. Do you have just a minute?"

"Uh, sure. Just a moment. Let me close the door," Brad said.

"Brad, is this the best number to reach you on? It's the only one I have."

"Yes, it is. It's the throwaway phone I got a couple of weeks ago. Very few people know of its existence."

"Good. Hey, can you tell me what kind of copy machines your company uses?"

"Well, that varies from department to department. We have a national account with several companies. Department heads are able to select the copier brand and style that meets their needs the best."

"I see. Would one of the companies be Yosheti?"

"Yes, we have some groups using Yosheti."

"How difficult would it be to determine what departments use that brand?"

"Well, we could search it pretty quickly in our invoice pay-ment system."

There was a pause. Betty said nothing and hoped Brad might offer the information.

"If I gave you a list of departments that use that brand, would that provide what you need?"

"It would be a helpful start," she said. "If it turns out we need more, I'll go through the proper channels. Thanks, Brad."

After she ended the call, she took some time to make notes for her file. Thus far, the strongest path of evidence suggested that any of the actions they were exploring could have been accomplished from within GCI. She didn't want to close the door on any other possibili-ties, but GCI kept coming up as a real option for culpability.

CHAPTER 26

FOLLOWING BRAD'S EXPERIENCE WITH PICKING THE MAN out of the pictures, Barb became concerned for their safety again. Brad tried to calm her fears by reminding her that the guy had never seen him during the session, and Detective Conner said he wouldn't know that Brad had identified him. Even if he did know, nothing good would come of harming Brad or Barb because they had already told the authorities what they knew. And should something happen, the man would be the first person the police would suspect.

Barb's fear seemed to subside a bit, but Brad had his own worries. Others could also be paid if this guy was just a hired hit man. Whoever hired him was doing a good job of staying in the shadows.

A couple of weeks later, Brad had a challenging morning at work. He needed some time to think through a few things, so he decided to take an extended lunch. He grabbed an Uber and headed to the Varsity.

The downtown Varsity was probably the most famous hot dog place in the world, a destination for tourists and locals alike. There were no servers, and everyone ordered their meal from a long counter. You could get any combination of hot dog, hamburger, chili, cheese, and slaw that you desired. Lunch was typically under ten or twelve bucks, but you were as likely to see executives there as blue-collar workers. Celebrity sightings were not unheard of. It was always crowded, but service was quick with seating for 800, plus car hop.

As he stood in one of fifteen lines to order his lunch at the counter, he heard a couple guys in the next line getting worked up about politics. "We need to shut those racist sons-of-bitches up so we can get something done in this country," one said.

"There needs to be a law against some of the trash they spew," said the other. Brad knew that twenty steps away there were probably people going off on the other side of the political spectrum. He saw no solution for the divide in the country.

He reached the front of the line. The gal behind the counter barked, "Whaddya have?" He ordered two chili cheese slaw dogs, onion rings, and a Coke. He found a table and sat down with his tray. The rhetoric he had heard stuck with Brad. He never thought he'd see the country in such a state of downright hatred between people. He wondered if everyone was going nuts.

His mind turned to the election fraud issue. If someone were able to manipulate elections as they may have in Pennsylvania, the country would soon be on a fast track to a place he hated to imagine. He thought about his daughters and their families and wondered what their lives would be like as they got older. What would his grandson learn in school? Would he grow up to experience the same America Brad had always known?

"Tillman! Fancy meeting you here," came a voice over the din of the crowded restaurant. "Mind if I join you?"

Before he knew what was happening, Brad was sitting face to face with Eric Blas. He froze, his mind racing in a hundred directions. He looked around to see plenty of people, all potential witnesses to whatever was about to happen. Should he stand and walk out? Should he call the police? He thought he might have a panic attack.

"Did I catch you in the middle of deep concentration or what?" Blas asked.

"Eric, how are you doing?" was all Brad could muster.

"I've never seen you here before. I eat here a lot."

"Uh, no, I just needed to take some time away from the office to think through some issues."

"Yeah, you accountants always have all those numbers flying around in your heads. Guess a guy needs to get away just to survive the onslaught!"

Brad stared at Blas. It seemed like everything the guy said could be taken a few different ways. *Get away to survive.* Was this some obscure reference to Brad having been on the run? Did he know that he had survived an attempted murder?

"Well, it's never the numbers. It's typically the people involved in the numbers that are tough to deal with."

"I guess so." Blas nodded as he took a bite of his hamburger. With his mouth still full, he went on, "Look, Brad, I guess I was a bit of a jerk at Al's funeral. I'm sorry if I offended you."

"I just thought that a service like that would be a time of appreciating Al and respecting his memory, as opposed to dwelling on negative things."

"You're probably right. I've never been accused of having too much tact," Eric said, smirking.

That doesn't surprise me, Brad thought. "How are you getting along without Al?" he said, trying to think of some way to make conversation with the man in front of him.

"It's tough, man. He was a solid project manager. Cathy's trying to replace him, but she's having some trouble."

"The company isn't letting her hire?"

This would surprise Brad. Typically hiring freezes came at his recommendation when he noticed challenges with the financials.

"It's not that. She's having a tough time finding a good fit. Says she may have to change our structure a bit if she isn't able to find someone. I wish she'd get on with it because I'm drowning in work, and it's taking me away from other things I should be doing."

"It must be difficult on your family."

"I don't have a family. My parents died when I was in college, and I never got married. I was almost there, but my fiancée died in a car accident a few months back."

Brad looked at him. He didn't seem nasty. He didn't seem angry. And this . . . what a gut punch.

"Eric, I'm so sorry. I had no idea you'd lost someone close."

"How would you have known?" Eric said. "We barely know each other." He sighed. "It's been a screwed-up few months for me. Losing Kathrine and then Al. It may not seem like it, but I did like Al and respected him. He did decent work and was someone who could put up with my crap, you know?"

That struck Brad as amusing. He wasn't sure if it was his nervousness or what, but he almost choked on the chunk of hot dog in his mouth. He was close to blowing coleslaw out his nose. When he recovered, he said, "Al said you were a guy with an attitude, but he spoke well of your capabilities. He respected you a lot."

"Yeah, that was mutual. I'd give him a ration of shit at times, but he'd never give it back for some reason."

Brad smiled. "He'd probably be happy to hear you say that!"

"Yeah, I suppose he would."

Brad was taken aback. He would never have considered a conversation with Eric Blas to go like this. Blas was a character for sure, but he didn't seem like someone who would hire a hit man. Brad was starting to feel comfortable, safe at least, so he started to probe.

"Al said you're politically active."

"I am at times. It just makes me crazy that people are dragging their heels as we try to take this country through the twenty-first century. The wealth in our society is outrageous, and at the same time we have working families who can't afford childcare. Teachers barely make a living wage. There needs to be balance in the system."

"What kind of things are you involved in?"

"Oh, I go to rallies and help on campaigns. They don't want me on the phone because I'm not the most patient with people who don't share our goals."

"You have a lot of expertise in technology. Do they take advantage of that?"

"Nah, I'm just a worker bee. There are technology companies that specialize in the political world. They don't need me for that."

"What else do you do with your spare time?"

"Don't have any of that these days," Eric said as he rolled his eyes. "I do a little work on the side. Mostly software development for small companies." Blas's look became serious. "I'd appreciate it if you wouldn't share that inside the company. I'm a long way from the point where I could support myself with this business."

"Okay," Brad said. He looked at his watch and saw that he needed to get back to work to prepare for a two o'clock meeting. His plan to ponder over lunch had been scuttled, but Brad wanted to continue this conversation. He wasn't sure why, but he was beginning to believe he had been wrong about Eric Blas. He wanted to be sure.

"Eric, I have to get back to the office, but there's something I'd like to talk to you about. Would you have time to meet for a beer after work?"

Eric shrugged his shoulders. "Yeah, I could do that. I don't drink, but I'll have my usual ginger ale."

They agreed on a time and place, gathered their trays and trash, and headed out.

"I have to make a stop on the way to work, so I'll need to go my own way," Blas said.

"Okay," Brad said. "See you later."

As Brad used his Uber app to get a ride, he thought about their conversation. Could he really have been that wrong about Eric Blas?

During the ride back, he wondered if he should bring Barb up to speed on what had happened at lunch but decided against it. She wasn't there to assess the situation herself, and she would worry. He would finish the conversation with Blas first and then get her caught up. He wanted to protect her from involvement. He knew she *was* involved but would prefer she become less so.

Then his mind began to take a different direction. Could Blas have known he was at the Varsity? Was he being tracked again? What if Brad was falling into a trap by inadvertently setting things up for Blas to meet him later in a less crowded place? If so, Blas was a particularly good actor. The thought of getting this issue with Eric Blas behind him, one way or the other, felt really good. He hoped he wouldn't regret what he was about to do.

CHAPTER 27

BRAD PHONED BARB TO LET HER KNOW HE HAD A LATE meeting that afternoon and to go ahead and eat without him. At a quarter past five, he drove out of the underground lot and headed out to meet Blas. The Bird Cage was a sports bar just north of downtown that specialized in wings. It was a fairly large place and typically had a decent crowd, but it normally wasn't hard to find a table. Brad didn't see any sign of Blas outside the entrance. He didn't see him inside either, so he asked for a booth for two. A waiter quickly approached the table for his drink order. He asked for a beer on tap and a ginger ale, explaining that he was waiting for someone.

A few minutes after the waiter delivered the drinks, Blas walked through the front door and looked around the bar. Brad stood and waved. Blas walked over and shook Brad's hand and sat across from him in the booth.

"Thanks for the drink. You must want something," Blas said with a deadpan voice.

Brad shook his head and smiled. "Just so you wouldn't have to wait."

Brad didn't have time at the office to think through how to proceed with this conversation. His afternoon meeting had taken all of his attention. He decided to begin with some simple security-related questions.

"How long have you been with the company, Eric?"

"Seven years," Blas responded quickly. "Why?"

"Were you in the tech security business before that?"

"Yeah, I got my degree in Cyber Security at Georgia Tech. I joined a small firm in Marietta out of school and was with them for four years doing research on potential approaches for safeguarding computer systems before GCI recruited me."

"I figured you must know your stuff. Let me ask you . . . what kind of person does it take to track someone by their cell phone, access their bank and credit card transactions, and monitor their comings and goings?"

"There are two ways to accomplish that," Blas began. "One would be to know the account access information and use it to change someone's account settings and get a notification via email when the person makes a transaction. If they had access to the person's phone, they could easily set up authorization to track it. Anyone could accomplish those things if they had access. The other way would be to go in through the service provider's system for the bank or phone account. There it would take a hacker with special skills. Of course, that would be illegal."

As Blas answered the question, Brad watched him carefully. He didn't know what to look for exactly, but perhaps some defensiveness or other indication that he understood the context of Brad's question. Brad didn't see any.

"Why?" Blas asked. "Do you want to monitor someone? I hope you're not wanting me to do that for you."

The waiter approached the table and asked for their order. Brad ordered a batch of wings and told him he'd have another beer. Blas looked up and said, "I'm fine."

"There was a period right after Al's death when someone was monitoring me. They seemed to know everything I was doing. They were definitely tracking my location," Brad said, again looking for some sign from Blas.

"They?" Blas asked. "How did you know *they* were doing all of this?"

Brad wondered if this was Blas's way of finding out how much Brad knew. His facial expression and voice didn't really show surprise, but then again, he hadn't shown himself to be a gregarious communicator. Brad decided he was in with both feet now, so he might as well get on with it.

"To answer your question directly, someone came to my home, under false pretenses, threatening me. I managed to escape and physically separate myself from the situation. Within minutes the guy located me, and, until I turned off my phone, got closer and closer, as though he knew exactly where to go. Once my phone was off, I lost him, but later he or they found me driving my car. I have since learned that my car had a tracking device on it. They also seemed to know when and where I used my credit card."

Now Blas's face showed a subdued look of astonishment. That was probably as demonstrative as the guy got. His lips drew in and he spouted a long low whistle as he stared back at Brad. "That sounds professional to me. Who's doing it? What do you have that they want?"

Brad took a deep breath. "I thought it might be you," he said matter-of-factly.

CHAPTER 28

ERIC'S FACE BECAME ANIMATED. "WHAT THE F—!" HE didn't finish the word, which was a bit surprising to Brad, but his mouth stayed open for a moment.

"I don't know why you think I would find you so fricking interesting, but you'd better get that out of your mind right now!" Eric appeared ready to come across the table.

Brad held up both hands. "Settle down, Eric. I *have* gotten that idea out of my mind. You would have to appreciate the full context of all of this to understand why I made the stupid assumption in the first place."

"Is this why you got me here tonight? To accuse me of this shit?" Eric had not settled down yet.

"Look, yes, I guess I had to feel you out on this, but after our lunch today I really didn't believe it was you. The bigger reason is I thought you might be able to help."

"Help? What can I do? It sounds like you should call the police."

"I have. The police have done some investigating and have identified the person who came into my house. The FBI is also involved."

Eric sighed. "Sounds like you've got some major problems, Tillman. You need to keep me out of it." He sat back against the booth and shook his head. Then his eyes widened. "Tillman, tell me you didn't tell the police I was the one monitoring you!"

Now Brad felt about two inches tall. He realized that he had really jumped to a conclusion based upon little evidence. "I'm sorry, Eric. I told them that they might want to check into you."

"Tillman!" Eric raised his voice. "Do you know what that could do to my career? How am I supposed to save my reputation if the police think that I am a cyber guy who's using his skills for illegal purposes? Have you said anything about this to anyone at GCI?" Eric was nearly hyperventilating now. He moved forward and put his hands on the table. Then he put his face in his hands and finally sat back in the booth again. "Brad, you have no idea what this could do to me! This could mean the end of my career in cybersecurity!"

Brad felt terrible. He hadn't even considered how such an accusation might impact someone. The waiter brought the food and Brad's beer. During the brief period of silence, Brad could see that Eric's mind was racing. Eric glared at Brad and then let out a breath and looked away.

"Look, Eric. Nobody at GCI knows anything about this. I'll go to the police and tell them I was wrong. I'll make sure they know you're not involved. I *will* do everything I can to protect your reputation. I can tell you that they told me you had no record, and nothing on social media suggested you might be involved in something like this."

"Crap! They're investigating me?" He sat back again, and his head rolled back as he stared at the ceiling.

"Eric, I will fix it!"

Eric glared across the table. "You'd better fix it, man, because if my career is impacted one iota, there's gonna be a huge defamation lawsuit coming your way!"

Blas's reaction worried Brad. He hoped he could get something from Detective Conner that would assure both of them that Eric's reputation would be undamaged by Brad's far-fetched accusation. "Eric, I will address this first thing in the morning and do whatever it takes to ensure this does not impact your career. I feel awful."

Eric said nothing.

"Look, I'd like to let you know what was going on so you can see that I wasn't intentionally trying to harm you."

"Just a minute," Eric said, motioning with his hand. He waved down the waiter and said, "I'll take a draft too, please."

Brad began his story once Eric had his beer in front of him. He told Eric about the document he had found in Al's briefcase. The columns of voting tallies by precinct in Pennsylvania. The full-page question mark. He told him about taking the document home with him.

Eric looked directly at him then. "This was a Pennsylvania special election?"

"It was."

"Pennsylvania is using our voting system," Eric said.

"So I understand," returned Brad. "Well, I didn't know what I had, but I did remember Pennsylvania having a special election after the former senator went to work in the President's administration. I went home and pulled up the Pennsylvania Secretary of State webpage and found that the results of the election were already posted. As I looked through them, I found that they were identical to the numbers on the document in Al's briefcase. I don't know much about the GCI voting system, but I do know that in our building the voting system division is heavily restricted. Al had also told me that few, if any, other networks can communicate with it. It then dawned on me that the document had to have been in Al's briefcase *before* the election. Al died before the election."

Eric's eyes narrowed. "Are you sure?"

"As sure as I can be. When Linda called me to go through the briefcase to see if there was anything the company needed among the files, I assumed she found it just as Al had left it. All I found were the folders that you ultimately got and that single sheet of paper. When you called to ask me if there was anything else, I didn't tell you about it because I thought it might involve voter fraud. You pressed me, and I began to think that you may have been looking for that document."

Eric sat with his elbow on the table and rubbed his forehead with that hand. "Holy crap! There is no way that the election could possibly have been manipulated. We made that system airtight!"

"You were on the development team with Al?"

"I was."

"Then how do you explain it?"

Blas simply shook his head.

"How could Al come upon the results of the election before it occurred?" Brad asked again.

"If it were possible, it would have to have come from inside the voting division."

"There's one more thing," Brad said. "There's a fairly good chance that Al's death was not an accident. I think he was murdered over this."

"You're shittin' me!"

"Because just a few days after I did a search for the Pennsylvania vote results, a thug came to my door with a gun and manipulated his way inside. The only reason I survived is because I had seen his van parked nearby a couple of evenings before and saw the gun before he could make a move on me. I shoved him down the stairs and ran."

Brad looked at Eric, whose eyes were moving all over the place, as though he were looking for something or someone. He seemed anxious. Had he, once again, misjudged the guy? Was he trying to figure out what to do with Brad?

Brad went on, "I got to thinking that if someone did have a way to manipulate elections, they would probably be willing to do almost anything to keep it secret. At that point I—"

Eric put up his hand and shook his head no emphatically. His eyes glistened. He kept shaking his head, faster and faster. "Oh shit! No!"

Suddenly he stood up and looked around the bar. He took off toward the restroom sign, almost in a sprint. Brad didn't know what was going on. He wasn't sure what to do. He stood and watched Eric as he rounded the corner. He looked at Eric's ginger ale and his beer. Neither had been touched. All Brad could think to do was to go after him.

Brad opened the men's bathroom door. He heard someone retching. He didn't see Eric at a urinal. He leaned in, moved his head forward, and peeked inside the first stall. There was Eric, on his knees, hugging the commode. When he finished, he just sat there on his knees with his forehead on his forearm. He was sobbing.

"Eric, what's wrong?" was all Brad could muster. "What do you need? What can I get you?"

A man came into the restroom and stood at the urinal. Brad felt awkward, standing in the middle of the restroom staring into a stall. The guy seemed to sense something was off and left without washing his hands.

Eric just sat there sobbing for a couple of minutes, which, to Brad, felt like an hour. Finally, he got up and faced Brad. Tears were streaming down his face, mingling with the remains of what had come up from his stomach.

"They killed her," he cried. "They killed my Kathrine."

CHAPTER 29

THE BLACK SUV PARKED IN FRONT OF LINDA JOHNSON'S home a few minutes before four o'clock. Inside, Special Agents Betty Finnigan and Chris Allan were discussing the voter fraud case. Betty told Chris that Jeff Unger had returned her call and said that he would need to talk with his legal department about providing details of updates on the Pennsylvania Secretary of State website.

When it was four on the dot, they knocked on Linda's front door. "Thank you for making the time to see us, Mrs. Johnson," Finnigan said warmly.

"Come in. May I get you something to drink, or a snack?"

Both agents politely declined and thanked her. As they sat down in Linda's family room, Finnigan said, "We know this is a very difficult time for you, Mrs. Johnson. We would like to make this as easy as possible."

"Thank you," Linda replied. "How can I be of help?"

Chris explained that Brad Tillman had said he found a document in Al's briefcase that was of great importance to the FBI. He told her that it was their objective to simply try to develop a documentable chain of custody for the document, if possible.

"Yes, Brad told me about it," Linda said politely. "I'm not sure that I can be of help, but I'll do what I can."

"Thank you," said Finnigan. "Brad said that he found the document in your husband's briefcase. Is that right?"

"Yes, he said that he found it there with some folders that needed to be returned to the office."

"Did he show you the document?"

"No, I don't think he even said anything about it at that time."

"Is that the briefcase?"

Linda picked up the briefcase that she had set out for the meeting. "Yes, this is it. I intend to give it to my son."

Allan took the briefcase from Linda and looked through it carefully. It was empty. He set it down and used his cell phone to take pictures of it.

"I'm sure your son will be proud to have his dad's briefcase. It looks like a really nice one," Finnigan offered. "Mr. Tillman indicated that you asked him to go through the case for you, is that correct?"

Linda nodded. "A person from the company came by to pick up Al's laptop and anything else that might belong to the company. It was obviously awkward for them, but I tried to be as cooperative as I could. I never even thought about Al's briefcase. We used the room where Al had his desk for company after he died. In preparing the room, I put the briefcase in my bedroom closet. I never even thought about it. Of course, my mind was not too sharp in the midst of all that happened."

"I understand," Finnigan assured her. "While it was in your husband's office or later in your closet, would anyone have been able to access it? Could someone have put something in it or removed something from it?"

Linda thought for a few moments. "Well, it was accessible before I moved it. My kids were around. We had a lot of visitors. People went to the bathroom, which was across from that bedroom. I suppose it is possible. I can't imagine any of our friends doing that, however."

"I understand. Mrs. Johnson, I'd like to focus on the Tuesday following your husband's death. That was an important day relating to the information on that document. Where was the briefcase on that Tuesday? Can you remember?"

Linda paused again to think. "Al's brother came on that Monday, so that was the day I moved it into my bedroom closet. It was there until the day I called Brad. I noticed it on Friday morning as I was getting ready for the day. It occurred to me that there could be something in it of interest to the company."

"When you noticed the briefcase again, was it in the same place as when you left it the Monday before?"

"Yes, I'm pretty sure it was in the same place."

"Thank you, Mrs. Johnson," Finnigan said as she reached for her own briefcase. "There is just one more thing. I would like you to look at a copy of the document in question." She removed it from the case and passed it to Linda. "Do you ever recall seeing this document in your home or elsewhere?"

Linda took the paper and stared at it for a moment. She lifted her head and stared across the room at nothing in particular. "It's possible that I did see it before."

"I see," Finnigan said evenly, as she glanced toward her partner. "Can you explain when and where you might have seen it?"

"Well, the week before Al died. It was on a Thursday night. I came home, and Al was in his office. I went in to kiss him hello, and he was sitting at his desk just staring at a piece of paper that looked like this one. There was no question mark on the paper, but it had columns like this. I remember because usually Al was on his laptop in his office. That night, his laptop wasn't even on the desk. He was just looking at a piece of paper."

"I understand," said Finnigan. "How can you be sure it was the week before your husband died?"

"I have a ladies' Bible study that I attend on Thursday nights. I had just returned. The study was canceled because the leader was sick that week of Al's death."

"Thank you, Mrs. Johnson. Is there anything else you can think of relating to this document or your husband's briefcase that might be relevant?"

"No, there is nothing that I can think of," Linda said. "Special Agent Finnigan," she added, her eyes beginning to tear up, "Did Al do something against the law?"

Finnigan reached out and took Linda's hands in hers. "No, Mrs. Johnson. We have no reason to believe that your husband did anything wrong." She smiled. "In fact, we believe he acted honorably.... You have been very helpful. What you have told us will be important as we continue the investigation. Thank you again."

The agents stood and gave her their cards along with instructions to contact them if she thought of anything else. They said their goodbyes. Once in the car, Chris looked at Betty and said, "It's not airtight, but it does seem to corroborate Tillman's story."

Betty said, "Well, it certainly doesn't refute it."

CHAPTER 30

BRAD STEPPED FORWARD AND HALF-HUGGED ERIC AND pulled him out of the stall and toward the sinks. Eric straightened his shirt and splashed cold water on his face. "We need to get out of here," Brad said. They walked back into the bar and toward their table. Brad tossed two twenties on the table as they hurried past.

He wasn't sure what Eric was talking about with regard to his fiancée's death, but he knew that the bar wasn't the place to talk about it. Eric had broken down as soon as Brad had spoken about the possible murder of Al Johnson. Why would Al's murder suddenly upset Eric quite so much? Brad tried to think. He didn't know this Kathrine or how she died. What if her death had not been an accident either? Was this something Eric had bottled up since her death? Had Brad been responsible for bringing it to the surface? So many questions were stirring around in Brad's mind, but above all he felt a wave of concern for Eric. He wondered what he could do to help him get through this.

Outside the bar, they walked away from the entrance. Brad stopped and turned toward Eric. "Eric, I'm so sorry for your loss. I'm sorry that our conversation brought up such painful memories. Let's finish this another time. Do you think you can get home safely? Do you need a ride? Would you like me to follow you?"

Eric looked at him with an expression that Brad had not seen before. It was fury. Eric was shaking. "You don't understand," he said with his eyes fixed on Brad's. "The people who killed Al killed my Kathrine. They must have killed my Kathrine."

Brad didn't know what to say. He had to find out what in the world Eric was talking about, but a parking lot was not the place to do it. Suddenly, he reverted back to his mindset when on the run. He had convinced himself that whoever had been threatening them before had drawn back, afraid to get too close with the police and FBI involved. Now, he looked around, wondering who was listening. He thought of his phone, his car, all of it. Might they be quietly tracking him again? He didn't want anyone to hear what Eric was about to say. He needed to find a quiet place for them to talk.

"Hang on man, we need to go somewhere else to talk about this," he said, awkwardly patting Eric on the shoulder. He looked around them. They were standing in the corner of the parking lot. The sports bar was an outbuilding on the corner of a small shopping center. They couldn't drive anywhere in case he was being tracked again, and nothing in the vicinity seemed to have possibilities. Brad scanned the streets all around them. Then, a block away to the east he saw a church spire. There was a car in the parking lot and lights on in the building. He turned to Eric and said, "Okay, we need to make sure we aren't being followed. Out of an abundance of caution, let's turn off our phones." He paused as they both did so. "Now walk with me."

They moved toward the main stretch of stores in the shopping center. When they reached the largest building with various small business suites, Brad turned and surveyed the lot, looking for any suspicious cars or people watching them. Seeing nothing, the two walked on and turned left on a side street towards the church. Brad surveyed the landscape again at the next intersection. Still nothing.

He grabbed Eric's elbow and led him across the street and through the church lot to the entryway. The doors were locked. He knocked firmly. Looking around, he saw a bell tower on their left with stained glass windows and a soft light. In fact, there were several lights on in the building. He banged on the door again, this time as hard as he could. He looked around to see if anyone was watching from afar. Then a young man approached from inside the church. He cracked opened the door.

"May I help you?"

"Yes, thank you so much," Brad said. "My friend recently lost a loved one, and we'd like to pray. Would it be okay if we came in and sat for a while?"

"Well, I don't know, the church is closed. I'm on the prayer team and here alone. This is my shift to offer up prayers."

"I understand.... This is particularly important," Brad countered respectfully. "My friend is quite distraught. Can't we come in and sit for a brief time? I can assure you we won't disturb your prayers."

"Well, I guess it's okay. Would you like me to call the priest to come and talk with you?"

Brad looked at Eric in a questioning way, seriously doubting that he would wish to talk to the priest. Eric shook his head. "That won't be necessary. We'll let you know if we change our minds, though. Thank you."

The man opened the door further to let them in. "May I pray for your loved one?"

"Yes, that would be very much appreciated."

"What was their name?"

Brad looked at Eric again and said, "Kathrine. Kathrine—"

"Cruise," Eric finished.

"Okay, I will include Kathrine in my prayers. Feel free to sit in the sanctuary and talk. I will be leaving soon, but I'll let my replacement know that I let you in."

"Thank you so much," Brad again said sincerely. "We'll let ourselves out."

"That will be fine. God bless you," the man said as he turned and walked toward the tower door.

Brad and Eric walked through a set of large double doors with glass panels and started down the aisle. About halfway down, Eric raised trembling hands and said, "This is far enough." They sat down in a pew. Brad gave Eric a minute to settle down. He looked around the church's sanctuary. There were a couple of ladders set up against the front wall where two large Christmas banners hung. A large pine tree, perhaps fifteen feet tall, stood on the left side of the room, but there were no ornaments on it. Apparently the church was in the process of decorating for the Christmas season.

Brad looked at Eric and explained his worry about the pursuers showing up again. "Now tell me about Kathrine," he said. "Tell me everything you think I should know."

"Okay." Eric took a deep breath. "Kathrine was a software developer at GCI. We met as I was about to transfer out of the election services group of the Special Projects Division before the voting software went live. I trained her and others on the system we developed.

For election security purposes, the people involved in developing the software needed to transfer out. They replaced us with a group of individuals that had very compartmentalized responsibilities. The idea was to ensure that the voting system could not be tampered with from the inside if nobody had access to all of the components. I thought it was a stupid move and that there should be a few people left who knew the entire system, but I wasn't consulted."

"So you and Kathrine hit it off?"

"Yeah, we did. She was a pretty tough cookie. She wasn't intimidated by me or my surly attitude. She gave it back to me in spades."

"I like her already!" Brad interjected.

Eric huffed and offered a small smile. "We knew that the company was paranoid about keeping original developers and managers away from the election software, so we thought it best that we keep our relationship a secret. We never spoke when either of us were at work. We never let anyone at GCI know that we were dating. When we decided to get married, we planned for her to request a transfer out of the voting division."

"Man, I can't imagine what it's like to lose someone like that."

Eric paused, his eyes watering again. "Well, a couple of months back Kathrine called me from the office. She said she had found something that, in her words, showed there was 'some serious shit happening here.' I told her she should know better than to call me from work. She ignored me and said she would make a copy for me to look at. I yelled at her again for persisting. I can't believe I yelled at her like that."

"So, you think that it may have been Al's document that she found?"

"It had to have been. That night, she called me from her cell phone. She said she had promised to spend the evening with her parents, but that she stopped by my office after work and left a copy. She said she had to get it to me."

"Had she ever been to your office before?"

"No. She knew what floor I worked on, but she didn't know any more than that. So of course, I ripped into her for going to my office. I told her she was going to get us both fired. Then she said that she gave the document to someone to give to me. She assured me that she did it in such a way that they wouldn't even know we knew each other."

"So, you're thinking that it could have been given to Al by mistake?"

"It must have been," Eric said softly, now beginning to sob. "I was such an asshole. She was doing the right thing, and all I could think of was keeping our relationship secret. I didn't trust her to know what was important."

"Eric, I'm sure she understood. Did you ask her about what she had left for you the next time you saw her?"

Eric shook his head. "That was the night she died," he said, tears flowing. "No, that was the night she was murdered!" he exclaimed with renewed anger in his voice.

"How do you know she was murdered for sure? Could it have been a coincidence?"

Eric again shook his head. "No. She died in a one-car accident. She hit a bridge abutment on the way home from her parent's house. She was a good driver. Her mom said she hadn't had anything to drink and didn't seem tired when she left. They killed her; I'm sure of it!"

Brad sat back in the pew and breathed out slowly. He thought for a moment. It was possible that Eric was right, but they still had to make a lot of assumptions for things to have happened that way. He had just been reamed by Eric for making a false accusation toward him. They needed to be careful that they didn't repeat the same mistake.

"Okay, Eric. Yes, it's possible that things happened that way. Keep in mind there could be other explanations, though. We should be careful not to jump to conclusions the way I did about you."

Eric ignored him. "I'm going to take them down," he promised with vengeance in his voice. "They will pay for this."

"Okay, okay," Brad said, trying to calm him. "But if you're right, these people will kill us both without batting an eye. We need to proceed carefully and make sure we bring the police into this. You could be really helpful for the investigation, knowing the election software as you do." He looked around them. "I wonder how they knew that Al had the document. How did they know that Kathrine had a copy? There are a lot of questions we need answered."

"We will get the answers. And then I will kill the son-of-a-bitch that did this," Eric said again.

They sat there for a long time. Brad was thinking about what to do next. He didn't know if his apparent adversaries knew about his and Eric's meetings at this point, but if they did, Eric could become a target too. His head was spinning. It felt good that they had more information, but his mind went back to the attempts on his life. Fear crept into his mind. Apprehension grew. He didn't want to go back to running. He knew that they needed to be really careful.

"Eric, if the wrong people have connected you and me, you could be in trouble. We need to work together on this, but we need to be vigilant that it's not in the open."

"What do you suggest?" Eric asked as he stared at the back of the pew in front of them. He seemed emptied of all emotion now.

"I suggest we take it slow. First, we need to bring the police and the FBI into the loop. And . . . if these people do know of your involvement, could you move around without being tracked? Could you get to a meeting place without our high-tech followers knowing?"

"I guess so. I can figure something out."

That wasn't too reassuring to Brad. He knew that Eric was in a frame of mind where he wasn't thinking very clearly.

"All right, let's do this," Brad said with some forcefulness. "I want you to do nothing tonight except go home and get some sleep. You've been through a lot and need to be able to proceed with a clear mind." He closed his eyes for a moment. "Okay. Tomorrow is Wednesday. I will have a cell phone delivered to your office. It is one of four that I bought when Barb and I were in hiding. Keep it charged and on. You'll get a call from me later tomorrow, and I'll tell you how the police suggest we proceed."

Eric nodded his head. He looked like he had been through the wringer.

"Tonight, when you go home, just be watchful to see if anyone might be following you."

Eric nodded again.

"We need to try to avoid anyone finding out we met tonight if they don't know it already. If they're following anyone, it would most likely be me. Why don't you stay here for another twenty minutes or so? I'll slip out of the church and go back to my car by a different route. If they're following me, they'll be gone when you return to your car. Okay?"

Eric nodded once more.

"Are you okay, Eric? We are going to get this resolved. Those responsible are going to get what they deserve, but we need to be careful."

"Yeah, I hear you. You sure know how to ruin a guy's frickin' day, Tillman."

Brad smiled to hear the surly Eric Blas returning. He lightheartedly punched him on the arm and said, "Twenty minutes."

"Twenty minutes," Eric repeated.

Brad walked into the entryway of the church and looked outside. With the lights on in the building, it was difficult to see into the darkness. He stepped back and looked down the width of the church and saw another set of doors to the outside. He walked to those doors and slipped outside. He stayed close to the building until he was away from the interior lights. Once he could get his bearings, he walked down the street in the other direction. He eventually returned to the main thoroughfare and to the parking lot where he had left his car.

CHAPTER 31

BRAD WAS BARELY ABLE TO FOCUS ON ANYTHING AT work. He was consumed by what had happened the night before. He had briefed Barb when he got home at nearly ten p.m., and they talked about how this would provide some solid information for the investigation. The possibility that Kathrine Cruise had stumbled across the document and been killed for it was conjecture, but he thought surely the police would investigate. He was also sure that Eric's knowledge of the election system would be invaluable.

As promised, that morning he had contacted a local courier service and sent a throwaway phone to Eric. He wanted to talk with him right away to gauge his state of mind but thought he should wait and call him after work. The extra time would also give Brad an opportunity to talk to the FBI.

He took some phone calls and went through his to-do list; he just couldn't devote his attention fully to anything. At a little after ten in the morning, he left a note on his door that he would be back by one-thirty. He left the building and walked two blocks to a coffee shop that he used from time to time for meetings. He ordered his usual medium roast black coffee and sat at a counter looking out to the street. He liked more frou-frou coffees too, but he could hardly justify spending seven bucks on one as a finance officer.

He took his throwaway phone from his briefcase and called Detective Conner. He said that he had pertinent information that could have a significant impact on the investigation. They agreed to meet at one o'clock at the coffee shop.

He then called Agent Finnigan and told her the same thing. She said that she was willing to set up a meeting in an out-of-the-way location with Eric. Brad thought it might be best if he be there as well. Finnigan had no problem with that if it would make the informant more comfortable. She suggested they take Bus 183 to the corner of Greenbrier Parkway and Fontainebleau for a ten-thirty meeting the following morning. She and Agent Allan would pick Brad and Eric up in a black SUV and drop them wherever they wanted afterwards.

At half past eleven, Brad walked to a park near the office. He sat on a bench where he could see people coming and going. At 11:42, he saw what he had hoped for. Jennifer Bradley, the administrative assistant for Al and Eric's department, was leaving the building with another woman. Brad followed at a distance and watched them go into a café, the same one he had bumped into her before. After about ten minutes, Brad walked in and looked around to see where they had settled. He placed an order for a club sandwich, fries, and a Coke. Once delivered, he took his tray and walked by the table where Jennifer was sitting.

"Well, hello Jennifer!" he said, feigning surprise.

"Brad! It's nice to see you. It's been a while," Jennifer said with a smile.

"Oh, you know, always more to do than time to do it!"

"Yes, we are really busy too, especially since Al hasn't been replaced yet."

"Actually, I'm glad to bump into you. Would you mind stopping by my table after your lunch? There is something I'd like to ask you."

She cocked her head a bit and said, "I'd be happy to. It'll be fifteen minutes or so."

"That would be great, no rush." Brad turned to the person Jennifer was having lunch with. "Please forgive my intrusion into your lunch. My name is Brad Tillman."

The woman smiled and introduced herself as Cindy Lawford. "I'm an administrative assistant to Cathy Hoover, the VP in Jennifer's department."

"Yes, I met Cathy not long ago. I'll bet she keeps you on your toes," Brad said. "As in most cases, I'm sure you keep Cathy and the department on track!" With that, Brad moved on to find a table. As he ate his lunch, he hoped that Jennifer would come over alone. He thought she might have been the person who Kathrine Cruise gave the document to that night.

As Brad took his last bite of sandwich, Jennifer and Cindy came by the table. Brad knew he shouldn't have introduced himself! They exchanged small talk for a moment, and Brad invited them to sit. He decided that his questions would seem innocuous enough to Cindy. "Jennifer, I talked with a friend recently who told me that he had asked someone to drop off a document for Eric Blas late one afternoon a month or two back, but it seems that it didn't get delivered. The woman felt certain she dropped it at the right place. Do you remember anything like that happening?"

Jennifer thought for a moment and said, "No, I don't remember that. My daughter's after-school care program is pretty strict about not being late, so I usually bolt right at five."

"Oh well, just thought I'd ask."

"Uh, excuse me, but I remember something like that happening," Cindy offered.

Brad looked at her with surprise. "Oh?"

"Well, this may be something totally different, but I was working late one evening and a woman came into the office, seeming a bit lost. I asked her if I could help. She said she thought there was someone who worked on our floor that used to be on the voting development team. I told her that there was. She handed me a large envelope and asked if I would put it on that person's desk. I knew that Al had been on that task force, so I put it on his desk."

Brad felt his heart pound in his chest. He tried not to show his keen interest in what she had said. He said, "Wow! What luck! Did the woman tell you her name, by chance?"

"No. I thought the whole thing was kind of odd, but she seemed happy that I could help. She just handed me the envelope and thanked me."

"So that's the reason Eric didn't get it." He looked at Cindy. "Both Al and Eric worked on that development team. She probably just forgot Eric's name and figured he was the only one."

Cindy covered her mouth with both hands. "I'm so sorry! I didn't realize that Eric had worked there too!"

"I'm sure it's not a problem," Brad said, his insides churning. "At least the mystery is solved." He tried to smile. "I'll let my friend know what happened."

Jennifer and Cindy stood to go. Cindy apologized again, clearly feeling guilty about her mistake. Jennifer said, "Well, I'm glad you found out what you needed to know. I wonder what Al did with it."

"We have no way of knowing, but with this information, I'm sure they can resolve the matter," Brad said. They exchanged goodbyes, and Jennifer and Cindy made their way to the door.

Brad couldn't believe his fortune that Cindy was the one who had received the envelope. He looked at his watch. It was 12:40 p.m., almost time for his next appointment.

CHAPTER 32

BRAD WALKED BRISKLY BACK TO THE COFFEE SHOP WHERE he had started his long break. He arrived about five minutes early and thought about ordering something, but he really didn't feel like more coffee. Besides, he usually didn't drink coffee after ten in the morning, but he thought he should order something for the meeting. When Detective Conner arrived, he asked him what he would like. Black coffee was the answer, so Brad ordered a large coffee and a smoothie for himself. Once they had their drinks, they sat at a table with no one else nearby.

"I learned of some new information that should be helpful to you, I think," Brad began.

"Oh? What have you come across?"

"Well, first of all, I feel certain that Eric Blas is not responsible for anything that we experienced since Al's death. I totally misjudged him. I'm also concerned that in doing so, I could have potentially damaged his career with my premature charges."

"Mr. Tillman, if you think that the police would toss his name around as a suspect with no more proof than you provided us, I assure you that we are incredibly careful about things like that. We realize that we come into contact with, and sometimes investigate, plenty of innocent people. The only time someone might know that an individual was being investigated would be if they were a witness or an informant such as yourself. Beyond that, the only time a person's name might come up in public would be if we charged them or a prosecutor brought them to a grand jury for possible charges."

"Good. I feel bad about jumping to conclusions. I guess a guy's mind goes off the rails when he feels threatened."

"I'm sure it does. We have no facts that have led us to consider Eric Blas a suspect in anything," Conner assured him. "Was that what you wanted to talk with me about, or was there something else?"

"Perhaps another murder."

Conner was about to take a sip of coffee but put his cup down and looked at Brad. "*Another* murder?" he began. "Oh, you're assuming Al Johnson was murdered. We haven't been able to determine that as of yet."

"Right. What I learned may also lend credence to that assumption."

"Okay, what have you got?" Conner asked, sounding a little bemused.

Brad began by telling the detective about his chance meeting with Eric Blas the previous day at lunch. Conner listened patiently as Brad described what had happened at the sports bar and then later in the church.

"What was the name of Blas's fiancée?" Conner asked as he pulled out his notepad.

"Kathrine, with a K, Cruise."

"So, she took this document to Blas; how did it come into Al Johnson's possession?"

Brad told him about what he had learned at lunch, just thirty minutes earlier.

This got Conner's attention. "So, the document was put in Johnson's office by mistake?"

"Well, I guess you could say that. Kathrine didn't want to specifically ask to have it given to Eric to avoid any questions about their relationship. So, she asked someone to put it on the desk of the guy who worked on the original election software design team. Both Eric and Al had, but the woman Kathrine gave the envelope to was only aware that Al had worked there. She put it on his desk."

"Who took the envelope from Kathrine?"

"Her name is Cindy Lawford."

"You're quite the detective," Conner teased as he printed the name on his pad. "When did you say Kathrine Cruise died?"

"I'm not sure of the exact date, but it was the same day she dropped the envelope off in that office. A couple of months ago."

"It won't be too hard to find that information. If we still have access to the wreckage of her car, I will have our people look over it carefully to see if there is any indication that another vehicle may have forced her off the road," Conner said.

He closed his notepad and looked at Brad. "Look, I know this is personal to you and that you may have been a target yourself, but you are not an investigator. If you aren't careful, you could get yourself killed looking into this mess."

"The information I got from Eric Blas was entirely by accident," Brad said, a little defensively. "Based on what I learned there, yes, I did arrange to bump into someone from his office to get more information. I thought it would be helpful to you."

"I understand. I just want you to be careful. You will be no help to me dead . . . and it will look bad on my case record," he finished with a wink.

Brad got back to his office a bit later than his note promised, but there didn't seem to be anyone looking for him when he returned. It was difficult getting his head back into his work, but he pushed through the rest of the afternoon.

CHAPTER 33

WHEN BRAD ARRIVED HOME FROM WORK CLOSE TO SIX IN the evening, he found a note from Barb. She had picked up an evening shift at the hospital, and he was on his own for dinner. This type of sudden schedule change with Barb's nursing job was routine. She seldom even called Brad anymore unless it impacted plans they had. He opened the refrigerator and considered the leftover situation. He really didn't feel like cooking nor did he like the thought of going out again. He just wanted to unwind from his day. He pulled out the last remnants of all the leftovers in the refrigerator: lasagna, mashed potatoes, and salad.

After dinner, he picked up his throwaway phone and dialed the one he had sent to Eric. Eric answered on the third ring.

"Yeah, I'm here."

"How are you getting along, Eric? How was your day?"

"How do you think my day was, asshole? I find out my fiancée is murdered, and I don't know who did it. Let's say I had an issue with concentration at work today."

Brad ignored the sarcasm. "I did too. I'm sure it was worse for you, especially not knowing anything more than what we talked about last night and having no place to go for answers."

"That's putting it mildly. You really know how to screw up a guy's life, Tillman."

Brad tried to comfort him as much as he thought Eric could tolerate, then he told him of the detective's assurance that there would be no repercussions from Brad's premature accusation. He apologized again. Eric seemed to be in a better place and took it all in stride.

Finally, Brad outlined the planned meeting with the FBI for the following day. He again emphasized that they needed to be careful for Eric's protection. Eric said he would pull up the bus route information online after they finished talking and find a place to hop on that bus.

Before Brad hung up, he remembered that he had not briefed Eric on what he learned over lunch that day. He said, "Kathrine did drop an envelope off; however, she was apparently being careful to avoid giving any impression that she knew you. She asked if there was 'a guy there who used to work on the voting software development team.' The person she spoke to said there was, and Kathrine gave them the envelope to put on his desk." Brad paused briefly. "Unfortunately, the person she gave it to was only aware of Al from the team, so she put the envelope on *his* desk."

"Who did Kathrine give the envelope to?" asked Eric.

"I'd rather not say. I got the information in a roundabout way, so she doesn't know who Kathrine was, what was in the envelope, or why it was important. Why does it matter?"

"I guess it doesn't.... I guess if she had put it on my desk, then it would be *me* who was dead and not Al."

"Eric, I've learned through all of this not to speculate about things like that. We don't know how they learned that Al had the document or why they decided to kill him. Shoot, we can't even be sure he was murdered yet."

"I guess," Eric said skeptically.

They wrapped up their phone call, and Brad sat and thought through all of the information that had surfaced over the last few days. It occurred to him that he had never gotten back to Agent Finnigan on the copier question. He had asked an analyst to do a quick search on copier invoices and give him a report, by department, of who used what brand. The analyst had put the report in a folder and placed it on his desk with a sticky note, but he had not opened it.

He wondered about the ethics of giving such information to the FBI without going through the proper channels. He wanted to be helpful to the investigators, but there was a part of him worried that this could cost him his job. Several weeks had gone by before this latest information from Eric, and it had felt like everything was behind him. Some normalcy had returned; now the stress was back. Once again, he was consumed by it. He just wanted it all to go away, so he could settle back into life as he knew it before Al's death.

Brad realized how exhausted he was from the last two days by eight o'clock. He went to bed and set his alarm to get up early the next morning.

CHAPTER 34

BRAD WAS OUT THE DOOR BY A QUARTER AFTER SIX THE next morning. He wanted to go to the office and take care of a few things before the meeting with the FBI.

He had successfully cleared most of his desk the afternoon before. He finished the rest and finally opened the folder that the analyst had left about the copy machines. It appeared that Yosheti was not a popular brand within the company. There were only two areas where they were used—the Executive Office and the Special Projects Division, both reporting directly to Jeff Unger. Brad called up the invoice payment system on his desktop and found the cost centers to review the invoices from Yosheti paid by those departments. He was surprised by the cost of only three machines. The price seemed to be double what was typical for copier services. He closed the folder and put it in his out-basket.

As he drove out of the parking garage, he stopped, picked up his cell phone and looked up the number of Karl Jennings, the director of the Special Projects Division. He tapped on the phone to call the number as he drove out of the underground parking area.

"Karl," he heard a delicate voice say on the car speaker. Despite the cadence of his voice, Karl's manner and behavior were very masculine. He was a professional and apparently very good at what he did. Unger relied heavily on him in the fields of cybersecurity and new software development.

"Hi Karl, this is Brad Tillman. I don't normally bother you with such things, but it's my nature to look for savings. I noticed that your group has a copier contract with Yosheti, and the price seems really high.

Have you considered shopping around the other service providers we have contracts with to get a better price?"

"Hi, Brad. We actually have shopped around, and this *is* our best price. The reason the price is higher than normal is that our copiers have special security features. Due to our need for enhanced security, we use machines that capture and store information on who is making what copies. We need to ensure none of our proprietary information leaves the premises."

"Ah, that makes sense. Sorry I bothered you with it, Karl. Have a great day!"

"No problem, Brad. Thanks for looking out for our profit-sharing bonus. Take care."

It really did make sense. They operated that Special Projects facility like a military SCIF, a Sensitive Compartmented Information Facility. Employees couldn't have their cell phones with them in the secured walls where the group worked. Nobody except those with the appropriate security clearance could go into the area without an escort. Brad sometimes wondered if this was really necessary, but he trusted Jeff Unger's judgment.

Brad, ready for the meeting with the FBI, traveled southwest out of downtown towards the bus stop. It was in a residential area; he parked his car on the street and walked a half block to the stop. The bus arrived on time. Brad hopped on and paid his fare. Turning toward the back of the bus, he saw Eric seated by a window halfway down. He took the seat beside him.

"Thanks for doing this, Eric."

"As much as I would like to just find out who did this and kill them with my bare hands, it seems like this may be a safer way to go for now."

"I'd say I know how you feel, but how could I know that? I do think that after you talk to Agents Finnegan and Allan, you'll feel more confident that they'll do the job."

"Why the FBI and not the police? Murder is a state crime."

"Yes, but the killer was probably hired by someone involved in some kind of election fraud. It is them that we need to get to. Besides, I'm sure Detective Conner from the police will want to talk with you as well."

They rode for another five minutes without comment. When they arrived at the designated bus stop, they looked around and saw a black SUV in the lot at a hamburger place behind them. It was not in a parking space but pulled over to the side of the road. As they approached, Agent

Finnigan stepped out of the passenger side. Brad introduced her to Eric, and she invited him to join her in the back seat of the SUV. Brad got in front and greeted Allan, who was driving. Allan started the vehicle and pulled away, leaving the parking lot and setting out for who knows where.

Brad spent the next ten minutes briefing the agents on all that had happened over the last couple of days. He told them how he and Eric had connected accidentally on Tuesday and went on to describe everything that had happened that day and night. He then explained what he had learned from the "chance" meeting with people from Eric's office.

Finnigan took copious notes throughout his briefing and then turned to Eric. She spent a minute or two offering her condolences and asking how he was. She voiced her appreciation for his willingness to meet with them and also thanked Brad for arranging it.

She then began her questions. Most of them seemed to be an effort to have Eric tell his story in his own words. She asked about Kathrine, their relationship, and the desire to keep it a secret. She asked why he believed she was murdered and whether it might be possible that the document Kathrine wanted him to see was not the document they were dealing with at all. Eric calmly answered the questions in his usual coarse manner and language. He told her that he knew the document was the same one but couldn't really offer any evidence to prove it.

At that point, Finnigan flipped the page on her notepad and moved to a different field of questioning. The focus was on Eric's experience in the development of the voting system. She asked how it worked and what security measures made the system so impenetrable. Eric's responses basically mimicked what Jeff Unger had told them several weeks before.

"It's been a few years since the system was put into use," Finnigan said. "Is it likely that it may have changed since you helped to develop it?"

"Little has changed. Kathrine would tell me what was happening with the system and how it was working," Eric answered. "She said it was working amazingly well. Other than adjusting to increase capacity as more states joined, there were few changes needed."

"At what point was the system subdivided so that only certain people could access particular sections of it?"

"About three quarters through the development process. At that point it became a pain in the ass because you had to sign in every time you wanted to look at something or make changes or whatever." Eric added nonchalantly, "I actually created a back channel to go around all of that security."

Finnegan looked up from her notes. "Did all of the developers use that back channel?"

"No, I didn't tell anyone about it. I figured Jeff would have a conniption if he found out."

"Couldn't others who were involved with the system bump into your back channel?"

"It's possible, but by that time there were millions of lines of code, so it would be pretty unlikely. Nobody found it while I was there."

"Do you think it could still be there today?"

"I would guess it is. Kathrine never said anything about them finding something like that while she was there. I doubt that they've found anything since."

"Do you think others involved in the development could have created back channels of their own?"

Eric huffed and smiled. "It's possible, but the others were pretty straight arrows. I'm a bit of a ... a renegade I guess."

"I see. Seeing as you were able to develop that back channel, do you think that someone else could have been able to find a way to manipulate election vote counts?"

Eric paused to think. "I would say again that it's possible, but to do something like that you would have to have access to the entire system. At this point, nobody has that authority. That's the reason they reassigned all of the original developers to other parts of the company when the system went live."

"Mr. Blas, are you telling me that nobody has that authority?"

Eric looked up at her and then at Brad, who was in the front twisted in his seat and looking back. Then he said slowly, "Jeff Unger. Jeff Unger is the system administrator."

Allan spoke up from the front seat. "Did he access the system regularly during its development?"

"Pretty regularly."

"Did he have a computer in his office to access the system?"

"Sure. Ever since we completed the system development, he has had two computers on his desk. One for his CEO work and one for the election system."

Finnigan glanced up and saw Allan looking at her in the rearview mirror. She said, "This question is for both of you. Do you think Jeff Unger would have the capability to change votes?"

Brad said, "That is really out of my domain. I'm a bean counter and have no knowledge of software development or computer security. But, I can't even fathom that he could be the one who did it. Especially if murder is involved."

Eric listened as Brad answered the question and then said, "It's feasible. In fact, with what I know, he would be the *only* one who could do it." Eric began to fidget in his seat. His breathing increased. His jaw tightened. His eyes bulged. "I'll kill the bastard!"

Finnigan jumped in, "No, you won't kill the bastard, Eric. We need you to help us get into the system and find out if he did in fact murder your fiancée. Do you understand me? If any harm comes to him, you will be the first person suspected. You don't need to spend the rest of your life in jail just to get vengeance. Help us take care of it instead."

Eric said nothing.

Finnigan pressed on. "Eric, will you continue to help us understand the system and access it at some point if we have a warrant?"

Eric looked her in the eyes and said, "Absolutely, I will."

Nobody spoke for a few minutes.

Finally, Brad said, "Uh, by the way, I did take a look at the copy machines used by the company. Yosheti machines are only used in two areas, the Executive Office and the Special Projects Division that reports to Unger."

"I see," said Finnigan.

Brad went on, "They are actually special machines that record and log every printout or copy made and who made it, as well as create an electronic copy."

"Really? Maybe two points for us!" said Allan in a display of enthusiasm that Brad had come to expect of him.

Finnigan smiled and then her face grew somber. "You both need to avoid doing anything that could be interpreted as investigating the company from the inside. If you are right, someone has killed two people and surely is willing to kill again if that's what it takes. Is that clear?"

They both nodded.

"We'll sit down with Detective Conner so we can compare notes on our investigations. If he contacts you, please cooperate, but be *careful* to maintain a low profile."

Brad and Eric nodded again.

CHAPTER 35

AFTER THEY DROPPED OFF BOTH BRAD AND ERIC, AGENTS
Finnigan and Allan drove back to the FBI office.

"Okay Chris, review what we've got." Betty liked for someone else
to give the facts so she could listen objectively and watch for bias.

"You've got the notes, and I'm driving," laughed Chris. "Maybe you
could get the ball rolling this time!"

"Fine," she said. He had a fair point. "Our copy machine could be
in either the Executive Office or the Special Projects Division. We should
probably act fast on that because someone could potentially delete the
record in their security database."

"We could have Jeff Unger in a lie regarding his access to the election system," Chris said.

"He also doesn't seem very cooperative about identifying the person who made the changes to the results on the Pennsylvania Secretary
of State's website. Neither he nor anyone else in the company has gotten
back to me on that." Betty turned the page in her notepad and started to
write. "Let's get a search warrant to focus on those three areas—the copy
machines and their records, the real story on Jeff Unger's access to the
voting system, and the changed numbers on the website."

"We may also know how the document came into Al Johnson's
possession. The copy records can help with that," Chris said. "If we *are*
able to confirm Kathrine Cruise copied that document, we will need to
interview Cindy Lawford in Eric Blas's office. We should ask him for a
picture of Kathrine."

Betty added that to her list. "It's time we pull in Conner to begin
full coordination between the voter fraud and possible murder investiga-

tions. Let's get a meeting set up." She chewed on the cap of her pen. "It's also time we do a full background check on the boss. Let's do everything short of interviews. I don't want him to learn of our interest in him just yet. However, we need to learn all we can about Jeffery Unger."

There was a pause. "I think those are our action items for now. Probably the top priority is coordination with Conner. We may get more information to help justify the search warrant," Betty concluded.

"Okay, I'll set up a meeting for tomorrow with Connor," Chris offered.

"All right," Betty said. "Make it after noon because I have a nine-thirty, and I'm not sure how long that will take. I'll put together a request for a search warrant. Why don't you get the background check rolling as well, Chris?"

"Will do.... Oh, and I'll reach out to Eric Blas to see if he can get us a picture of Kathrine Cruise."

Chris pulled into the garage and parked the car in the carpool area alongside several others like it. They headed to their respective offices to get to work. In her office, Betty pulled the one-page form for organizing a search warrant request. It would be nice if she could just fill in a few blanks and take it to a judge. She would need to provide sworn affidavits from herself, Chris, and possibly Brad Tillman and Eric Blas to prove to a judge that there was adequate reason for violating a company's right to privacy.

She thought about how corporations don't have the same Constitutional right to privacy as individuals. But, they do have some privacy rights. The corporation's right is subject to a balancing act as to whether the requested information is reasonable considering the likelihood that it may lead to the discovery of admissible evidence. Betty always tried to err on the side of privacy when she put together a search warrant, and she had never had one refused. She began writing an outline of the facts she would present for this one.

CHAPTER 36

DETECTIVE JOHN CONNER HAD CONTACTED THE PEOPLE at the fifth precinct involved in investigating the accident and was pleasantly surprised to learn that Kathrine Cruise's demolished car was still accessible to the police. Because the vehicle was involved in a fatality accident, the salvage yard could not move it out without police authorization. The investigation had apparently been closed, but fortunately no one from the fifth had authorized the removal. Conner printed out the accident report. He picked up Warren Gregory, an investigator from the department's Crime Scene Investigation Unit. Gregory and his associates were trained to apply forensic science to investigations where fatalities were involved. They drove to the yard.

After they showed their badges, the attendant led them to the corner of the lot where the crumpled vehicle sat. Seeing the totaled Toyota Corolla left a sickening feeling in the pit of Conner's stomach. It was obvious that the woman was traveling at least fifty miles per hour when she hit the concrete support. Almost the entire engine was inside the passenger compartment. Airbags or not, nobody could survive a crash like that.

Gregory, briefed on the possibility that the vehicle had been forced off the road, looked over the still-accessible side panels to search for clues. He spent extra time studying the right front door and fender. Parts of those surfaces were gray in color rather than the powder blue that covered most of the car. He removed a small pocketknife from his hip pocket and two sterile plastic bags from his jacket pocket. Bending down, he scraped his fingernail across the gray shading and found that it came off easily. He used his pocketknife to scrape a good-sized sample into the plastic bag. Then, he pulled some of the blue paint off of the car. That did not come off easily. It was important to get a sample of each in case they found a vehicle that may have collided with this one. It would likely have some paint or primer from the Corolla on it.

He motioned Conner over and said, "It looks as if this car was involved in an altercation with another vehicle at some point. It is a bit unusual, however, because there's no paint from another vehicle here, only primer. It would be easy to miss, because without a close look it appears that the gray is the Corolla's primer. In fact, the primer is on top of the car's blue paint."

The detective looked at the accident report. He saw that the concrete the car struck was between an unusual left off-ramp and the three lanes of the main highway. It would be feasible for someone to bump the Toyota from the right, pushing it into the concrete abutment. The driver of that car could just continue down the highway, get off at another exit, and disappear into the night.

After a complete exterior overview of the damaged vehicle, the two returned to the shack at the lot's gate. Conner told the attendant that they would need to hold on to that vehicle for a while yet. "It's likely that we may move it to a police lot for security," he said.

On the way back to the office, Conner contacted the fifth precinct again, letting them know that there was a possibility of foul play. Since it was evidence, he recommended that they move the vehicle to a police inspection station so that it was not tampered with. He asked that they allow Gregory to work with them on further analysis of the car.

Conner thought that there shouldn't be too many cars driving around coated with primer instead of paint. He would submit a request that all north Georgia police officers, sheriff deputies, and highway patrol officers be on the lookout for a vehicle that had damage to and primer on the left side.

Upon returning to his office, he found a message from Chris Allan at the FBI. He returned the call to learn that they were interested in an information exchange and expanding cooperation on the case. He agreed to a meeting at the FBI office at two the following afternoon.

He wandered over to his Captain's office, thankful to find him there. Going to Captain Hughes directly was bypassing multiple levels of authority above him. However, anytime there was a joint investigation with the FBI, the Police Chief had made it clear that he was to approve it. Conner wasn't prepared to jump that many levels, but with little time before the meeting he knew that information through the normal chain of command would never reach the Chief in time. He figured he would get to Captain Hughes right away and let him determine the best way to get the Chief's authorization. Connor would communicate to those between him and the Captain later. Fortunately, those officers were understanding and trusted his judgment.

Swanson went directly to the Chief, who tentatively approved the expansion of cooperation. He wanted Swanson to attend the meeting with Conner, however. This meant that Swanson would need a full verbal briefing from Conner before the meeting the next day. Back at his office, Swanson set a meeting time with Conner for the next morning. There was no time for coordinating schedules. Conner would have to do whatever was necessary to get there.

CHAPTER 37

THAT NIGHT BRAD BRIEFED BARBARA ON WHAT HAD TAKEN place during the FBI interview. She was grateful that the FBI was taking this seriously and hoped the police were as well.

They spent some time watching the news. The general election was nine months away, and election politics were beginning to consume the cable news networks. Primary season was almost over; presidential nominees would be selected before too long. Brad cringed at the rhetoric. Words remained testy between the primary candidates, but references to the opposite party were downright nasty and over the top. All of the candidates promised to win big in the fall and sweep in a wave of senatorial and congressional winners that would ensure their side would seal the deal on putting the country firmly "on the right track," from their perspectives.

Democrats promised a nation that cared and would provide free childcare, free college, and an actual single-payer health care system, not to mention racial equality. Republicans promised to stop giveaways and reduce government spending and work toward keeping taxes low while balancing the federal budget. They also assured their base that they would seal the southern border once and for all and sustain an up-to-date military that would assure national security. Law and order, drug policy, and education were big topics for both parties.

Brad felt like the differences between the two sides were becoming starker and clearer. For voters who paid attention to policy, there was less and less room in the middle. Independents like Brad would almost be forced into one camp or the other because there really was no middle ground to speak of anymore. He thought that the upcoming election could well be the one that would lock the nation into a single direction for a generation or longer. It would be for all the chips, so to speak. Both houses of Congress were pretty evenly split. A successful presidential candidate could sweep enough representatives and senators into the legislature to make it relatively easy to pass their agenda. If either side were to make significant strides toward what they desired for the country, it would be difficult for future administrations to reverse course. This made it even more vital that the election process be fair and accurate. Brad thought about the investigation. The people of the United States should make the decision as to where the country would go, not an individual with the ability to manipulate voting results.

He got up and fixed Barb and himself each a dish of ice cream. They turned off the television and enjoyed their dessert and companionship. This little ritual had become a routine for them, and Brad thought it was a wonderful way to keep communication lines open. They talked politics. They talked about their kids. Ultimately, their conversation led back to the possibility of voter fraud and potentially murder.

"Brad, I know you're happy to see more information surfacing for the investigation, but I'm scared. They've come after you before. I worry that they'll do it again....Maybe we should just quit our jobs and move," she suggested. "I can get a job anyplace. We could live on my salary until you get situated."

"We can't just walk away from this. I feel a sense of responsibility to see it through. With the FBI so heavily involved and developing some strong leads, I'll bet someone is starting to get really nervous right about now. But hurting us won't help them."

"Brad, they may want to take us out for sheer vindictiveness. I wouldn't think someone who would kill two people would have a lot to lose by killing another. Can't we leave here?"

"We could, but you know that someone with the capability these people have would find us anywhere if they wanted to. Here, we have a direct relationship with the police. They will protect us. Don't worry; I'll be careful. I'll leave the rest to the police and the FBI. Okay?"

"Yes. I just want to get past this."

"I do too, sweetie. Believe me, I do too."

It was true that Brad wanted to leave things to the authorities and get their own lives back to normal; still, he decided he needed to avoid briefing Barb from here on out.

CHAPTER 38

AGENT FINNIGAN WAS PLEASED WITH HOW THE MEETING
with Detective Conner had gone. The police had agreed to full cooperation
and had shared information on Conner's investigation of Thomas Everett,
the suspect who he believed had entered the Tillman home. Finnigan
agreed to do an interstate check on Everett to see if they could find
anything not evident in standard background checks. She had Allan do
the groundwork to begin that expanded check.

On Monday Finnegan reached out to Brad and Eric. She apologized for contacting them on Christmas Eve but asked if they might each
come by after the holiday to review and sign an affidavit that would clearly cover the information they had provided to the FBI. With those documents, she would be prepared to take her search warrant request to a judge.

Brad stopped by on Thursday morning to read the affidavit. He
was surprised at how thorough it was. He didn't realize that the recording
of their discussions would be fully transcribed. While the information
was plucked out of what he had told the agents, there were a few things
that he thought may have been misunderstood. Based on his explanation,
some statements were eliminated and a couple of others rewritten. After
the changes were made, he signed the document.

While Brad was there, Finnigan took the opportunity to talk with
him about his role at GCI. Upon learning that Brad had access to the
highest levels of information on company financials, she asked, "Mr. Tillman, could you please give me a picture of how financial responsibilities
work within the Special Projects Division that reports to Mr. Unger?"

"Well, they work in the same way that the rest of the company does. Team members develop a budget each year. Then we track their performance to budget."

"How large a group is it?"

"I think the last time I looked they had forty-five full-time people. They also utilize consultants a good bit."

"Is there anything different between them and other departments?"

"Well, yes and no. We use the same financial framework as with other departments, but they are pretty terrible about achieving budgeted levels."

"Is that because the group may be poorly managed?"

"No, I wouldn't say that. The director of the group, Karl Jennings, has always appeared to know his division well and to have good answers when I have asked him questions. I seldom ask questions relating to their expenses, however."

"Oh? Why is that?"

"All of the basic line items in their budget are typically met well. It's ad hoc electronic purchases and paid consultants where they go over. A vice president or above must approve these, which in their division is Jeff Unger. Early on, I would challenge Unger on those purchases at times, but he would just smile and say, 'this is what it takes to be on the leading edge.' Over time, I quit asking. He seems to really trust Jennings and the group, regardless of what they are spending."

"So, Unger spends from his own budget and potentially from the Special Projects Division budget."

"I guess you could say that. If there was something special that he wanted to do, he could assign it to Jennings and then sign off on it personally. In the corporate world, anything with the CEO's signature on it goes through swiftly, with few or no questions asked."

"Thank you, that is helpful information," Finnigan said thoughtfully. "Would you do me a favor and review the last six months' expenses of the Executive Office and Special Projects Division to see if anything appears to be out of the ordinary to you?"

"I could do that," Brad told her. "I just don't believe Unger is involved in this."

"I understand. You may be right. However, it's important to eliminate some individuals from the suspect pool. This allows us to focus our time on others."

Brad paused for what seemed to Finnigan to be a long time. "Special Agent Finnigan, I want to support this investigation in any way I can. I am, however, a bit torn. I'm afraid that my doing this in secret could ultimately cost me my job."

Finnigan paused for a moment and then stood. "Brad," she said, although she had never used his first name before, "I understand your concern. The fact that you are concerned reinforces that you are a good person wanting to do the right thing for your company as well as law enforcement." Pacing a bit across her office, she went on. "I cannot force you to help us in the ways I have asked. I may be able to arrange payment for feeding us information, although what I have asked is discoverable by a search warrant or subpoena. Your cooperation does save us time, which seems especially important, since someone appears ready to kill in order to protect what they are doing."

"I don't want money. I guess I'm just wondering if we should bring the GCI legal department into this."

"I'm afraid if we approach the company's lawyers, our investigation will be stifled at every turn. It is not that they are bad people, but they are there to defend the company legally. It will be their job to put up as many roadblocks as they can to delay us. I would hope that leadership in the company would be alarmed enough by our investigation to initiate an internal investigation; however, one never knows how companies will respond."

She sat down next to Brad again. "To answer your question, yes, you could lose your job for providing us information. That would be the company's prerogative. While we would do our best to convince them that you were really working in their best interest by helping us, we would have no authority in such a matter."

Brad leaned back in his chair, tilted his face to the ceiling, and closed his eyes. "Is there a drinking fountain nearby?" he asked, to buy time.

Finnigan could have easily gotten Brad a bottle of water, but she understood he needed to think. She directed him to the fountain in the hallway near the restrooms.

Brad made his way into the restroom. Barb's words from the other night returned to him. If necessary, they *could* live on her salary. His job may be on the line, but, more importantly, their *lives* may be on the line. There really was only one thing to do here.

He returned to Agent Finnigan's office. "This is more important than my job. I will provide any information I can."

"Thank you, Brad. You're doing the right thing," Finnigan assured him. Pausing briefly, she said, "Brad, keep this very low profile. No calling people to ask questions. There is a good chance that someone out there is engaging in criminal conduct. We know that information is much more accessible if the perpetrators don't know we're looking for them. Continue to use your throwaway phone to contact us, as long as you are confident that it has not been compromised. If you ever sense that someone is beginning to act differently toward you, contact us immediately. Understood?"

"Understood."

CHAPTER 39

BRAD TOOK VACATION TIME BETWEEN CHRISTMAS AND
New Year's Day since it was an administrative slow period. They didn't go anywhere; in fact, Barb worked most of that time. When he arrived in the office on the following Wednesday, he pulled up twelve months of general ledger data for the Special Projects Division and the Executive Office. He placed them in an unmarked folder and put them into his briefcase.

When he arrived home that evening, he went straight to his home office and spent an hour going through the reports. He wasn't sure what he was looking for, but this is what Finnigan had asked him for. As he went through the Executive Office numbers, things appeared quite normal, even routine. No unusual charges. Travel and entertainment costs were similar from month to month. He couldn't see anything there.

In the Special Projects Division, it was more challenging. Salaries were normal; travel and entertainment costs were consistent. Technological equipment purchases were up and down. The division had made most of the big purchases nearly a year ago. Brad recalled some hardware upgrades from that time to increase processing speed. Their processing capabilities needed to match the growth in business, or it would take longer to manage even typical computer activity.

Consulting fees were not too unusual either. He looked at the consultants that the group was using. He knew nothing about any of them, but he did recognize most of the names because he had seen them in these reports, on and off, for several years. There was one company that was new to him, but Cyber Tech Consulting Group sounded like the kind of company the Special Projects Division usually hired. The consultants they used were typically specialists in a very particular area. It cost the company less to hire a consultant for a few months than to recruit, hire, and train an employee with special skills for limited needs. Hired employees might run out of work within six months or so, and then they would either need to lay them off or underutilize them in some other capacity. Consultants were sometimes companies that assigned a task force to work with the client company, but often they were individuals. Either way, GCI paid them handsomely for a specific task and then let them go. It saved them money in the long run.

Cyber Tech Consulting Group was paid for the first time three months ago. There were two details that were unusual about it: the contract seemed to be new, and the amount GCI was paying was lower than normal. They had been paid 9,950 dollars per month since coming on board through last month. Brad didn't know about the current month because the monthly financials hadn't closed out, and there was no general ledger report yet. Temporary consulting fees were typically much higher than this and rounded off to an even dollar figure, such as 25,000 dollars per month. That was the only detail Brad saw that he thought was different within the past six months. It wasn't necessarily that it was unusual on its face, but it was novel.

He turned to his computer and started to type the name of the company into his search engine. Then he froze. Could they be monitoring his computer? All this seemed to start after he pulled up that Pennsylvania Secretary of State's website from home. He backspaced, erasing the one word that he had typed. He decided that the next day at work would be safer to look into the company finance system to see when this new consultant had started. He thought anything beyond that should be left to the FBI.

The next day Brad confirmed that the first time the consultant was entered into the company vendor system was three months prior. He wrote down their address. It was a P.O. Box, but there was also a street address listed. He took a minute to open the accounting system to see if there was a current payment. There was. He didn't know if such information would be helpful to the FBI but decided that he would call Agent Finnigan with his findings. He just hoped he wasn't potentially creating grief for some poor company that had just received a nice contract with GCI.

CHAPTER 40

ERIC BLAS HAD ALSO GONE TO THE FBI OFFICE BETWEEN Christmas and New Year's Day, as requested, and edited and signed his witness affidavit. With the statements and other items she had pulled together, Betty Finnigan felt good about going to a judge for a warrant. It was also good to have waited until a week into the New Year. Judges bothered over the holidays can be cantankerous. Now, with the holidays behind them, she asked for a date to present her request.

Chris Allan tapped on her door, though it was open, and said, "Have you got a minute?"

"Sure, Chris. What have you got?"

"It seems that our Thomas Everett has a thing for buying and selling cars. The thing is, he almost always buys them in states other than where he lives."

Betty stared at him. "What other states? How many cars?"

"He has cars purchased in North Carolina, South Carolina, Tennessee, Florida, and Alabama. Sold some in the same states."

"Can you tell me more?"

"Let me get my file."

While Chris got his case file, Betty remembered that the police briefing indicated that the guy had purchased his van in North Carolina, but it hadn't been registered here or there. After they picked him up, he was released on bond. He proceeded to register the vehicle in Georgia. She wondered why anyone would need so many cars.

Chris returned and sat at the table with Betty. "A year ago, he bought a Honda Pilot in South Carolina. That fits the description of the car that followed Tillman after the forced entry at his house. A couple of months later, he bought the van in North Carolina. Six months ago, he bought and sold a Lincoln in Florida within a single month. Technically he never registered it, but his name was handwritten on the back of the title and noticed by the state Department of Motor Vehicles when the buyer went to register it. Three months back, he bought a fifteen-year-old Cadillac in Alabama, and he sold it there about a month ago. Same approach: not properly registered, but the information was captured by the state from the back of the title. I'll bet these states are calling foul and looking for some sales taxes from Everett."

"Hmmm.... Why in other states? Why the turnover? Let's have field agents talk with the people on the other end of those transactions and see what details we can learn about the vehicles. I'd like to know what condition they were in when purchased and when sold. Have them notify Conner with the information and copy us."

"Will do."

After Chris left, Betty got a call about a court date at nine the next morning to present her request for a search warrant. She figured she'd better start pulling together a team to pay GCI a visit once the search warrant was in hand.

CHAPTER 41

FIVE DAYS LATER, FBI SPECIAL AGENTS BETTY FINNIGAN,
Chris Allan, and their team approached the security officer in the lobby of the GCI building. They asked to see the Chief Counsel for the company. John Erikson was in the lobby within five minutes, greeting the agents and asking how he might be of help.

When presented with the search warrant, Erikson's demeanor changed. He asked the agents to follow him into a small conference room on the first floor that the company used for meeting with contract employees without taking them into secured work areas. He offered them water or coffee and said that he needed to inspect the search warrant.

Erikson spent the next ten minutes reading the document. Looking at Agent Finnigan, he simply said, "I don't understand what this is about; however, everything seems to be in order. I will need to contact the department heads to escort you and assist you with getting what you need."

"I understand, Mr. Erikson. Please do so in our presence."

Erikson didn't know contact numbers for everyone. He called his administrative assistant, gave her the list of department heads, and asked her to send them to the conference room. He also asked that she notify Jeff Unger that the FBI had just served the company with a valid search warrant.

Unger was there before any of the department heads. He recognized Finnigan and Allan and approached them immediately. "What is this all about? I told you to contact me if you needed further information. Why such formality?"

Finnigan responded professionally. "Thank you, Mr. Unger. We find that doing things this way is much more efficient in search of vital information. I appreciate your desire to cooperate."

Unger's face reddened, although he seemed to be at a loss for words. Maintaining his composure, he nodded briefly and turned to Erikson. "Did you know about this, John?" he asked, clearly irate, but subdued.

"I just learned about it this morning when they arrived in the lobby."

The department heads for the In-house Computer Support, Client System Security, and Special Projects Divisions started to arrive. As Unger watched the managers coming into the conference room, he said firmly, "Tell me what's going on, John!"

Erikson looked up and told the department heads to please stand by for a moment. Turning to Unger, he said quietly, "They have a search warrant that gives them legal authority to discover three things. The first is they want access to the copy machines and all security data tied to them in the Executive Office and the Special Projects Division. Secondly, they want to know all information related to the updating of the Pennsylvania Secretary of State webpage between November first and December first of last year. Finally, they want information and access to both computers on your desk."

Unger turned and stepped toward Finnigan. "Why didn't you just meet with me and ask me? Do you know what kind of disruption something like this has on a business?" Not waiting for an answer, he turned and stormed out of the conference room, calling back, "John, call me when this is over!"

Erikson turned back to the department heads and asked for their attention. He began to introduce and brief them. He pointed and said to the agents, "This is Mary Simmons. She is the director of Client Service Support." He looked at her. "Mary, we are to provide details on any changes made to information on the Pennsylvania Secretary of State website for the month of November of last year."

He said, "This is Stan Haley. He is the manager of In-house Computer Support. Stan, they need access to both computers on Mr. Unger's desk, and they want to know what the capability of each is."

Finally, he gestured at the third manager. "This is Karl Jennings. He is the director of the Special Projects Division. I'm sorry to drag you into this, Karl, but I wasn't sure who else to give this to. They need access to all Yosheti copiers in the Executive Office and the Special Projects Division. This includes any records from each relating to what copies were made and who made them in the last six months."

Speaking to all three, he said, "This warrant is very specific as to what information they need. You are to fully cooperate with them in providing them access as I have described." He raised his right hand and pointed his index finger at them. "This is everything requested. Do not provide any information beyond this. If they decide they need more later, they will have to go to a judge to have their search warrant amended. If you have any questions in this regard, you can contact me in my office. Am I clear?"

All three nodded.

Finnigan thanked Erikson and introduced the agents pre-designated to each of the three managers. She then smiled and thanked the escorts. "The FBI thanks you for your cooperation. We will do everything possible to avoid disrupting your workplace." They split up into three teams and proceeded with their inquiries.

Erikson followed the team to Jeff Unger's office and then made sure he went in first. "Jeff, they're going to need access to your office. Why don't you come down to mine for a few minutes?"

Unger glared at him, slammed his laptop computer closed, and stormed out of the office, following Erikson.

By the time the FBI left the premises at around three p.m., they had removed the three Yosheti copiers, including the hard drives on each that contained the record of copies made. They had also taken the laptop computer from Unger's desk used to access the election system. They promised Erikson that they would be back to get access to all records relating to Unger's access to the system.

Unfortunately, they did not have the information they needed on who changed the voter tallies on the Pennsylvania website. Mary Simmons was surprised to find that some sort of glitch had apparently wiped out that tracking mechanism; no web change information was available after September of the previous year. None of her people were able to locate any information on the changes made or maintenance done on the website. The investigators asked how that could happen and none of her people be aware of it. She said that if there was no need to check that information, then no one would know that it was no longer available. Neither Simmons nor key staff members in the Client System Security team knew of any other way of getting the information the FBI needed. Simmons was asked to spot check other states to determine if such a glitch had impacted them. After checking with John Erikson, she did the check and found that none of the states they audited had similar problems.

Betty asked Chris to stay on top of the situation and get her any details as soon as he had them. "It appears we may have a case for destruction of evidence. Let's begin looking at how we might prove it."

"Okay, I'll run with that. I'll get you a summary of what we find relating to our three objectives as quickly as possible. I'll also work with the team to determine what we need to know to investigate the destruction of evidence question."

CHAPTER 42

DETECTIVE CONNER OPENED THE CONFIDENTIAL REPORT
that the FBI sent him on Thomas Everett. His eyes widened as he
leaned in toward his computer screen. He was amazed about the pace
and quality of the information that the Bureau had provided him. The
report indicated that they had done a check on state records in each of the
contiguous forty-eight states. In addition to the criminal record search,
they had combed the Department of Motor Vehicle and Department of
Revenue records. Not only had they found multiple transactions in which
Everett had bought and/or sold vehicles, but they had also contacted the
other parties involved in the transactions.

As soon as he heard of Everett's penchant for buying and selling
vehicles, he suspected that Everett could well be a killer who used au-
tomobiles as his weapon of choice. Both Al and Kathrine had died in
automobile accidents, of a sort, that had yet to be adequately explained.

Conner saw that Everett owned a Honda Pilot. That fit in with
Tillman's claim that someone in that type of car followed and chased
him until he managed to get himself arrested.

The Lincoln that Everett purchased in Florida was sold to Everett with no damage to speak of. When he sold it a month later, there
was front end damage on the vehicle. He told the buyer he had hit a
deer. The buyer said he got a good deal on it and immediately had the
front end fixed. This could be the vehicle that had hit Al.

Conner wanted to get in his car and drive to Tallahassee, Florida
immediately. Two things stopped him. First of all, he knew that he
was a bit of a control freak who wanted to be directly involved in everything. Sergeant Swanson also knew of that tendency and had been

after him to utilize the help of others so he could be more effective. This was a perfect opportunity for that. He had multiple transactions to investigate, and he couldn't be everywhere at once. The second thing that stopped him was that the Lincoln had been repaired. He needed a forensic specialist to check it out. The only way the vehicle could be tied to Al Johnson's murder would be to find remnants of Johnson's blood or hair on it. It would be pure luck if such evidence still existed.

The information on the Cadillac cinched the deal. It was an old car that someone had done some repair work on and then primed in preparation to paint it. They ended up selling it to Everett before they finished the job. It was later sold to a junkyard for scrap and parts. The buyer confirmed that there was indeed damage on the left side. Better still, the vehicle continued to sit in the same junkyard in Auburn, Alabama. Conner immediately arranged for another investigator to head west to examine the Cadillac. If the investigator came back with good news, they would have plenty for an arrest warrant for Everett and a search warrant for his home.

This was the part that Conner hated. Now he had to wait. He always got antsy waiting for information. He went back to his case file to see what more he could work on, but he was too distracted by what he was waiting for to concentrate on anything else.

CHAPTER 43

BETTY FINNIGAN RETURNED TO HER OFFICE AFTER AN early meeting and found a phone message. She had received a call from Brad Tillman while she was away.

"Good morning Brad, Betty Finnigan returning your call."

"Hi, Agent Finnigan. I just wanted to follow up with the results of my review of the financial records for the two GCI departments over the past year."

"Thank you. What did you find?"

"Most of what I found was normal. There is only one thing that was, uh, not so much out of the ordinary, but I would call it new. Three months ago, the Special Projects Division hired a new consultant. They have three or four companies that they typically go to when they need help. Occasionally, they will hire someone new if the others don't have the technical capability to meet their needs."

"I see," said Finnigan. "Do you have any idea why they hired this new consultant?"

"I really don't. I didn't want to probe too deeply at this point."

"That's smart. What is the name of this company?"

"Cyber Tech Consulting Group. I was going to do an online search on them to find out more, but I was concerned that someone could still be monitoring my computer. It's not much, but it is all that struck me as different." Brad gave her the information he had, such as the address and phone numbers for the company. Finnigan thanked him and assured him that he need do nothing else. They would check into it.

Finnigan called a young intern, Tammy Dawson, into her office. Dawson was a student at the University of Georgia who was considering a career in law enforcement. Her career counselor had informed her that the FBI would be interviewing for internships midway through her junior year. She jumped at the opportunity and had been working with Betty Finnigan for two weeks. She had a bubbly personality and was easy to be around, but she also took her work seriously.

"Tammy, I'd like you to do some research on a consultant that GCI has recently hired. We know nothing about them and have no reason to believe they are involved in anything illegal. We just want to know more."

"Sure, thanks for the opportunity. Can I contact them directly?" she asked.

"At this point, I don't think that would be a good idea. I'd like you to find out when they registered with the Secretary of State's Office and do an online search to see what kind of work they do: is there a specialty, that sort of thing. If you are unsure about an avenue of research, talk to me before you pursue it. What questions do you have?"

"No questions. I'll get right on it."

"Good. Let's see what you can come up with by three this afternoon."

When she saw the detailed report on each of the cars Everett had purchased, Betty knew things were going to come together quickly now. That is the way most cases were. She would feel like she was spinning her wheels for months, but once a couple of key elements came together, the rest fell into place rapidly.

The phone interrupted her thoughts. It was Chris Allan, who told her he was ready to go through the information from GCI whenever she liked. They set up a meeting from three to four for that purpose. When the time came, they sat in a conference room and went through everything item by item. Betty invited Tammy Dawson to join them.

They had confirmed through their lab that the document that started all of this was copied on one of the copiers in the Special Projects Division. They also found in the security documentation that Kathrine Cruise had copied the document at 1:32 p.m. on the day of her death. They were close to having a clear chain of possession from the copier to Kathrine Cruise, to Cindy Lawford in Eric Blas's office, and to Al Johnson. What they didn't know was where Kathrine had gotten the document and how someone knew Al Johnson had ended up with it.

They knew for sure that Unger's second computer was directly connected to the election system. At the very least, they had him for lying to the FBI.

"What did you learn about Unger's access to the election system?" Betty asked. Chris had gone back to GCI to get more information about what Unger had been up to.

"We received a sort of log from their internal system security people, but it is difficult for us to decipher. I was going to arrange to sit down with them and have them walk me through it. Another option would be to ask for Eric Blas's help," Chris said.

"That's an interesting idea. Yes, let's get with Blas and see how helpful he can be. It would be good to get a feel for how much he knows about the system."

The next item on the agenda was the changes on the Pennsylvania website. Chris indicated that they had found no way to learn who had changed the numbers. That information could potentially point a big red arrow at the person behind all this. It was the one piece of information that Unger knew they wanted, because Betty had called him about it. He said he would get back to her after he talked to the company attorneys, but he never had.

Betty turned to Tammy. "What did you learn about Cyber Tech Consulting Group?"

"I'm a bit stumped by it," Tammy replied. There is no company with that name listed with the Georgia Secretary of State's Office. In an online search, I found only two in the United States. Would you like me to reach out to those to see if they have ever done work for GCI?"

Betty thought for a moment. "Yes, why don't you give them a call? Ask if they have an Atlanta office, or if they have ever heard of GCI. Nothing more. Just tell them that we are validating some information."

"Okay. I also learned that the P.O. Box is really not an official Post Office Box, but a mailbox in a shipping store in Lilburn." Lilburn was a suburb in the northeast part of the metro area. Betty was pleased with Tammy's work and told her so. Now they needed to determine who was paying for the mailbox.

After the update Betty asked Chris, "What are our next steps?"

Chris began, "We need to arrange a meeting with Cindy Lawford. I have a picture of Kathrine Cruise so that we can confirm her role in the custody of the document."

"You may want to touch base with Brad on that. He wasn't exactly truthful when he talked to her about it."

"I agree. I'll let him know," Chris said. "I think we also need to set up some interviews with others inside GCI, including John Erikson, regarding your request to Unger about Pennsylvania's website. Karl Jennings, the director of the Special Projects Division, is another one. It would be interesting to find out exactly what Unger's interaction with his division is like. Formal, informal, that sort of thing. We need to find out if anyone else saw the document or knows where it may have come from."

"Yes, let's get that completed before we talk to Unger again."

"We could have someone talk to the owner of the packaging store about the mailbox renter," Tammy offered.

"Thank you, Tammy. You're right," Betty said. "I would also like to know where the consultant's bank account is. Unfortunately, we really don't have the facts to pursue that sort of information on them. The consultant company is probably just a bunch of college whiz kids who know nothing about how to set up a business. They've done nothing that would justify the FBI investigating them." She paused. "Is there anything else?"

"I'll contact those out of state companies like we discussed," Tammy said.

Chris said, "Yeah, and I'd like to know where Conner is on his investigation."

"Good idea. Things are moving quickly. Let's get another information sharing meeting set up."

Betty adjourned the meeting and prepared to brief her superiors. Every indication at this point was that Jeff Unger, the head of the nation's new, tamper-proof voting system, was involved in voter fraud. This could seriously shake the confidence of the American people in the integrity of the national election system.

CHAPTER 44

DETECTIVE JOHN CONNER ARRIVED IN HIS OFFICE AFTER lunch. There were a couple of phone messages awaiting him, including one from Agent Chris Allan. He returned the call and tentatively agreed to another meeting the following morning at ten. He placed a call to the sergeant to check the time with him. Considering this case potentially had national implications and could become highly publicized, Swanson decided he should attend all of these meetings to stay on top of things. They arranged a nine a.m. briefing session before leaving for the FBI office.

Conner updated Swanson on what they had learned regarding Thomas Everett's buying and selling cars out of state. They were close to confirming that one of the cars was used to push Kathrine Cruise's car out of her lane and into the concrete abutment at fifty miles per hour. Their investigator had extracted flakes of primer and blue paint residue from the vehicle and had given them to the lab for comparison with the primer and paint on Cruise's car. Conner also discussed the possibility that another car, purchased and sold, could have been involved in the hit and run that killed Al Johnson. He was awaiting a report from that investigator. Swanson responded by ordering that someone locate and follow Thomas Everett so they could pick him up when the information came in.

The meeting with the FBI was beneficial, just as the first one had been. Circumstantial evidence indicated that Everett was likely hired by someone involved in the voter fraud case to eliminate people who had access to the document Kathrine Cruise had copied. During the meeting, Conner got an urgent text from his investigator who had gone to Alabama. He asked that they take a brief break.

He immediately returned Warren Gregory's call.

"What have you got, Warren?" Conner said abruptly when Gregory answered the phone.

"We've got a match," Gregory said. "The primer and paint chips on the Cadillac bought and sold in Alabama match those on Kathrine Cruise's car."

"Fantastic. Thanks, Warren. Perfect timing. Please do whatever it takes to get Cruise's car into the crime lab garage. We need to go through it with a fine-tooth comb and get any evidence documented."

When the meeting reconvened, Conner updated the agents. Finnigan asked that the FBI be present in the search of his property. They agreed that if they could confirm his whereabouts, the team would meet to make the arrest at two that afternoon.

Betty asked Chris where they stood on setting up interviews with GCI employees. He said that a block of time was set up for the following day. Erikson was cooperating and had arranged for a couple of conference rooms on site for the interviews.

"Okay," she instructed Chris, "I want to meet with Jeff Unger as soon as possible after we finish the interviews. We have confirmed that murder is involved. We need to wrap this up and get the person responsible off the streets."

CHAPTER 45

THE SURVEILLANCE TEAM HAD BEEN FORTUNATE ENOUGH to find Thomas Everett at home. He lived in a lower middle-class neighborhood; homes were about sixty years old, most mid-century modern in design. Everett's house was one of the smaller houses on the block. His Honda Pilot was parked in the driveway.

Two plain-clothed cops parked down the street and around the corner with a view of the house. Another car parked a block away in the opposite direction. Both had access to pictures of Everett. About an hour after the police had arrived, Everett backed out of his driveway and turned north. The car around the corner followed him from a block away, and the other vehicle started moving in the general direction, staying well behind.

Once Everett moved onto a main thoroughfare, the two unmarked cars alternated keeping an eye on him. Everett turned into a large shopping center and parked in front of a fitness center and went inside, carrying a gym bag. The two surveillance cars parked nearby.

At a quarter to noon, thirty minutes after Everett had gone inside, the team received word to make the arrest. Jeanette Price, the lead officer, notified dispatch of their location and requested two additional cars to position themselves close by but out of sight. She thought the best plan would be to approach him in the parking lot as he walked back to his car. They should be able to take him quickly and quietly. Hopefully, he would not be armed. Even if he was, she felt sure that with the element of surprise they could have him disarmed and under control before he knew what hit him.

Plainclothes officer Jack Wallace went into the gym and asked to speak to someone about a membership. He watched Everett as he moved around to the different machines. At twelve thirty, he walked into the locker room. Wallace thanked the person who was showing him around and asked if he could wander around the gym for a few minutes while he thought about it. He went to the empty waiting area and took out his phone.

"He just went into the locker room," he whispered. "If he takes a shower, he will probably be hitting the door in fifteen minutes. If not, it could be anytime now."

"Okay," Price replied. "We will be positioned on either side of the door. When he walks out, I will approach him immediately. You come from behind and lead him to the left where there are no windows. Chet Winston will take the bag out of his hand."

When Price contacted dispatch for back-up, she had asked that John Conner be updated. Conner, now out of his meeting with the FBI, headed to the shopping center. Unfortunately, road construction along his route had taken out a lane, and traffic was a mess. Conner's blood pressure rose as he sat there waiting, sometimes taking three lights to get through an intersection. They didn't need him, but, as usual, he wanted to be there.

At ten after one, before Conner arrived, Everett walked out of the locker room and headed for the door. Wallace followed close behind.

As soon as Everett was through the door, Price took two steps toward him and flashed her badge. "Thomas Everett, police. Please walk to your left and away from the door. We would like to talk with you."

Before the man could utter a word, Wallace firmly took hold of Everett's left arm, placed his right hand in the small of his back, and turned him so that he was facing the wall. Winston, Price's partner, took hold of the bag. "I will hold that for you, Mr. Everett," he said.

Everything happened so fast that Everett barely had time to react. He just stared at them in disbelief. Price had her right hand on her gun in the event it was needed. With her left hand, she keyed her mic to call the back-up patrol cars to move into position.

"Please place both hands behind your head, Mr. Everett," Wallace said as he began patting him down. He wasn't armed. Wallace placed a handcuff on his right wrist, moved that arm down behind his back, and did the same with the left.

The police car pulled up to where they were standing.

"Mr. Everett, you are under arrest," Price said as they moved him into the backseat of the car. She read him his Miranda rights and asked him if he understood.

"I want to talk to a lawyer," he said.

The entire process took less than ten minutes. Price called Conner to let him know that the arrest had been made and Everett was en route to the station. Conner banged his hand against the steering wheel. Thanking her, he moved out of traffic and headed back toward the station.

Agent Betty Finnigan was pleased with how the arrest of Thomas Everett had come together. She wasn't pleased to learn that he refused to talk; she wasn't surprised either. His rights were there for a reason, and she respected that, but it would make their jobs much more difficult.

The combination FBI and police search team combed through Everett's residence for six hours. They collected six boxes and four bags of materials to be carefully inspected. Finnigan offered to send the materials to the FBI evidence lab and assured Conner that she would request top priority. Their search found over twenty-four thousand dollars in cash and a mailbox rental agreement from a packaging store in Lilburn. This was the link to GCI. Everett's mailbox number matched the address of the new consultant that GCI had hired around the same time people started dying.

They also found a rental agreement for a small warehouse nearby. Expanding their search to that location, they found several vehicles, but little else. He seemed to be using it as a garage.

CHAPTER 46

AFTER THE POLICE ALSO CONTACTED ERIC BLAS TO LET him know that a suspect in Kathrine's murder was in custody, he immediately called Brad. He told him that the Police Victim Services unit visited Kathrine's parents to inform them that Kathrine's death was not an accident. The unit assured the Cruises and Eric that the suspect was in custody and that an ongoing investigation may implicate others. They would not go further than that in their explanation and could not yet reveal the killer's motive, but they promised to keep them informed. The police assured them that Kathrine had done nothing wrong.

Brad felt a little bit of weight lifted; he could only imagine how Eric felt. He wondered if the person arrested was responsible for Al's murder as well. His mind went to GCI. Was someone at GCI arrested? He had heard that the FBI were in the building a few days before, but he'd decided to stay out of it. He was doing his best to get his life back to normal. He hadn't even told Barbara about it.

He received another phone call. "Hello Brad, this is Chris Allan at the FBI."

"Hi, Agent Allan. Eric tells me that you found the person responsible for Kathrine's death. That is good news. Was he also responsible for Al's death?"

"I'm sorry, but I don't have any information on that. In fact, we are keeping things pretty close to the vest right now. We are making progress, though."

"Glad to hear it."

"Brad, the reason I called is to let you know that we are about to contact Cindy Lawford to see if she can identify Kathrine Cruise as the woman who dropped off the envelope that went to Al Johnson. I thought you would want to know."

Brad sighed. "I guess I knew you would need to contact her at some point. I'll get in touch with her and tell her to expect your call."

After he hung up, Brad dialed Cindy's number. She told Brad that she had been told to be available at work the next day to meet with the FBI. She had no idea why they wanted to talk with her. Brad told her briefly that it was related to the envelope she had accepted months back. He apologized for being less than truthful with her and assured her that she was not in trouble. She should just tell them what she knows.

The FBI team completed all of the interviews as planned the following day. When Finnigan and Allan met with the team to review the information from the new interviews, they learned of Cindy Lawford's confirmation that Kathrine Cruise was the person who had given her the envelope. Cindy had put it on Al's desk on October 20th, the evening that Kathrine was murdered. The agents had probed her for anything else she could remember about that evening, but she couldn't recall any other details other than Cruise approaching her very near the elevator. She had gotten up to make a copy, and Cruise had come out of the elevator as Cindy walked by on the way back to her cubicle.

More evidence was pointing to Jeff Unger. He had never asked his General Counsel about assisting the FBI with information on who changed the website. "Did Karl Jennings provide some helpful information?" Finnigan asked Agent Chip Bell, who had led the team's interviews.

"Not a lot. When we asked him about the new consulting company, he told us that he didn't know what sort of services they provided. He said that Unger said he hired the company to help him understand what promising technologies were on the horizon so he could assess future opportunities for GCI. Jennings said he was a bit surprised that he wasn't included in those meetings, but he didn't complain to Unger," Bell said.

"That's interesting," Finnigan said. This is the company that doesn't exist." She looked at Chris Allan. "Tammy contacted the two companies with the Cyber Tech Consulting name. Neither of them have ever done any work for GCI."

Bell waited to see if that would draw a response, but it didn't. Then he went on, "Jennings also said that Unger was very hands-on in the management of the Special Projects Division. Apparently, he drove innovation for the company. He especially kept up with the election services group. That was his baby. He was a genius who understood everything right down to the programming. Jennings said Unger would walk through these areas several times a day just to ask someone a question or kick around new ideas. He carried a notepad with him and used it frequently. He seemed to have a lot of respect for Kathrine Cruise and visited her cubicle often."

"Was he suggesting that something inappropriate was going on between Unger and Cruise?"

"No. We asked the same question. He said it was all business. She was one of a few who he liked to bounce ideas off of."

"Okay. What else did you learn?"

"Marty Paris, one of the programmers, made an interesting comment. When asked how often Unger came into the area, he laughed and said he usually made one more visit than he needed to. He said he often gets so engrossed in talking to different people that he sets his portfolio notepad down and returns to his office without it. Then he comes around looking for it an hour or so later."

"Hmmm, anything else?"

"Everyone we spoke with said that they didn't know how a person could change votes in the system. Most of their work was to ensure something like that couldn't happen."

Finnigan looked at her watch. It was Wednesday. She told the team that she wanted all of their documentation completed by three the next day. She and Allan would use it to develop questions for Jeff Unger's upcoming interview.

CHAPTER 47

ON THURSDAY MORNING, CAROL BEHMER ARRIVED TO work at half past seven, her usual time. She always tried to get in before Mr. Unger so she could restock the small refrigerator in his office and start the coffee brewing. That day, she could tell through the opaque glass window in the door that his light was on, so she supposed he had come in early, as he occasionally did. All of this hoopla with the FBI seemed to have him on edge. She assumed he probably couldn't sleep, so he came in to work.

Normally, when he got to work early, he made his own coffee. She opened the door slightly and saw that he had laid his head down on his desk. She didn't want to bother him, so she quietly closed the door and went about her work.

At 8:15 a.m. John Erikson called. Carol answered the phone in her usual manner. She told him that Jeff had come to work early and appeared to be sleeping. Erikson said that it was important, so Carol pressed the intercom and announced that John was on the phone. She heard no response. She got up and slowly opened the door to Jeff's office.

"Jeff?" she said. "John Erikson is on the phone for you and says it's urgent."

He didn't respond, and she continued into the office. She hadn't taken two steps when she noticed a pool of congealed blood on the floor in front of his desk.

"Jeff!" she shouted. "Jeff! Are you all right?"

She continued walking toward him, and only then did she realize what she was seeing. There was a gun in Jeff's right hand, resting on the desktop. His head was also on the desk. There was a small hole in his temple. Blood was everywhere on the desk, and a spray of blood and flesh coated the carpet to his left.

"Jeff! Jeff!" she screamed as she turned and ran from the office. Those in the area looked up to see her pick up the phone and scream, "He's dead, John. Jeff is dead!" She laid the phone receiver on her desk and sank down into her chair, sobbing. "Oh Jeff, what did you do?"

Everyone in the executive suite was up and running toward her. Other administrative assistants went to Carol's side, while the company's officers went straight into Jeff's office to see his limp body and the mess left behind.

Cathy Hoover walked out of his office and back to her own. She picked up the office phone and called 911. First responders, both police and fire, were in the office within seven minutes. Within fifteen minutes, every GCI employee had heard the news that Jeff Unger had taken his own life.

CHAPTER 48

IT DIDN'T TAKE LONG BEFORE WORD CAME TO JOHN
Conner that Jeff Unger had been found in his office with a gun in his
hand and a hole in his head.

Conner immediately contacted dispatch and asked that one of
the responding officers call him. His phone rang within four minutes.

"Conner."

"Yeah, this is Tony Pirelli. I'm the lead at the GCI situation. You
wanted a call?"

"Thank you for the call, Officer Pirelli. You need to be aware that
the subject, Jeff Unger, is a person of interest in a criminal investigation. It is extremely important that the FBI and I be involved in any
interviews conducted in this case. I will be there in less than fifteen
minutes. I'll get the FBI there ASAP as well." Conner didn't want to
get in the officers' way, and he definitely didn't want to take over their
investigation. However, if they could participate in the questioning, it
would save the employees having to sit through two sets of interviews.

"Okay, we will make sure everyone is aware. There's plenty to
do before we begin talking with people here. So far, we've just been
assisting the medical team."

After hanging up, Conner immediately called Betty Finnigan.
By half past nine, Finnigan, Allan, and Conner had joined the gaggle
of activity in the executive suite.

The GCI members present weren't too helpful. Most of them
suggested that Unger had not been himself since the FBI probe came
to the building earlier in the week. However, none of them believed
him capable of taking his own life.

Investigators looked through security video to find that Unger had returned to his office at eight the previous evening. There was no sign of him on video again. The building security guards had a shift change at midnight, and neither guard heard the gunshot.

After investigators cleared the site, they removed Unger's remaining computer CPU and brought it to the FBI evidence lab. Once the tech professionals at the lab connected a keyboard and monitor to it, they turned it on and began their work. They determined that the only programs that had been open were his email and word processor. They opened the word processor and found that the computer had automatically saved the unnamed document that had been open. They clicked to reopen the document and found a series of notes written by Unger.

To Amber and my family, please forgive me for leaving you in this way. I love you and have made sure that you are taken care of.

To my colleagues and employees, you are the finest group of professionals that I have ever worked with. I'm sorry that I used such poor judgment in manipulating the amazing system that you developed and maintained for counting votes. I did it with good intentions, but things spun out of control, and I did not handle that well. I was saddened and sickened by the division in our country. It seemed to only be getting worse. It was my intent to adjust votes from time to time just to ensure fringe candidates were never elected. I wanted to keep our country in the center, politically, just until politicians were able to work together again.

To the families of Kathrine Cruise and Al Johnson, please forgive me. I thought that what I was doing was a noble act for the 360 million citizens of the United States. Unfortunately, I convinced myself that one and even two lives would be a small price to pay for our country's well-being.

To Brad and Barbara Tillman, I am sorry for what I put you through and happy, now, that I was unsuccessful in doing you further harm.

To my board of advisors, please take care of my company. Don't let my mistakes lead to its downfall. The work we do is important to protect IT systems everywhere.

~Jeff

CHAPTER 49

JEFF UNGER'S DEATH WAS A SHOCK TO ALL. HE HAD developed a reputation among politicians, businesspeople, and the public at large as a brilliant entrepreneur who loved his country and had taken great strides to make it better. News channels put together five-minute montages of news footage, photographs, and interviews with other notable businesspeople talking about Unger's importance to the world of technology, business, and especially the election system.

On Friday morning, Agent Betty Finnigan felt overwhelmed by Unger's death and the attention instantly generated regarding the case. At eight-thirty, she and Allan met to talk through the developments.

"It looks like our case just wrapped up," said Allan.

"It may appear that way," said Finnigan. "But there is something about this that is unsettling to me."

Before Allan could respond, Rick Christianson, the Special Agent in charge of the Atlanta Field office, knocked on Finnigan's office door and entered without waiting for an answer. "Hold off on everything," he said. "I just got a call from the Justice Department. They are all over this and have ordered that we stop everything until they arrive."

The U. S. Justice Department had moved in and shut down any possibility of the truth about Unger's death coming out before Finnigan knew what had happened. The last thing the Justice Department wanted was for voters to believe that the election system was tainted in any way. They believed that outrage and panic would result; violence would almost be a certainty.

The FBI never shared Unger's suicide notes with anyone, including those they were written to. They only shared it with Detective Conner and others on the force who needed to know. Finnigan told the police and the Georgia prosecutor's office that Justice Department lawyers would assist them in putting together their case against Everett in a way that would not compromise national security.

The official story was that Unger apparently had some internal demons that nobody was aware of. Rumors within the company spread that his death had something to do with the FBI investigation, but his employees could not believe that Jeff Unger was capable of criminal activity. The rumors were inconsistent and simply died away over time.

Three days after Unger's death, the police and FBI had a final joint meeting regarding the investigation. It was a bit different than the others. The police commissioner and every level down to the Captain were there with Detective Conner. On the federal side, fourteen people were present, including the Assistant Attorney General for the U.S. Department of Justice.

Detective Conner shared that the investigator had found blood splatters inside the engine compartment of the Lincoln, which was sold with front end damage. The forensics lab matched the DNA to that of Al Johnson. The detective explained that Thomas Everett didn't want to go down alone and was willing to cooperate.

"But," Detective Conner said, "Everett doesn't seem to actually know who his contact person was. The phone number he used was to a throwaway phone purchased in Baltimore, but the number is no longer in service. A search of cell tower records confirmed that the phone was only active in Atlanta, much of the time in and around the GCI building."

Following Detective Conner's report, Robert Gomez, the Assistant Attorney General, took over the leadership of the meeting. "I want to thank all of you for the important work you have done in this case. You defended our country from the potential loss of confidence in the most cherished right the American people have: their right to vote. I am thankful to the Atlanta police and the FBI for your excellent work in solving the related murders."

Finnigan remained silent.

After his opening comments, Gomez, a large man both in height and stature, paused, as though for effect. He looked around the room with eyes furrowed and a slight frown. "As for the election fraud investigation, it is finished. Those involved in the investigation are to wrap up your cases without further communication with anyone and send your closed case files to the FBI Director's Office. Should anyone who has been involved ask, you are to tell them that the case was solved with Unger's death, period. Does anyone have a question?"

Finnigan raised her hand. She couldn't keep quiet any longer. "Sir, I believe that for proper case resolution, we may want to look into a couple of things."

Gomez glared at her. "What is your name, ma'am?"

"Special Agent Finnigan, sir. I am the lead agent on the case."

"Special Agent Finnigan, you are to wrap up your case without further communication with anyone and send your closed case files to the Director," Gomez repeated forcefully. "Do I make myself clear?"

"Yes, sir."

Neither Finnigan, her local superiors, nor anyone at the FBI spoke further at the meeting. Gomez made it very clear that the voter fraud case pursued by the FBI was considered closed. He simply reiterated that the FBI had done a tremendous job ensuring that the integrity of the election system was preserved and that there was no risk of this sort of fraud in the future. In closing the meeting Gomez pronounced, "The details of this investigation are to be sealed for national security purposes. Anybody involved who shares details of the case will be prosecuted."

At the conclusion of the meeting, Finnigan and Allan quietly left the conference room.

"Can they do that?" Chris Allan asked his boss.

"They just did. Justice be damned! We can't trust the people of the United States to handle the truth!" she said with all the sarcasm she could muster. They returned to their respective offices to gather all documentation of the case to hand over to the Department of Justice.

CHAPTER 50

BRAD AND BARB TILLMAN WERE ALSO STUNNED BY Unger's suicide. Brad knew enough to understand that Unger was a logical suspect, but Brad had always believed that there was no way he was a murderer. Yet, his suicide seemed to be a confession that, indeed, Jeff Unger had been responsible for everything that had happened. Brad saw that, although Barbara was surprised as well, she seemed relieved more than anything. For the first time in months, she began to relax. Neither of them had realized the level of stress they had been feeling until it was lifted.

Brad and Barb went to Linda Johnson's house as soon as they could after the truth about Al's death came out. Linda told them about how the FBI Victim Services unit had contacted her to break the news. They assured her that the investigation was complete and that those involved in Al's death were either under arrest or deceased. They never mentioned Jeff Unger by name. They asked for her cooperation in not talking to others about the details of the document and the FBI's investigation; they were truthful with her about their desire to protect the integrity of the election system. She accepted their request because Al had been part of the system's development and had felt strongly that it was worthy. She said that she felt justice was being properly served.

There was no apparent government misconduct that she could see, so she signed a non-disclosure agreement. In order to make it a legally binding agreement and to show their appreciation, the US Government deposited $100,000 into her account.

"I would think the money could be helpful to you and the kids," Barb said.

"The money is meaningless to me," Linda replied. "No amount of money will bring Al back to us."

Brad and Barb nodded, Barb feeling a bit embarrassed by her comment. "Linda, this must feel like ripping a bandage off of an old wound," Brad said.

Linda looked at them both with a fire in her eyes that Brad had not seen before. "I am so angry that I could spit!" she said with a rasp that showed she was actually holding back the scream that she wanted to let out at that moment. "The kids are too. It feels like a boulder has been dropped on us. To think that someone would hate Al so much as to kill him! We were starting to accept his death and develop a new sense of normalcy. Now, it's like we've been dragged back to the first day he died. This time, we will not move on until we see that his murderer is convicted and never sees the light of day again."

"Linda, there is nothing you can do now. It is up to the prosecutors to take him to trial and convict him," Brad said. Barb nodded, resting her hand on her friend's shoulder.

"That may be, but I will be there for every hearing, every day of trial, every witness statement. I will be there at the sentencing. And I will make sure Al's presence is felt throughout."

CHAPTER 51

BRAD AND ERIC ARRANGED TO MEET AFTER WORK ONE
evening to talk about the truth surfacing. The FBI had offered them similar agreements to Linda's. Brad and Barb changed the amount to $15,000 and signed the agreement. They didn't want to be "paid off," as such, but this would cover the costs that they had incurred while on the run. Eric took all the money and signed. The two men couldn't call their get-together a celebration because there was nothing to celebrate. However, they thanked one another liberally for their roles in seeing justice done. Brad knew that Eric had the same emotions as Linda to deal with. Eric just said that his only regret was that he couldn't destroy those responsible.

"I'm feeling like I need to get out of here. Find something new," Brad shared. "Maybe not now, but soon."

"I'm with you on that. Unfortunately, my small business can't support me yet. I'll need to stick around for a while," Eric said. He paused. "Cathy Hoover has offered me a promotion."

Cathy Hoover, VP of Product Development, had been tapped by the GCI Board of Advisors to be the interim CEO and take over Jeff Unger's role in the business.

Unger's wife, Amber, not only had to deal with her husband's suicide, but the business as well. She was on record as his sole partner in the corporation, although she had never taken an interest in the company and was not involved in its operation. Unger had set up the board of advisors to help him in growing the business. The advisors were all from outside the company; most were executives in different industries. Amber Unger, because of her limited knowledge of the business, gave the board of advisors full authority to make decisions on her behalf for the continued operation of the business until further notice.

"A promotion! That's great, Eric." Brad said, touching his arm. "Cathy Hoover's old position?"

"No. She knows next to nothing about the election system. She wants to work toward taking the election services group out of the Special Projects Division and making it a new division. She asked me if I would take the reins of the group and prepare for that."

"You should take it. It's perfect for you!" Brad exclaimed.

"I don't know how perfect, but I can hardly afford not to take it. She offered me the new position with a salary of $225,000 per year and a half million-dollar bonus after three years if I stick around."

Brad's eyes widened. He said, "You're kidding me!"

"No, it's true. She said she wants two things from me. First, to provide stability to the election system. Second, to work with her in developing a succession strategy that would ensure that there is a bench of talent to draw from for future leadership in the new division."

"Wow. That is some responsibility."

"Yeah, can you see me developing new leaders?" Eric asked as he rolled his eyes. "I'd rather figure out a way to get out.... I told her I'd let her know next week."

CHAPTER 52

BETTY FINNIGAN CONTACTED BRAD AND ERIC BOTH AND
asked to meet with them, informally and off the record. They met in a
quiet bar that she recommended at a table that was well away from traffic.
She ordered hors d'oeuvres and their drinks of choice.

Once left alone, a somber expression overtook her.

"What I am about to tell you cannot leave this table, do
you understand?"

She looked first at Eric and then at Brad.

Both nodded, somewhat apprehensively.

"I am not happy with the way this case has been closed. My gut
is telling me that something is very wrong."

Brad's eyes widened. "Well, why did you close the case then?" he
said incredulously, while Eric stared at her.

"I did not close the case. The U.S. Department of Justice closed
the case in order to protect the public perception of the strength of the
election system."

"Yes, we were both approached and signed an agreement for the
same purpose. I do understand why they would want to avoid negative
publicity for the system," Eric said.

"What concerns do you have?" Brad asked.

She looked at them both and said, "I will lose my job and end
up in jail if you ever tell someone what I am about to show you. Can
I trust you?"

Brad and Eric looked at each other and then at her. "Yeah, I'm
with you," Brad said.

"Me too," Eric added.

Finnigan reached into her folio and pulled out two copies of the same document and handed one to each. "Read this," she said.

The document was Unger's suicide note.

Brad and Eric both read through the letter. Eric became angry.

"If I had access to that son-of-a-bitch's body, I would shove this thing right up his ass!" he said, quietly.

Brad put his hand on Eric's arm. "I could have done without seeing this. Why are you showing it to us?"

Finnigan said, "I have been doing this job for nineteen years. My instinct tells me when things aren't right. This is all too neat and tidy. This is not how criminals behave. Cases never conclude like this. It's like someone wrapped everything up for us and topped it off with a nice, pretty bow."

Brad looked at her and then at Eric. "So, you think Unger wasn't responsible?"

"He may have been involved, but I would be willing to bet that he didn't type that letter."

"Well, reopen the case!" Eric said.

"Reopen the case," Brad parroted.

"It's out of my hands. The Department of Justice is so happy that things were so conveniently concluded that they sealed the file and threatened that if I don't drop it, I will be fired from the agency, or worse."

Brad didn't know what to say. "You told them your concerns and they threatened you? Did you tell your superiors?"

"I did. The story is the same."

Finnigan reached out and took the copies of the note from each of them.

"I want you to keep your eyes open and watch your backs. I wish I could offer more than that, but I can't."

Eric's face deflated. He looked at her and asked, "What are we supposed to do?"

Both men looked at Finnigan for an answer.

"You should do nothing other than your job as you normally would. Just be aware, that's all. And keep my phone number."

Brad rolled his eyes. "I thought we were through with this," he grumbled.

"Gentlemen, I wish I could do more for you, but I can't. I just couldn't in good conscience turn my back and say nothing to you at all," she said as she stood and threw two business cards and forty dollars on the table. "Keep my number," she said again, and she walked away.

"We need to get out of GCI," Eric moaned.

Brad thought for a minute. "No, you need to take that job. That will put you in the best position possible to see if the election system is still compromised. If someone else was involved in Kathrine's murder, that's the only way you can find out."

Eric glared at him. "Tillman, this is *bullshit!*" He stood and left the bar.

CHAPTER 53

BRAD TOLD NOBODY ABOUT THE MEETING WITH FINNIGAN, including Barb. She was in a better mood than he had seen her in months. He remained busy at work, in large part because of the financial issues generated by the changes to the organization the board of advisors implemented. The Chief Financial Officer left the company, and Brad's boss, Keith Hughes, was promoted to that position. Brad had a new position, Director of Financial Controls, but his responsibilities were not significantly different from before.

Over the spring Eric and Brad met after work on occasion to compare notes. Brad learned that Eric had accepted his new position reluctantly. He was now working directly for Cathy, as Al had. She was incredibly busy in her new role as CEO, and her old VP position remained open. All of the officers were working together to keep everything covered, but Cathy was looking for someone with a unique set of skills for the position. Nobody inside the company met her standards. Consequently, Eric was on his own. Cathy's first task for him was to find Unger's mechanism for manipulating votes and to get rid of it.

He told Brad that he found the task harder than he had imagined, but he was able to retrieve Unger's laptop from the FBI. It was the one that Unger used to access the election system; it would provide him equal access. Of course, the laptop would do him no good until he could get into the cyber-protected system. The program required a thirteen-digit password with sixty-two possible characters for each digit. It also required multi-factor authentication that sent a code to Unger's cell phone to allow access. Fortunately, Eric was in the cybersecurity business. With Cathy's help, he was able to get his hands on Jeff Unger's cell phone. In addition, Cathy contacted Amber Unger and asked if Jeff had a thumb drive among his possessions. Amber dropped one off that Jeff had kept on his key ring. Eric found that the thumb drive operated as a token, which basically entered the password information for him. Once Eric had those items, he was in within minutes.

Cathy gave him an office one floor down from the executive suite with a dedicated phone line with access to the election system. For the first two months, Eric went directly into the software code himself to try and locate Unger's window for manipulating votes. He was unable to find it among the millions of lines of code. He next had the programmers who worked with the system look for it. After two more weeks, still nothing. His motivation began to decline, and he began spending more time developing a proposal for bench strength in future leadership. The search never left his mind, though. At the end of August, he sought help from someone from the Special Projects Division who worked on more advanced systems that would ultimately replace the current one. Nobody was able to identify how the system could be manipulated.

In early September, Brad and Eric met for a drink after work.

"Are you still looking for Unger's means of manipulating votes?" Brad asked.

"I am. Unger was a genius for sure, but I just can't figure out how he was able to access the system without anyone knowing it. How can he have had a window to the system that nobody else can find?"

"It's less than two months until the election. I hope you find it before then."

"Me too," Eric said. Of course, if Unger had buried it that deep, I suppose nobody but he could access it anyway. If we can't find it, there is little chance that someone else could. It still haunts me, though. I feel like I have to find it before the election."

"Have you run across anything that suggests someone threatening is still out there?" Brad asked.

"No, thankfully. You?

"I haven't either. It may be that Finnigan's gut was wrong this time."

"Yes, I expect you're right," Eric said.

Brad met Eric less frequently throughout the fall. Both men settled into their jobs and spoke little about what Finnigan had said, though it was never far from either of their minds.

CHAPTER 54

BY MID-OCTOBER, THE NATIONAL ELECTION WAS JUST A few weeks away. Eric followed the polls, which reflected that the Republican candidate for President was comfortably ahead. Still, the polls had been notoriously inaccurate for the past decade. Eric realized that the candidate for the Democrats was a far-left progressive, and it was unlikely that there were enough voters to elect her. She was farther left than Eric preferred, but he would much rather have her than the Republican. He had been so busy that he had not been involved in any campaigns during this cycle. At this point, he almost considered using the portal, if he found it, to boost the progressive. It didn't matter. He hadn't found it, and he was beginning to have a "don't give a shit" attitude about the whole thing.

However, the closer the election got, the more Cathy Hoover pressed him about finding Unger's manipulation mechanism. Her pressure helped to refocus him. He was still at a loss but continued to think about it, almost obsessively. He knew that Unger had been a genius in cybersecurity, but it was Eric's field as well. Unger couldn't have used something that had yet to be invented. Why couldn't Eric find the trick?

One day during the fourth week in October, he left the building and took a walk. It was a blustery day, though, and he turned back toward the office to get out of the wind. He had to wait to cross the street because a large box truck drove by. On the side of the truck was a sign that said, "AAA Shredding Service: We shred personnel documents, accounting documents, or whatever you need destroyed." Suddenly, an idea came to him. It was like a eureka moment. A triple-A server! he thought. It had to be!

AAA stood for Authentication, Authorization, and Accounting. A triple-A server was like a gatekeeper into a computer system. It was set up so only specific individuals could access the program. A password protected individual had to be on a specific computer, which had to be plugged into a specific jack or port for access. It was usually used for accounting systems to ensure that only certain users could gain access.

Eric picked up the phone and called Cathy. "I think I may have it!" he announced.

"What, Unger's way in?"

"Yes! A triple-A server!"

"If it's that simple, we should both be fired!" Cathy mused.

"Listen, I'll see if I can locate the server, but would you mind if I accessed your office tonight to plug into the port that Jeff used? I'm leaving for a meeting now, but I can come back later.... The election is only ten days away. I would love to solve this mystery before it gets much closer."

"Sure, stop by on your way out and pick up a key from Carol." Eric headed over and retrieved Cathy's office key. After he pulled out of the parking garage, he used his hands-free system to call Stan Haley, the Computer Support Manager.

"Haley," he heard on his car's speaker.

"Stan, this is Eric Blas. Cathy is looking for a server that Jeff may have had special access to. Would you have any idea where such a server might be physically located?"

"Yeah, he had a server dedicated to himself. He wouldn't let me help him with it at all. He said he would be responsible for regular maintenance and keeping it clean."

Eric smiled to himself and shook his head. *I'm such an idiot.* "Sounds promising. Where is it located?"

"It's down in the Special Projects Division in a locked closet."

"Thanks, Stan," Eric said abruptly and hung up.

Eric completed his business meeting, which actually was related to the small business he had on the side. He grabbed a hamburger and headed back to GCI. By half past eight, he was in Cathy's office. He ran a USB cable from the jack in the floor to the laptop, now laying on Cathy's desk. He opened the laptop and entered the security code. Once online, he went to the File Explorer folder and clicked on "Network." Bingo! There it was. A server that he had never seen before.

He clicked on the server; a password command came up. Here we go again! he thought. He scrambled down to his office to get the thumb drive and Unger's cell phone.

Within thirty minutes he was in. He assigned a new password to the server and opened the program. "*Yes!*" he said out loud, pumping his fist like a young Tiger Woods making a putt.

The screen that popped up had fifty-one tabs on it, one labeled "U.S." and one for each state in the Union, listed alphabetically. He clicked on the U.S. tab and saw a reference to each state. Beside each state was a number. Eric suspected that the numbers represented total votes or registered voters for the state.

For Arizona, the number was 4,357,000.

He clicked on the Arizona tab and found an entry labeled "Percent of registered voters voting." The amount "fifty-six percent" was on the top of the page. Below that was a label called "Desired Outcome." There were two fields listed under that: "Republican" and a blank entry space. Below it there was a line labeled "Democrat." Following that, the percentage entered was "+1.2%." Then there were a series of numbers that appeared to be the state's precincts. They had a burnt orange background, where the percentage had no color inside the cell. He tried to click in the precinct number cell but could not; that cell was locked and couldn't be changed. Then he clicked in the white percentage number cell, and his cursor landed there. He double-clicked on the percentage number to highlight it and typed in "1%," and the number changed.

Beside each of the precincts was a number of votes for Democratic candidates and a number of votes for Republican candidates. He tried to click on those numbers, but those cells were locked as well. They were probably the result of formulas based on the percentage number and the totals entered at the top of the page.

Eric returned to the main U.S. tab and jotted down the total number for Arizona. This had to be registered voters. He was able to change the number to 3,000,000. Upon opening the Arizona page, all of the numbers had gone down considerably. He changed the desired outcome to "Republican +10%" and deleted the percentage after "Democrat." He pressed the enter key. All of the numbers changed accordingly.

This was it, he thought to himself. It was so simple. Unger just created a program that would mimic the GCI computer that collected all of the votes and dropped them into the counting system, by state. All Unger had to do was create fictitious vote entries and, after the actual votes downloaded, redownload the fabricated ones. They would overwrite the actual vote counts. No wonder they hadn't found it in the larger system. He had simply developed a new system to connect momentarily to download the desired vote totals. That asshole was brilliant, Eric thought to himself. It was so fundamental but also so simple. Eric said out loud, "You're not so smart, Jeff Unger. Eric Blas has found your ruse, and he's gonna shut it down!"

He went back to the U.S. tab and saw that California had no number recorded. He clicked on the tab and found blank entries. Eric thought, if a state is likely to be a safe state, the system would not re-place the actual—.

He heard the creak of a door and jumped. He looked up. Nobody was there. He turned and looked behind him just in time to see the door from the office to the stairwell close the last two inches. He turned his chair fully around and asked himself what he had actually seen. Had the door really closed? He got up and walked slowly to the door. He wasn't sure he wanted to open it, but he did it anyway. He stepped onto the concrete stairway and looked across and down. He saw nothing. He tried the door handle on the stairwell side. It was locked. Holding on to the door handle, he stretched his left arm out as far as it would go and walked to the middle of the stairwell. He looked down. He saw and heard nothing.

Eric returned to the office and closed the door. His heart was pounding in his chest. Somebody closed that door, he thought. Who was it and how long were they there? He decided he needed to protect what he had found and get out of there. He walked through the front door at the other side of the office and into the executive lobby area. He scanned the room but saw no one. Returning to the office, he sat back down, clicked back on both the Arizona and U.S. tabs and changed the numbers back to what they had been. He looked carefully to see if there was a save button. There did not appear to be one. He closed the program and File Explorer.

Finally, he closed the laptop as well and sat for a moment to think about what he should do. A surge of paranoia set in, and he decided that he needed to hide the information, now. Walking out of the office again, he went to the copy room. He pulled a couple of pieces of paper from the copier and returned to Cathy's office. He sat down again at the desk, took a pen from the pencil holder, and wrote a note.

Found Lenger's portal!
— Laptop must be plugged into open jack under desk
— Explorer will show a network named u-drive
* User name: unger
* Password: tig65.my@8tcup
!! Someone may know about this!
I will hide this and brief you first thing in the AM.
Eric

Eric stood up and looked around again. He needed to hide the note in case he was found out. He folded it and walked over to Cathy's personal coffeemaker that sat above her mini refrigerator. Opening the tray for the filter, he was glad to see that someone had removed the grounds. He placed the thumb drive and the folded note into the basket and closed it again.

Looking around, he tried to think of a place where he could hide the laptop too. He went out to Carol's desk and looked around. The cleaners had already been there; the trash had been emptied. Pulling the wastebasket out from under the desk, he loosened the trash liner, leaned Unger's laptop inside the inner edge of the wastebasket, and pulled the liner back over the edge. He pulled out Carol's chair, placed the wastebasket directly in front of it, and pushed the chair back in. Eric figured that when she moved the wastebasket, the weight of the laptop would make her look inside.

Eric closed and locked Cathy's office and returned to his own. He picked up the phone and called Brad. "I found it," he said.

"You found Unger's access to make changes? That's great! Congratulations!"

"I'm kind of hyped up right now, though. Someone could have seen me. I'm not sure. Could we meet and talk? I've got to tell you about it."

Brad looked at his watch. It was eleven p.m. "Sure, Eric. Where are you?"

"I'm at the office, but we shouldn't meet here. How about the Bird Cage?"

Brad said, "Sure. I'll be there in twenty-five minutes."

Eric grabbed his jacket and headed for the elevator. He would feel better after he was out of this place, for good. He pushed the button to the second level of the parking garage. The doors opened. He walked toward his car.

A voice came out of the darkness, "Eric! I'm so glad you're here. I'm working late and my battery is dead. Do you have a set of jumper cables?"

Eric looked up and saw someone in a black hoodie walking toward him. He recognized the voice and was about to let him know he didn't have cables when the man's left hand reached out and grabbed the front of his jacket. A ten-inch knife blade was thrust under his ribcage and up into his heart.

Eric crumpled immediately, his face distorted by shock and terror. The man who held the front of his jacket tugged his limp body behind a concrete pillar. He bent down and took Eric's watch, wallet, and two cell phones. Rising, he walked slowly out of the parking garage in the same manner he had entered it. He moved onto the street and then into an alley nearby.

CHAPTER 55

BARB WAS IN BED BECAUSE SHE HAD AN EARLY SHIFT THE next morning. Brad left as quietly as he could so he wouldn't disturb her. It only took him twenty minutes to get to the Bird Cage. He walked in, got a table, and ordered a beer. He sat for twenty-five minutes, checking his watch often. He finally called the throwaway phone he had given to Eric and got no answer. He went ahead and tried Eric's regular cell number. No answer.

Brad began to panic. He remembered Eric saying that someone may have seen him. He paid his tab and drove to the office. He pulled into the parking garage and drove around and down, looking for Eric's car. He found it on the second level. It didn't appear to be tampered with. He parked his car and went into the building using his work ID card. He took the elevator to Eric's floor. His office was dark and locked. "Eric," he called out softly. No response. "Eric," he said more loudly. There was still no answer.

He tried to think where Eric might be. He took the elevator to his own floor and checked there. Nothing. A chill ran down his spine as he wondered what was happening. He returned to Eric's floor. He stood absolutely still and listened. He heard nothing except the whisper of the heating system. He went back to Eric's office. He took his cell phone out and turned on its light. He shined it in the office window but saw nothing out of the ordinary.

Finally, Brad took the elevator down to the lobby to talk to the security guard. "I'm Brad Tillman from the Finance Department," he said as he showed her his ID. "I was asked to meet Eric Blas here tonight. He is not here, but his car is in the parking garage. Have you seen anyone come or go since eleven?"

"No sir," she said. "I took over at eleven. I haven't seen anyone come or go through the lobby. There is nothing at all in my shift log." She took his ID and printed his name in the log. "I wish I could help you."

Brad thanked her and took the elevator to the parking garage to retrieve his car. He drove out of the garage and pulled over to the side of the street. He tried both of Eric's numbers again. There was no answer. He remembered that Special Agent Finnigan had told them to call her if they needed her. He looked at his watch and saw that it was 12:50 a.m. He called the number that she had given them.

"Federal Bureau of Investigation," a voice said.

Brad introduced himself and explained that he had helped Special Agent Betty Finnigan with a case and that she had asked him to call if something came up. He told the person that he needed to talk with Finnigan immediately; it was an emergency. The woman on the other end of the line took his phone number and said that she would contact Finnigan and give her the message. It would be the Agent's decision as to whether to call him immediately or not.

Brad thanked her and hung up. He decided that there was not a lot he could do. He headed home. Just five minutes later his throwaway phone rang. "Brad Tillman," he answered.

"Brad, this is Betty Finnigan. What's up?" Her voice sounded a bit scratchy from being awakened at one in the morning.

"Betty," he said, taking some liberty with her name that he hadn't before. "I'm concerned about Eric. He called me at eleven tonight and told me that he had found Unger's method of manipulating votes. He said someone may have seen what he was doing. He asked to meet at a bar where we had met before. I got to the bar just before eleven-thirty, and he wasn't there. He never showed, so I went to the office, where he had been when he called me. His car was in the parking garage, but he was nowhere to be found. I tried to call him several times on both of his phones. I got no answer."

There was a pause. Her breath during the silence was amplified by the phone. "He told you that someone may have seen him gaining access to the information?"

"Yes. He sounded kind of . . . jumpy."

"Okay. Thank you for calling me, Brad. You did the right thing. Go home and get some sleep. I'll take it from here."

Brad obeyed and returned home. It took him an hour to get to sleep. Once he did doze off, he slept the rest of the night restlessly.

CHAPTER 56

AS SOON AS SHE GOT OFF THE PHONE WITH BRAD, Finnigan contacted the police department and told them who she was. She reported that Eric Blas, an important witness, might be missing. She explained where he had been at last contact and that his car was still there. After hanging up the phone, she looked at her watch. It was a quarter after one in the morning. She took a shower and put on her work clothes. She didn't leave home yet, though. She figured she should allow the police to take a look around.

The call came an hour later. The police had done a careful search of the parking garage and had found the body of a male victim. He had been stabbed. They said it appeared to be a robbery. He had no wallet on him, no watch, and no phone. His body had been dragged behind a pillar in the garage.

Finnigan thanked them and immediately drove to the scene. She asked for one of the police officers heading up the investigation. She was introduced to Detective Rich Graham, who had just arrived. His hair was a mess. He had a deadpan expression on his face and talked in a monotone voice. It sounded like he had been awakened out of a deep sleep and was not happy about it. She explained why she was there. The detective showed her the body, and she was able to confirm that it was Eric Blas. She told the detective that there could be more to this than appeared. She described the phone call that the deceased man had made to Brad. She told him that she had been working the connected case with Detective John Conner. She said it would be helpful for the police to get Conner involved.

Conner was there by half past four. He and Finnigan went to the security guard on duty and asked if she had seen or heard anything unusual. She told them about Brad Tillman asking her something similar and showed them her logbook. Conner said that they needed to speak with a representative of GCI. Finnigan asked if she could find out who owned the building, assuming GCI was leasing the space. The guard promised to contact GCI right away and would work on getting the other information. They walked away from the security guard.

Finnigan stopped and stared at nothing in particular. "I would give anything to find out that Blas's death is unrelated to the GCI case."

"It would be quite a coincidence based upon Tillman's description of last night," Conner replied.

"I knew it was premature to close the case. I should have pushed back harder."

"You pushed back. Any more and you would have lost your job. How would that have helped?"

She looked Conner in the eye but said nothing. As she walked away, she thought about Brad. Was he in danger too? What would Robert Gomez at the Justice Department have to say now?

At just before five, Conner spoke with the director of HR for the company. He told the director that Eric Blas's body had been found in the parking garage and asked how they might get access to the security camera footage. The director said that the building owner was responsible for those cameras; the cameras inside the offices were the responsibility of the manager of Computer Support, Stan Haley.

It took a couple of hours of back and forth with the building manager, but finally they had access to the video footage in the garage. Detectives Graham and Conner sat in the conference room with Finnigan to watch the video from the garage cameras. The garage entry camera showed that someone wearing an oversized, discolored hoodie walked into the parking garage from the street and went down the drive aisle toward the second level.

"What time was that?" Conner asked the property manager, who was playing the video on a laptop computer. He pressed a function key and the time appeared in the upper right corner of the picture.

"10:51 p.m.," Finnigan said. 'There's no way to see the face for the hoodie. Could this person be homeless?"

The person then appeared in the second-floor camera view. "It seems like they are walking with purpose," Graham said. "They went right to the shadow of that pillar and waited."

"It's possible that they were hoping to see the owner of one of those cars come out. If they live around here and walk the area regularly, they would know that the garage is typically empty this time of night," Conner said. "It could indicate a robbery motive."

The computer operator sped up the video and they continued to watch in high speed as the person waited in the shadows. When Blas came out of the elevator, the camera operator slowed down the video. The person approached him and immediately thrust a knife into him. The hooded individual then dragged him into the shadows, out of the view of the camera.

"Either our killer is a man or a very strong woman," Finnigan said. "He had very little trouble moving Blas into the shadows." As they watched, the person in the hoodie reappeared and walked out in the same direction as he had come into the garage. "Back that up," Finnigan directed. "He appears to be putting something in his pocket as he comes out of the shadows." The rewind confirmed that. Then, the person was picked up by the entry camera again, walking out of the garage and back out to the street.

The only other activities the footage showed were a couple of people coming and going. At 10:37 p.m. someone, eventually identified as Karl Jennings, the Director of the Special Projects Division, came out of the elevator and drove away. At 12:25 a.m., Brad Tillman drove into the lot, parked, went into the building for a short amount of time, and then left as he had described. "Well, it's not a lot of help, but it's something," Conner sighed.

At seven-thirty a.m., Finnigan placed a call to Brad Tillman. "Brad, this is Betty." Finnigan began. "I'm afraid I have bad news."

"What is it?" Brad said, even though he knew. His voice was soft, almost hesitant.

"Eric's body was found in the parking garage not too long after you called me. It was behind a pillar. Probably there when you came and went last night." Finnigan heard nothing. "Brad, are you there?"

"Yes," he said, his voice cracking. "Do you know who did this?"

"Not yet, but we have some leads. Brad, I want you to be really careful. Maybe you and Barb should go visit your kids for a few days."

"Okay. We'll see," Brad said, not even considering it.

"Brad, do you know someone in Eric's family that we might contact?"

He cleared his throat. "Uh, no. Eric told me that his parents died several years ago. I don't know if he has—*had* any brothers or sisters. He never mentioned any to me."

Before ending the call, Finnigan told Brad that if he remained in town, he needed to keep a low profile, wherever he was. She said it would probably be best if he only went to work or stayed at home. She told him not to go out to lunch, not to run any errands, not to do anything else, until he heard from her.

CHAPTER 57

BRAD DECIDED NOT TO TELL BARB ANYTHING UNTIL HE knew more. He didn't want her to worry. She had left at half past six in the morning while he was still asleep, well before the phone call came from Finnigan. He felt like an emotional wreck—Eric's death hit him hard. Finnigan said that, at this time, the circumstances surrounding Eric's death were inconclusive, but Brad knew he had been murdered because of his discovery. In addition to feeling guilty for convincing Eric to stay at GCI, he became almost overwhelmed by the thought that this mess was still not over. People continued to die. Would he be next? Was Barb in danger?

He went to work at about ten a.m. The parking garage was closed off by the police, so he paid to park in a public parking lot a couple of blocks from GCI. When he got to work, he was in a daze. Of course, everyone was talking about Eric Blas's murder, even though they had no idea what they were talking about. Most of the people in his department didn't even know Eric.

He spent the day cleaning up emails and straightening up his files. He simply could not think about anything for more than a couple of minutes at a time. His mind constantly went to Eric. He thought that someone at GCI must still be involved in this; the murderer was in the building last night. At four in the afternoon, he went home. He tried to be more aware of vehicles around him. He felt like he needed to hide again, like before.

Barb was at home and just starting dinner when he arrived. She knew immediately that something was wrong. She asked, but Brad would say nothing. He sat in front of the television watching the news, staring blankly at the screen.

Finally, she walked in front of him, turned off the TV, and said, "Tell me what is bothering you. We don't keep secrets from one another!"

Brad teared up and put his face into his hands. "Eric Blas was killed last night."

Barb's eyes widened. She covered her mouth and sat down on the coffee table in front of him. "What do you mean, he was killed? Was he in an accident?"

"No, he was murdered in the parking garage at work." Brad's face contorted, and he released his tears completely.

"Oh, dear Lord, let this not be!"

Barb hadn't really known Eric, but she knew that he and Brad had become friends through the voter fraud ordeal, which she had thought was behind them. "Oh Brad, I'm so sorry!" She leaned forward and put her hands on his thighs. He leaned forward and they embraced for a long moment.

"Do they know who did this or why?" she asked.

He shook his head no, truthfully. He did not share his thoughts or even tell her of Betty Finnigan's hunch regarding the fraudulent vote case. She didn't need to deal with this. She had been through enough.

Just getting his emotions out made him feel a bit better. They ate dinner without saying much. Barb was really ready to leave Atlanta now, but this was not the time to get into that. Brad took care of the dishes after dinner and cleaned up the kitchen. He went into his home office and thumbed through a magazine, but, still, nothing could keep his attention for long.

At 7:24 p.m., he got a text message on his regular phone. He didn't recognize the number.

Mr. Tillman, Eric Blas asked me to meet with you and share some information that he had, a.s.a.p. Could you meet me at the Adam's Apple Lounge in Lawrenceville at nine tonight?

Brad just stared at the message. He was almost too anxious to process it. He wrote, *Who is this?*

I don't want to say. I'm afraid for my own safety. Can you please meet tonight?

Brad rubbed his hands across his shaved head. It had to be a trap. Or...might Eric have put something in a coworker's inbox asking that it be shared with Brad in the event that he died? It was possible. He texted, *I'll be there.*

CHAPTER 58

BRAD WALKED BACK INTO THE LIVING ROOM AND GAVE
Barb a kiss. "Thank you for being you," he said sincerely. "I'm so blessed to
have you as my wife."

She gave him a hug and simply said, "I love you."

"I love you, too," he said. "I need to go out for a little while. I should
be back by eleven. Don't wait up."

"Where are you going?"

"A friend of Eric's is having a challenging time," he lied. "I told him
I would meet with him. It'll be okay."

"Well, you be careful." He kissed her again and headed out the door.

As soon as he was driving down their street, he reached for his
throwaway phone to place a call to the FBI. It wasn't in his pocket. Realizing he must have left it at home, he took out his regular phone and made
the call. A call agent answered the phone again.

"Hi, this is Brad Tillman. I have an important message for Special
Agent Betty Finnigan. Could you please get it to her right away?"

"I would be happy to. What is the message?"

"Please tell her that Brad Tillman called. I am meeting someone at
nine tonight at the Adam's Apple Lounge in Lawrenceville. They say they
have some information that Eric wanted me to have."

She repeated the message. "Is that all you would like to say? Does
she have your number?"

"Yes, that's it. She has my number."

Brad pushed the end button and pulled over to the side of the road.
On his cell phone, he found the address for the lounge in Lawrenceville
and entered it into the GPS. As he drove on, a wave of tremors crossed

his upper body as he shook in fear. *Brad, you're an idiot*, he thought. He stopped the car once more and called the FBI again. It was a different agent this time, but she told him that Finnigan had been contacted by the previous agent.

Due to heavy traffic, he didn't arrive to the lounge until five after nine. He walked inside, not knowing who to look for or what to do. Nobody approached him, so he looked around a bit. This was a dive if there ever was one. The walls were dingy. The bar looked like it hadn't been cleaned in a while. The people he saw didn't appear to be people he would normally socialize with. He chastised himself, mentally, about being so judgmental. There was a large gathering at one end of the place that looked like a party of some sort. He looked at the opposite side of the bar and saw a table that was slightly set apart from the rest. He walked over slowly and sat in the chair that faced the door.

Several people came and went over the next ten minutes. A guy who appeared to be a regular walked through the door—at least the bartender called him by name as he sat at the bar. A woman also came in the door and looked around, like she was looking for someone. After a walk through the place, she threw her purse on the bar, not far from Brad, and sat on a barstool. She looked like she was trying a little too hard, a full-chested woman in a red knit sweater one size too small and a thick layer of bright red lipstick. Brad watched her for a moment as she checked her phone and chatted boisterously with the bartender. Others came and went.

Brad ordered a beer. He was even more tired than he was nervous, though the tremors were back. At this point, he figured he was either going to find out something that Eric had wanted him to know, or he was about to meet the killer. He felt a flood of exhaustion overtake him. He almost didn't care either way; he was just ready for it to be over. He sat there, almost amused with himself.

He wondered how he would know this person he was to meet. He decided that if the guy, or gal, wasn't there by nine-thirty, then he was leaving.

A man walked up to the woman at the bar and asked if he could buy her a drink. She smiled and said, "Thank you sweetie, but I'm meeting someone." The poor guy walked away, looking embarrassed. Ten minutes later, a middle-aged man walked in the door. Brad thought he might be coming toward him, but he stopped at the bar. The woman smiled and put her arms out. "You did come, you devil you," she said as she hugged him. He settled into the stool next to hers, and they began talking softly.

At 9:25, the door opened again. This time it was someone he knew. Karl Jennings entered with a jacket draped over his arm. He looked around a moment until he saw Brad. He smiled and nodded his head as he walked over and sat down at the table.

"Brad, thank you for meeting me," he said quietly.

"Karl," was all Brad said in response.

"You know, it's really hard to find a place to meet someone in private anymore. This place is typically pretty dead; it was the only place I could think of."

Brad's mind was reeling. He hadn't expected it to be Karl. Of course, he hadn't known what to expect. There was something about Karl's demeanor. He didn't appear nervous or in fear for his safety, as he had said in his text. Brad felt his face grow red. "You have something for me from Eric?" he said, not taking his eyes off the man.

"Relax; we'll get to that." Karl said in a calm, almost soothing tone.

Not liking his answer, Brad demanded, "Did you kill Eric Blas?"

"Brad, is that any way to greet a coworker?" Karl said, ignoring the question. The server approached and asked what Karl wanted to drink. "Thank you so much, but I can't stay."

She asked if Brad wanted another beer. He also declined. She shrugged and walked away. "Well, I suppose I'm next," Brad said matter-of-factly. "So, what is my demise going to be? An accident or death by an apparent homeless person?"

"Brad, let's don't talk about that," Karl said in that soft, almost syrupy voice.

"Okay, well, why don't you tell me how you and Unger came up with this little voter scam of yours, then."

"Oh, don't give me credit for that. It was all Jeff's set-up from the start. Such a noble guy. He really did think he was doing his country a favor. His big mistake was trusting me with his little secret. Correction, his *really* big mistake was leaving his little voter tally sheet laying around in my department for others to find."

"You can say that again. He had to go through a killing spree to cover up that one."

"You must be kidding. Jeff was such a nerd. He couldn't possibly hurt another person, let alone himself."

Brad said nothing for a moment. He looked up at the bar to see the guy nuzzling the woman's neck. "So, you did his dirty work, huh?"

"Brad, Jeff Unger never even knew the deaths were anything more than an accident. I had Kathrine and Al taken care of. That would have been it if you hadn't let your stupid curiosity get the better of you."

"Well then, what *did* you do for Unger?"

"I maintained his secret access to the voter count system. He and I became quite good friends, you know. I guess he was so proud of his little project for protecting America from itself that he needed to brag to someone."

"So, if he didn't kill Kathrine and Al, why did he confess to their murders?"

"Brad, you are really slow, aren't you? I wrote Jeff's letter on his computer while he was out at dinner that night. I knew he wasn't going to be able to handle the stress of the FBI investigation. I figured suicide would be a fine way out for him." Karl paused for effect. "You see, I have a back door key into Jeff's office. Again, the value of earning the man's trust!" He smiled proudly. "While he was out, I decided we could put the investigation into Kathrine's and Al's deaths to bed at the same time. But the part about the reason for creating his little tool was exact. I heard it from him ad nauseam."

"And you killed Unger as well."

"Yes, this one was difficult for me. I had never really killed anyone before."

"What do you call Kathrine and Al?"

Karl ignored his remark. "If I may say so, I think I did an excellent job of it. You see, Jeff trusted people too much. He often left his desk un-locked. I knew he kept a pistol in the desk, so I removed it after I finished his suicide note. I returned his screen to his email, where I found it, and then put his computer to sleep.... Jeff and I were to meet that night. I let myself in the back door as I often did. He typically ignored me when I came in, at least until I took a seat in front of him. He was logging into his computer when I got into his office. I took two steps forward, put the pistol to his head, and pulled the trigger. The actual job wasn't as hard as I thought it would be. Plus, it tied up so many loose ends. Anyway, I put the gun in his hand, his finger on the trigger. I left the way I came in."

"It sounds like you enjoyed it."

"It does give one a sense of, you know, power."

Brad grimaced. "And Eric?"

"Oh, I enjoyed that even more. He was a contrary sort of guy. He also knew too much. What bad luck that he was in the wrong place at the wrong time. There are so many homeless people out there. The company really needs to provide better security in the parking garage."

Brad couldn't believe Karl's arrogance. He couldn't stand to hear any more. He began to rise.

"I think you'd best stay put," Karl said, his voice tightening as he slightly lifted the jacket that was over his right arm, now resting on top of the table. Brad saw the gun in his hand before the jacket fell back over it.

Brad sat again and breathed. "Why was it so important to you to hide the voter manipulation system? It was Unger's baby."

Oh no, there you are wrong! That system was solid gold. Do you know how much some countries are willing to pay for influence like that? Well, I'll tell you how much," he smiled broadly. "I found a country that paid one hundred million dollars for Jeff's little toy. What's more, I was able to completely copy the system for my buyer. Eventually, I'll train them on Jeff's system so they can get one of their agents to drop vote tallies into the system right after the actuals get put in."

"You betrayed our country to line your pockets," Brad said accusingly.

"You're damn right!" Karl hissed back. He cleared his throat and his honeyed tone returned. "Once I get them trained, I will resign and disappear. I just have to take care of one more issue."

"Oh, that would be me, right?"

"Brad, your incessant attention to detail got two people killed. I'm sure it weighs on your mind. Once again, suicide will remove that stress forever.... No more questions. I think it's time for us to go now. Why don't you drive?" Karl stood with his jacket still draped over his arm. He put his left hand in his pocket and pulled out a couple of ten-dollar bills and threw them on the table.

"Drinks are on me," he said. "Let's go."

Brad tried to think of what to do. Would he have an opportunity to get away? If he ran, would Karl shoot? What if someone else got hurt? He stood and walked toward the door, Karl close behind. Just in front of him, the couple from the bar were also approaching the door. The man opened the door for the woman. Seeing Brad and Karl approach, he stepped back and held the door for them as well.

Karl thanked him cheerfully. As Brad cleared the door frame, the woman grabbed his right arm and jerked him clear of the door. At the same time, the man holding the door grabbed Karl's right arm and gave it a rapid twist. The gun fell. In a moment, Karl was face down on the hood of a car parked in front of the door. The man had him in handcuffs faster than anything Brad had ever seen, all while barking orders. Others, seemingly more FBI agents, approached to help.

Brad had lost his balance and crashed to the concrete when the woman pulled him out of the way. Now he looked up at the woman and asked, "Can I get up now?"

"Yes sir," she said professionally. "I hope I didn't hurt you."

Brad stood and rubbed his shoulder with his left hand. "Yes ma'am, it hurts a lot. But I wouldn't trade it for anything."

At that moment, Agent Finnigan walked up to Brad. "So, you stopped answering your phone?"

Brad's face cringed. "Sorry," he said. "I guess I left my throwaway phone at home. Then he looked at her, closed his eyes and said deliberately, "Thank you."

She smiled and introduced him to Special Agent Darcy Simpson, who had nearly yanked his arm out of its socket. Brad thanked her again, still rubbing his shoulder.

Brad turned back to Finnigan. "Karl is responsible for all of the deaths, not Unger."

"So we heard," she said and nodded toward Simpson. "Agent Simpson had a camera and mic in her purse and placed it on the bar, facing your table. She had an earpiece and monitored the entire conversation."

"And you wouldn't have let him hurt me?" he asked.

"We knew he wouldn't do anything in front of that many people. Everything he has done up to now has shown he was not interested in getting caught."

When Brad arrived home after hours of questioning, Barb had fallen asleep while curled up on the corner of the couch, waiting for him. She woke up and looked at him with relief. "Where have you been? Why are you so late?"

Brad hugged her and apologized. He said, "I feel better than I have in a year, but I need some sleep. Can I tell you about it in the morning?"

Barb smiled apprehensively but nodded after a moment. She put her arm around him, and they headed to the bedroom for much-needed sleep.

CHAPTER 59

THREE WEEKS LATER, BRAD AND BARB ATTENDED A meeting at GCI. Cathy Hoover led the meeting. Amber Unger was present, as were Agent Betty Finnigan and Detective John Conner. This was an exclusive meeting. Besides Brad and Barb, the only other attendees were Kathrine Cruise's parents and Linda Johnson.

Cathy began by expressing her heartfelt sorrow for the losses that those present had experienced, and for the dangers that Brad and Barb Tillman had faced. She continued by recognizing each person who had lost their life for their courage and commitment to doing what was right. "Kathrine and Al did not know what they were dealing with, yet they sensed something was wrong and sought to find out more. Eric Blas worked tirelessly to find out how our nation's voting system had been compromised and probably rescued the recent election from fraud, maybe even chaos."

She turned and faced Amber, who was standing next to her. "Amber, we are all devastated by the death of Jeff. He was your husband, and he was our leader and mentor.... In spite of this lapse in judgment, he was a good man. We were all blessed to work with him." She turned back to face the Tillmans. "Brad, your persistence in exploring all of this saved GCI's reputation and perhaps the company itself. You nearly lost your life as a result.

"Amber and I wanted to meet with you today to give you our sincerest thanks for your sacrifices and to let you know that your loved ones did not die in vain. Their actions did as much for the liberty of our nation as have other fallen heroes who have died in the line of duty. We asked

Special Agent Betty Finnigan and Detective John Conner to be here to help answer any questions you might have."

Finnigan and Conner took turns briefing them about the investigations that were still underway. Both assured the group that the evidence against Thomas Everett and Karl Jennings was overwhelming. While they couldn't presume to know what sentence each would receive, they were confident that neither of them would leave prison alive.

Brad, hands folded on top of the table, lifted his finger to catch Cathy's attention. "How did Eric communicate what he had found before he died?"

Cathy told them where Eric had hidden his notes and his laptop. "He was extremely careful to make sure we had the information before he left the building. We were able to see, from cameras, that Karl Jennings came to work at five the following morning. While we don't have cameras in the stairwells or in the CEO's office, we feel certain that he went in to make sure that Eric had left nothing behind.

"The information that Eric provided, taken with what we learned when Brad met Karl, gave us a clear picture of the system's vulnerability. Our software engineers have since been able to go into the vote counting system and ensure that no vote, once dropped in, can be overwritten."

At that point, Finnigan spoke up. "As most of you know, our United States Department of Justice has been anxious that the recent risks to the integrity of the voting system be kept confidential. While I was uncomfortable with that situation before, I do now concur. We are absolutely certain that we have held those responsible for its vulnerability accountable. We are also greatly confident that the system is now secure. To make this case public would only serve to heighten the doubts and divisions in the minds of our citizens for no purpose. Recently we shared this issue with the Cruise family, and they have also signed a non-disclosure agreement. I hope you will each follow through on your agreements as well."

Everyone nodded.

Linda Johnson asked, "What about the person, or people, who paid Karl Jennings for the program that could change votes?"

"I have to be honest with you. It will take a multi-agency effort to find all who were involved. For the FBI's part, we have two teams of agents working full-time on it. Agent Chris Allan is heading one team, and I am heading the other. I'm not at liberty to say more than that. We will eventually figure it out. I can tell you that we have been able to locate some of the money paid to Karl Jennings as a result of his carelessness. You can be sure, we will get to the bottom of it."

Amber Unger stepped forward.

"I want to thank Special Agent Finnigan and her team, as well as Detective Conner and his associates, for clearing my husband's name in the murders of your loved ones. This has been exceedingly difficult for me; my emotions have run the gamut. I do want to acknowledge Jeff's guilt in creating the opening in the system that started all of this. I'm both shocked and ashamed," she said as a tear trickled from her cheek.

She bit her lip and pressed both sides of the bridge of her nose to hold back her tears. "You may or may not know that since my husband's death, I have become sole owner of GCI. My first major decision is to authorize the payment of one million dollars, by my company, to the Cruise and Johnson families. Since Eric Blas has no surviving family, we would like the Cruise family to select a charity for a similar payment in his name." She didn't say that they would also ask each family to sign an agreement that would absolve the company of further liability, but they would cross that bridge when they came to it.

"Additionally, I happen to know that it is Brad and Barb Tillman's desire that Brad leave GCI and get a fresh start in a new location. Now, I would love for them to change their minds, but I do respect and understand that decision. I have authorized a payment to the Tillmans of $150,000 to defray their cost of relocating and getting settled in a new place.

"My final announcement is that I have been quite impressed by Cathy Hoover's handling of an incredibly arduous situation, including her frankness and honesty in dealing with me through all of this. For this reason, I will be announcing tomorrow that I am taking the "interim" out of her title. Cathy Hoover is now the permanent CEO of GCI, and I have every confidence that she will do a stellar job of leading us into a strong future."

As the meeting finished, Brad and Barb walked over to the Cruises and introduced themselves and offered their condolences. Brad told them that Eric was very much in love with Kathrine and was devastated by her death. They were gratified to hear this and said so. They also stopped to talk with Betty Finnigan. "Agent Finnigan, thank you for your tenacity throughout all of this, especially when your hands were tied by the system," Brad said.

Tears welled up in Barb's eyes. She squeaked, "Thank you for saving Bradley's life. We will be forever indebted to you."

"Stop, or you'll have me crying," Betty said with a smile. "I'm glad that we finally got everything resolved, with a good deal of help from Brad, I might add." Her mood became serious. "I feel horrible that we lost Eric."

"I carry some guilt for having suspected Eric, early on, and getting him involved in all of this," Brad said.

"Neither of you were responsible for Eric's death. You know that," Barb told them.

Brad and Betty nodded.

"Please give our thanks to Chris Allan as well. I can't tell you how reassuring it was to have you both on our side," Brad said.

"That's why we're here," Betty said. "I hope you never have to call on us again in any official capacity." Brad and Barb held out their arms and wrapped them around the agent. They didn't care if it wasn't professional; they wanted her to feel their affection.

On their way out, Brad and Barb also talked with Linda and asked how she was doing with all of this. She assured them that she and the kids would get through it. "I wish you weren't leaving, though," she said. "Where will you go?"

"Brad will finish the year with GCI. Then, we are going to take some time to travel and see where we might end up," Barb said. "Wherever that is, we will expect you to visit regularly!"

As they finally left the building and walked to their car, Barb stopped and turned to Brad. "Are you going to miss this place?"

"No," he said thoughtfully. "GCI has been good to me and good for us. I really hope it continues to do well moving forward. But nothing seems the same anymore. It almost feels like I don't fit in, now."

She smiled and took his hand. "Well, it sounds like you're ready for a new adventure."

Brad took a step back and gave her a funny look. "I'm ready to explore new possibilities with you. But I could do without any more adventures."

COMMENT FROM THE AUTHOR

Thank you for taking time to read Wayward Patriot: Preserving the Vote. I hope you enjoyed it.

The topic of election integrity has been on my mind for over 20 years. In November of 2000, watching the Florida recount when that Presidential Election was contested, I thought it would be a cool backdrop for a thriller. Anyone over the age of 40 will remember watching election workers in Florida looking at dimpled chads and hanging chads on computer punch cards, trying to discern the intent of the voter.

Fast forward 23 years, election accuracy and integrity are still on people's minds. State voter rolls are typically out of date. From time-to-time instances are documented of dead people voting. Most of us have heard the cute quip, "Vote early and vote often!" We all get a chuckle out of that. Many people aren't aware that nearly all the voting processes in the United States actually are open to fraud in one form or another. Following every national election in this century candidates and political workers, both Democrat and Republican, have expressed concern over election integrity.

Wayward Patriot: Preserving the Vote provides a glimpse into another potential issue with elections. The latest technology doesn't necessarily protect us from election fraud. The workings of the technology must be open and transparent to ensure votes are properly counted. Proprietary systems can be very secure from external manipulation but those who write and maintain the software can do what they wish with it because nobody can see how it works.

Election integrity is important for our republic. If you would like to learn more about bi-partisan concerns regarding election integrity, check out the following web sites.

Election Integrity Project of California
https://www.eip-ca.com/who-we-are.htm

More Proof That Voter Fraud is Real, and Bipartisan (Heritage Foundation Commentary)
https://www.heritage.org/election-integrity/commentary/more-proof-voter-fraud-real-and-bipartisan

ACKNOWLEDGMENTS

I sincerely appreciate the help that so many people gave me in this endeavor.

Several people were helpful in some technical aspects of the story. My friend and neighbor who wishes to remain anonymous, Paul Malchow, Jason Meyer, and others, were great teachers and sounding boards when I needed their expertise. I hope all will forgive me for instances where I strayed from reality in the name of author's liberty!

Thank you to friends and family members who read early drafts and provided feedback on areas that might be improved. A special thanks to Catherine Wells for a fiction writer's input. The book became better because of all of you.

Thanks also to my friend, Chuck Hughes, who worked with me from start to finish. His feedback was invaluable as he read each chapter, did preliminary edits, polished the writing and gave his honest feedback. Having him work with me was both encouraging and motivating.

I truly appreciate the work of Carrie Cannella, my editor, who pointed out opportunities to make improvements in the text. Her feedback and suggestions have also made the book better.

Finally, when my sister Nancy referred me to a publishing strategist, I listened. Karen Bomm patiently shepherded me through the complex publishing and promotion process. Her knowledge and guidance have been invaluable to me. I now have the confidence to proceed with books two and three of my Wayward Patriot series.

ABOUT THE AUTHOR

Jack Meyer is a retired businessman and author of the new suspense thriller, *Wayward Patriot: Preserving the Vote.*

He received his Bachelor of Science Degree in Aviation Management from Embry-Riddle Aeronautical University and an MBA in Global Management from the University of Phoenix. He also attended two years at Martin Luther College where he received a certification in Staff Ministry.

Meyer's career included work with a multi-national corporation, time facilitating leadership and team building training simulations and six years in full-time ministry. Overlapping that career he spent 30 years as an entrepreneur, of sorts, owning two different franchises.

Through much of his career, he has paid a lot of attention to politics although he wouldn't consider himself a fanatic. He has written in support of campaigns. Most of his political writing has been opinion pieces for various online publications.

In his Wayward Patriot series, characters may be conservative or liberal but he strives not to be judgmental. His books are not about the ideology of his characters but about the human experience, faults and all. His main characters tend to be everyday people who are in situations that they are not accustomed to. He strives to develop characters that his readers can relate to. It is his desire that his books be enjoyed by people from all political perspectives.

Meyer and his wife, Barbara, divide their time between their homes in Colorado Springs and Tucson. He stays busy remodeling his homes, playing golf and writing his next book in the Wayward Patriot series.

THE WAYWARD PATRIOT SERIES

Note from the author:

There are many patriots in our great nation who sincerely want what is best for the United States of America and are willing to work diligently for her good. Unfortunately, innate within every citizen is an original sinfulness which, when tempted, may give in to ethical lapses. These lapses may go contrary to the American spirit, principles and laws that the country was built on. They may even be tempted to set aside morality itself for the "greater good." Sometimes, when this happens, there are unintended consequences.

The Wayward Patriot Series does not follow a specific character but instead follows well-intended, everyday people who meet these temptations. I hope you will enjoy the series as much as I am enjoying writing it.

Visit WaywardPatriotBook.com and sign up to be the first to know when the next book in the series is released!

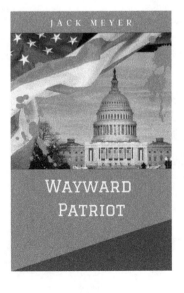

Watch for the next book
in the series
WAYWARD PATRIOT:
SERVING THE NATION
set in
Washington D.C.

CPSIA information can be obtained
at www.ICGtesting.com
Printed in the USA
JSHW022023140323
38952JS00001B/3